Hemingway's
Chair

Also by Michael Palin

Nonfiction
Around the World in Eighty Days
Pole to Pole

Fiction (with Terry Jones)
Ripping Yarns
More Ripping Yarns
Dr. Fegg's Encyclopeadia of All World Knowledge

Screenplays
The Missionary

Plays
The Weekend

Children's Books
Small Harry and the Toothache Pills
Limericks
The Mirrorstone
Cyril and the Dinner Party
Cyril and the House of Commons

Hemingway's Chair

Michael Palin

St. Martin's Griffin
New York

The goings-on in this story are entirely fictional, and none of the characters, outside of Hemingway's world, ever existed. The names of the companies mentioned, both solvent and insolvent, are also fictional.

First published in Great Britain by Methuen London, an imprint of Reed Consumer Books Ltd.

First St. Martin's Griffin Edition: June 1999

10 9 8 7 6 5 4 3 2 1

For Helen

'Neither snow, nor rain, nor heat nor gloom of night, stays these couriers from the swift completion of their appointed round.'

On the façade of the General Post Office, New York City

One

Marsh Cottage stood a little way back from a road that led to a cliff top and then stopped. It had once run out to a headland where there had been a small village, but the sea had clawed away the soft sandy cliff and the houses had long since disappeared. Now, apart from Marsh Cottage itself, the road served only a pair of holiday chalets. It was neglected and full of potholes.

On either side of the cottage lay flat countryside, tufty grassland on the landward side and on the other grazing marsh running a half-mile down to the sea. The house had been flooded several times since it was built in the early 1930s but more recently the local council had raised the sea defences in an attempt to create an extra beach or two, and since then it had been safe from the spring tides.

Marsh Cottage looked what it was. The unsuccessful prototype for an abandoned housing estate. Redbrick walls two storeys high ran up to a pitched slate roof. A suburban bay window faced on to the road with the front door to one side. Beside the house was a detached garage alongside which a passage led round to the back. In the seventies a white-painted wood and glass extension had been added to the rear of the house and framed the old back door.

On this Thursday morning in early September Marsh Cottage looked particularly vulnerable as it took a westerly wind full in the face. An unhealthy yellow sky offered worse to come as a bobble-hatted figure emerged from the garage, wheeling a bicycle. He secured the door of the garage behind him, patted the pockets of a sky-blue anorak, checked the

I

fastenings on a pannier basket and, mounting the bicycle with care, negotiated the short, bumpy driveway and turned southwards in the direction of the town of Theston, two miles away. Martin Sproale had made this journey, on various bicycles, for most of his adult life. He was now thirty-six, a little over six feet tall, with a round, soft face and light reddish hair. His skin was pale and prone to rashes, and his hands were long and fine.

Elaine Rudge, who worked at the post office alongside Martin, was still at home. She lived in the centre of town and could walk to work, and in any case she didn't have the responsibility of opening up, which brought Martin in on the dot of half past eight. Hair-grip between clenched teeth, she was standing before the kitchen mirror, concentrating on herself and a vital quiz question on the *Dick Arthur Breakfast Show*.

'*The capital of Indonesia is Jakarta, Mombasa or Rio de Janeiro? The capital of Indonesia . . .*'

As the voice from the radio came again, Joan Rudge, a trim, energetic woman in a padded nylon housecoat, gave a short dismissive laugh. 'Well, it's not going to be Rio de Janeiro, is it. That's in Brazil.'

Elaine took the grip from her teeth and thrust it into the back of her head. 'Mum, I'm trying to listen.'

'Soft, these questions.'

'You've still got to work out if it's Mombasa or – what was the other one?' Elaine said, reaching for a piece of paper.

'*Jakarta, Mombasa or Rio de Janeiro?*' repeated Dick Arthur obligingly.

'Must be Jakarta.'

'Well it'll not be Rio de Janeiro,' her mother said again. 'That's definitely in Brazil. That's where Uncle Howard ended up.'

Elaine bit her lower lip for some time and then wrote down 'Mombasa'.

2

She returned to the mirror and stood a little back from it. She'd chosen her clothes with more care than usual this morning, as it was a Thursday and she and Martin always had a drink at the Pheasant on Thursdays. The pink cotton blouse was simple but sophisticated, not figure-hugging but very feminine. She looked in the mirror and flicked the collar up. Then she flicked it down. She wasn't pretty, she knew that. She was a hefty, well-proportioned young woman, but on some days she could look oddly beautiful, the way Ingrid Bergman did when they photographed her nose right. Her thick head of copper-brown hair needed work but repaid the effort. She'd woken up with an ominous tenderness on her lower lip and was relieved to find on closer examination that it was nothing more than the tiniest of pimples which she would have no trouble in disguising. Unless of course Martin was in one of his touching moods. The other evening they'd been together down by the beach huts and he'd run his fingers very gently over her face, paying special attention to her lips. Elaine was curious to know where he'd learnt this, but didn't like to ask. She had concluded that it must have been from a magazine, or one of his books. She hadn't liked it much, as the tips of his fingers smelt of postal adhesive.

The next question on the *Dick Arthur Breakfast Show* concerned nocturnal animals. '*That's animals that only come out at night,*' Dick Arthur added helpfully, though most of the question had been obscured by the noise of Frank Rudge's Dormobile pulling into the yard. Through the window Elaine could see him wince with discomfort as he slid the door open and extracted himself gingerly from the driving seat. Thursday was market day at Norwich and he'd been out on the road before dawn. Paul, his latest acquisition from the Youth Training Scheme, checked his spiky blond hair in the wing mirror and by the time he'd got down, Elaine's father already had the back open and was reaching for the first of the long, flat boxes of Spanish lettuce.

Theston post office was part of an uncompleted 1930s development in the centre of the town. It was the work of Cedric Meadows, the Borough Architect, who had left for Malaya a year later, leaving undisclosed debts. On a good day, when Martin cycled into North Square he saw the redbrick walls, the asymmetric stone-dressed tower, the steeply gabled roof and portentous curved steps up to the bulky oak front door as a rather splendid mess. On a bad day he barely saw the post office at all, his eye being drawn unwillingly to the neon-bordered, poster-plastered window of the video store on its left and the jumble-sale jolliness of the Save the Children shop on its right.

As he had done every morning, forty-eight weeks a year for the last sixteen years, Martin cycled around two sides of the square and turned into Echo Passage. If there were no unwelcomely parked cars he would slowly raise his right leg, transfer his weight to the left-hand pedal and, braking as he did so, glide balletically into Phipps' Yard, coming to rest, precisely, alongside the back steps of the post office. Ernie Padgett, the current Postmaster, a title he had privately refused to relinquish when postmasters had been officially renamed managers four years earlier, lived on the premises. He would normally have opened up and had some tea on, but recently he had been unwell and with retirement imminent had seemed to be losing interest in the job. Highly irregularly, he had entrusted his assistant, Martin, with a set of keys and these Martin had to use today.

As Elaine arrived there was already a brace of regulars waiting outside the main door. At their head was Harold Meredith, a small, sturdy man with a walking stick and a head of closely trimmed white hair, more often than not concealed beneath a tweed cap. He took care over his appearance and wouldn't dream of leaving the house in anything less correct than a hound's-tooth jacket and an Army Pay Corps tie. His pale, smooth-skinned complexion showed little sign of age, though he was known to be over eighty. Since his wife's death five years earlier, the post office had become his adopted home.

'You're up with the lark, Mr Meredith,' Elaine called jauntily, because that was the way he liked it.

'I'm up for a lark any day,' came the ritual reply.

'I'm too old for you, Mr Meredith,' Elaine protested and fluttered her eyelashes as she reached the top of the steps and pressed the doorbell for Martin to let her in.

Elaine and Martin refrained from any physical contact whilst they were on post office premises. Even when there were just the two of them in the back kitchen they only ever touched accidentally. Elaine had begun to entertain increasingly elaborate fantasies of coffee-break passion but Martin remained the complete professional and, once he was inside the building, his sole relationship was with the public. No enquiry, however fatuous or ill informed, failed to receive his full attention, nor was any irrelevant personal information treated as less than engrossing. Even Mrs Harvey-Wardrell, whom Elaine thought the most vile creature imaginable, could not dislodge his mask of professional affability.

Pamela Harvey-Wardrell was the self-appointed queen of Theston society. She was a snob's snob, a woman of such epic and ineffable unselfconsciousness that, if born poor and unwelcome, she might well have been certified mad. She was another early riser. A keen ornithologist, she could often be seen on the marshes at dawn, glasses raised, scouring the reed-beds. She was over six feet tall and from a distance, in her deer-stalker, Barbour jacket and matching thigh-length waders, she could easily be taken for a small tree.

Though she could wait for hours on a jacksnipe or a water rail she had no patience for humans and this particular morning her

5

restlessness was almost tangible as Martin explained slowly and laboriously to Harold Meredith the intricacies of the Pension Income Bonds, something which he had to do on more or less a weekly basis. Mr Meredith nodded earnestly as he listened.

'So would you like a leaflet?' Martin asked him.

'Oh, yes please,' he returned, eyes lighting up.

Martin leant down to the cupboard and, flicking it open with his right foot, withdrew a small pile of them. He detached one and handed it to Mr Meredith. 'Here you are. Pensioners' Income Bond Booklet, Series 2.'

'D'you want it back?'

'No, you hang on to it, Mr Meredith.'

'How much is it?'

'Oh, for God's sake . . .' came quite audibly from behind him.

'Morning, Mrs Harvey-Wardrell.' Martin offered a placatory smile.

She didn't seem placated.

'I'm in a dreadful hurry.'

'Yes, I'll be with you right away. That should answer all your questions, Mr Meredith.'

'How much is it, Martin?'

'Completely free. Compliments of the Post Office.'

Mr Meredith's eyes swam with emotion. 'I can remember when you could send a letter to Hong Kong for a penny halfpenny,' he said somewhat at random.

Mrs Harvey-Wardrell exhaled threateningly. In paisley silk headscarf, thick-ribbed turtleneck sweater, body-warmer, tweed skirt, lisle stockings and lace-up brogues, she was looking about as feminine as Martin had ever seen her.

'I could have *walked* to Hong Kong by now,' she snapped and, using her substantial weight advantage, began to edge Mr Meredith along the counter. Harold Meredith knew this tactic and had his own way of dealing with it.

'Thank you, Martin,' he said, deliberately slowly. He

6

gathered up his various documents, picked up his tweed cap, unhooked his walking stick from the edge of the counter and moved unhurriedly across the post office to the public writing desk. Here he set out his papers, then tried to engage Jane Cardwell, the doctor's wife, in conversation. Having failed to do so, he reread the latest brochures on Parcel Force rates, live animal export regulations and forwarding mail to a private address.

Mrs Harvey-Wardrell began briskly. 'What I need,' she announced in ringing tones, as if addressing an open-air rally, 'is two postal orders. One for Sebastian who's just got into Eton with one of the highest Common Entrance marks they've ever had at Waterdene and the other for dear Charlie who's nowhere near as bright but I can't leave him out. Have you anything appropriate, Martin?'

'Postal orders are all the same.'

'No. I don't mean postal orders, I mean those sort of gift voucher things.'

'Well, we've got these.' He withdrew two cards, swiftly and expertly, from his sliding drawer.

'Those are ghastly,' said Mrs Harvey-Wardrell.

'Well, that's all we have at the moment.'

'They had dozens of them in Cambridge. All sorts of designs.' She looked down disparagingly at the two examples Martin had laid out on the counter. 'I can't send a boy wrestling with the problems of adolescence a bunch of pansies.'

'Geraniums, I think,' volunteered Martin.

'And what's this one?'

Martin examined the card. He wasn't too sure himself.

'I think it's a ship in trouble.'

'Artist in trouble, I should say. Who chooses these things?'

'Well, Mr Padgett does the ordering.'

Mrs Harvey-Wardrell lowered her voice to a whisper, which rang around the post office. 'How is he today?'

'Much the same.'

She leant across the counter. There was something damp and musty on her breath, like the smell of an abandoned house.

'The sooner there's some young blood in here the better, Martin. I'll take two ships in trouble.'

Everyone was waiting for Ernie Padgett's retirement. He had been Postmaster of Theston for twenty-three years and Assistant Postmaster for twenty years before that. 'Padge', as he was universally known, had long been at the centre of Theston life, twice Mayor and, like his friend Frank Rudge, on and off the council for as long as anyone could remember. Half a dozen years ago, Padge and Frank had laid plans for a property business, a two-man Mafia to revitalise Theston's fortunes after the collapse of the local fishing industry. Investment was promised but all that was raised was expectation and, amidst recriminations, Frank Rudge became a greengrocer and Padge remained a postmaster.

From then on expert Padge-watchers – and there were many, for the relationship between post office and community is close and pervasive – detected the start of a decline. He seemed to withdraw into himself, indeed on occasions to be downright surly. He developed a constant bronchial cough. He found the new, computerised systems no match for his voluminous memory, which he once boasted could retain the serial number of every new pension book issued over a six-month period. He relied more and more on Martin to get him through the last few years until he could retire and claim a pension for himself. But he was too proud a man ever to admit this and Martin remained in word, if not in deed, only assistant manager.

'They're sending three of them,' announced Padge in the lunch-hour.

'Three what?' asked Elaine, glancing up from her cross-word, grateful for a respite from 14 across, 'Hebrew prophet (5)'.

'Three from area headquarters.'

'What for?'

Padge tapped the letter he was holding, impatiently.

'For the – you know – for the farewell dinner.'

'Dinner now is it, Padge?' asked Martin between mouthfuls of bread and cold chicken. 'I'd heard it was cheese and pickles . . . you know, something lean and mean and ready for privatisation.'

Martin knew there was a dinner. He was the one who'd suggested it in the first place. Head Office had only offered sherry and a presentation, and now here they were muscling in on an occasion which was supposed to have been a surprise anyway. Padge took another look at the letter.

'Still, three of them,' he said, with a touch of pride. 'Shows they must consider it an occasion of importance.'

'Penny?'

'What?'

'For your thoughts? What's occupying that big brain of yours?'

Elaine and Martin were sitting together in the beer garden of the Pheasant Inn, at Braddenham, a modest village fifteen minutes' drive inland from Theston. Its thatched roof and quaintly angled half-timbered façade dated back to the late 1970s when it was rebuilt after a fire. The beer garden was little more than an outside space, a lumpy slab of lawn confined by a quick-growing cypress hedge. Half a dozen metal tables hugged the wall of the pub for protection. They looked out towards swings and a climbing frame which were to Ron Oakes, the publican, a Kiddies' Grotto, and to most of his regulars another way of recycling old tractor tyres.

But now autumn was approaching and families with young children came only at weekends. Soon the swing would be chained and padlocked and the wind and rain would see to the paint on the climbing frame.

Elaine preferred to sit in the garden if she could. In her experience, once inside a pub it was hard to keep a man's attention. He would find other men and they would start to argue over things that were of very little interest to her, generally football or fishing or cars or the inexorable decline of standards in almost every area except pub conversation.

Human relationships were what interested Elaine. They were such an endlessly rich and fascinating subject, an all-year-round phenomenon. A twenty-four-hours-a-day, seven-days-a-week phenomenon. Men could talk about passion and elation and despair if they happened within the confines of a league match, but for Elaine such emotions were too important to be squandered by football commentators. She was a romantic. She yearned and felt and sensed with an intensity which she had never yet been able to share. She had had boyfriends and they had said that they loved her, but she knew they loved go-karting and windsurfing just as much, and she wanted to be more than just an exciting evening out. Martin was different from the others. He wasn't gregarious, and he had no interest in sport.

Though he was still reserved and uncomfortable in talking about his feelings, she was convinced that beneath it all Martin felt the same way she did, which was why she was attracted to him, why she persevered with the relationship. At least it was a relationship. Until the Christmas before last it had been two people sitting beside each other behind a post office counter. Now he touched her face and sometimes took her hand.

Elaine watched him conduct some private battle with himself. He thrust his lower lip forward and drew in the muscles tight around his eyes.

'You're quite pensive.'

'I was thinking about the future,' he said.

'Well, no wonder you were pensive. Which bit?' asked Elaine.

'Which bit?'

'Of the future.'

'Oh . . .' He smiled bleakly. 'The nearest bit.'

'Am I in it?'

She knew this would irritate him and she was right. He took a studied sip at his beer and set the glass down before answering her.

'As a matter of fact, no. Just me and a large public company.'

'Beginning with P?'

'How did you guess?'

'There aren't many left to choose from,' she said.

Martin smiled ruefully.

'Are you not getting on well together, you and the Post Office?' she asked him.

Martin's frown deepened. A shadow of a breeze came from somewhere and ruffled his fine, soft, red hair. 'I don't know. That's the damn thing. I don't *know*. Padge is going in a fortnight and no one's written to me or got in touch with me. I mean, you'd think they'd have said *something*.'

'Well, you know what they're like at Head Office. They've got lots on.'

'Too much to bother with us?' Martin was indignant. 'We work in a Crown office. Who runs it matters.' There was real anger in his voice, and it quite aroused Elaine.

'You'll get it. I know,' she said.

'*You* know, but what do *they* know? I know my job. There's nothing I don't know about running a post office. But oh no, that's not enough any more. Now it's all management training stuff. I hated that seminar in Ipswich. Role-plays. Making business plans. Couldn't think of a word to say.'

To Elaine there was little more exciting than an angry man confessing a weakness. She grasped the remains of her piña colada decisively. 'Look, let's finish our drink, go back via Omar's, get two cod and chips and take them down the harbour. It's a lovely night.'

She watched Martin for a moment. The hairs in his nose needed clipping.

'Kiss me,' she said.

Martin glanced quickly round the garden.

'Not here.'

'No, here.' She pointed to the soft white skin at the bottom of her neck. 'Here.'

She thrust her chin high and pushed herself towards him.

'I still think they should have confirmed it. They would in any other business.' He leaned across and put his lips lightly on the side of her neck. It smelt soapy.

Elaine sighed. 'Be nice if you could do that without having to look round first.'

'I've got to be conscious of my public role. Specially when I'm Manager.'

'It would be nice to have a drink from our own bar in our own living room without having to come out here every Thursday.'

Martin nodded to himself. 'I think I'll contact the union. Check the legal position.'

Elaine reached in her handbag and brought out a bottle of cologne.

'I'm thirty next year, Martin.'

'There must be prior requirement of notification,' he said.

'You know what I mean.' She dabbed the scent below her ears and around her neck. 'Don't you, Martin?'

Martin looked up warily. 'You wouldn't want to be married to an Assistant Manager.'

'No, you're right.' She leaned across and kissed his cheek. 'But I wouldn't mind being married to a Manager.'

Two

By the time Martin got home that night he felt slightly ill. Fish was not Omar's speciality and it was always tainted with a hint of shish kebab. He parked his bike in the shed, let himself into the house, shut the door on the smouldering remains of a sunset and made his way up the stairs. His mother appeared in the hallway, accompanied by the sound of television.

'Is that you?' she called.

'No, it's the Duke of Kent.'

She seemed satisfied and went back into the living room. Kathleen Sproale was approaching sixty. She had a long, sad face, greying hair and deep-set brown eyes. She had been a domestic science teacher at the local girls' school, but when her husband had died, suddenly, nineteen years ago, she had retreated from the world. Now she stayed mainly at the cottage, earning a little from curtain-making and sewing the odd wedding dress.

Martin pushed open the door to his room. Once upon a time he'd thought of locking it but his mother was the only other person who ever went into it and she didn't seem to mind. Elaine had been there once or twice. Her visits had not been a success.

Martin shut the door.

He pulled open his Italian army first-aid cabinet, Milan, circa 1917. He reached along the crowded shelf for a bottle of grappa. He had two of them, but he chose the dark and pungent Amarone. Having poured himself a shot, he raised his glass to the huge black and white photograph, carefully mounted on board, that took up most of one wall from the mantelpiece to the ceiling.

13

'*Salute*, Papa.'

Ernest Hemingway looked back at Martin. He wasn't drinking. He was writing. More accurately, he was pausing in the act of writing. He was standing up, the way he preferred to work. His left arm rested on an angled wooden writing board that lay on top of a chest of drawers with scroll handles. Beneath the lightly clenched fist were several loose sheets of foolscap typewriter paper covered in his handwriting. In his right hand, held just below the waist, he loosely clasped a pencil. He wore a thick check sports shirt with flaps over both breast-pockets. His face was still powerful. It was framed in white, above by wavy hair brushed forward to disguise baldness, and below by a well-trimmed beard, growing with a leftward lean. About the eyes there was a look of age and sadness. Or so it seemed to Martin.

Of the many photographs in his possession (Hemingway with fish, elephants, typewriters, bottles, film stars, children, soldiers, guns, bullfighters) it was the only one in which the Great Man seemed not to be performing or posing. Instead he had the almost deliberately vulnerable gaze of one who wants not so much to be looked at as understood, who is, after a lifetime of running the show himself, appealing to someone out there to witness the reality of what happens when a legend becomes ill and old and lonely. This was why this particular photograph had pride of place in Martin's room. It allowed him in, permitted Martin to feel that he could have been of some use to his hero – not just another onlooker sharing him with the world but, just possibly, the only one who really understood him.

Martin never used to read stories much at school, his talents, such as they were, tending towards the science subjects, and the curriculum tending to keep it that way. He was not good enough at anything to enjoy the camaraderie of sport (though he had been official scorer for the cricket XI) so he had grown to envy the boys who were. They seemed to have more fun. They seemed to know more about everything that was important, like how to make friends. And hardly any of them did science. In his first year in the sixth form he took a decision and enrolled himself on a General Studies course, in which there was an English option.

The book they were given to study was Hemingway's *For Whom the Bell Tolls*. Martin was seventeen. That was when his father died. He was taken out of school for three weeks just as the course was beginning. But he took the book home with him and began to read it and, as he did so, the power of its writing shut out his grief. He followed Robert Jordan across the mountains and valleys of Spain. Jordan's 'red, black, killing' anger was an outlet for the anger Martin felt at his own loss. Hemingway's hero became, for a while, the only man he could trust. From that time on he had devoured everything Hemingway had written: ten novels, over sixty short stories. Then, much later, came the desire to read about the author himself. And in the letters and the thick biographies of Carlos Baker (which he liked) and Kenneth S. Lynn (which he loathed) and those of Myers, Reynolds, Mellow, Anthony Burgess and others he discovered that to all intents and purposes Ernest Hemingway and Robert Jordan were one and the same person. This only increased his appetite for the man.

Meanwhile he began to fill his room with memorabilia. Theston was not a collector's paradise. The best he could find were either replicas – the collection of Hem-style hats behind the door; or approximations – a bullfight poster, Pamplona 1971, genuine but fifty years too late; a Corona Number 3 portable typewriter, not the exact model Hemingway used, but a later one, barely changed. He also acquired a First World War gas mask of Italian design, a billhook (possibly Cuban), a punch bag, a kudu horn trophy, a German army belt of the kind worn by Hem in later life.

'I've made some tea. D'you want a cup?' It was his mother

calling. Reminding him of the rituals of life outside. 'I've put it in the kitchen, Martin!'

Martin shook his head sadly. Tea-drinkers, mothers, post office administrators, would-be fiancées. Little people with little minds. When would they realise that only through confrontation with danger could life be lived to the full? On the other hand he *was* thirsty after all that salt and vinegar.

He finished the grappa, slammed down the glass, threw a punch at the light switch and went out.

'Coming,' he called.

Three

Mr Padgett's 'occasion of importance' came round on a Friday, a dark day of storm warnings and squally showers that set the bowlines cracking against the masts of bobbing yachts and the north cone swinging in the wind outside the coastguard station. More than two hundred people squeezed into Theston church hall. It was mid-September by now and the town had been reclaimed from the summer visitors. The season had been a good one and the shopkeepers and landladies had grumbled at the hours of work, but quietly put away a bit of money, though they would never admit it to each other. So there were a few smiling faces beneath the balloons and the bunting, and conversation was excited by the weather.

A rich voice boomed out behind him. 'Grand turn-out, Sproale.'

It was Lord Muncaster, who didn't often come into the post office, but always turned out at town do's like this, dispensing feudal benevolence though it was no secret that only three months ago he had done a markedly un-feudal business deal, selling his Jacobean house to an Anglo-Saudi insurance company and renting it back from them, right under the nose of English Heritage.

'I must say these are the most damned decent set of people. I mean this is the backbone of England, I honestly think . . .' He gazed out over the throng, his warm and generous eyes watering with the kind of hazy sentimentality that affects only the truly out of touch.

Martin muttered something deferential and moved swiftly away. His main aim was to remain in visual contact with the three visitors from Head Office. He recognised two of them, his local boss and his area boss, but not the third. They stayed in a group together, all three in sober suits, blending uneasily with the heterogeneous town crowd. They were currently making heavy weather of a conversation with Padge, who was coughing badly in the hot smoky atmosphere. It was clear from their faces that none of them knew, or probably cared, what their retiring Manager was saying. Elaine came up and squeezed Martin's hand.

'Ooh, you're hot.'

Martin pulled away sharply.

'Sorry, I didn't mean to surprise you.' She leaned in close. He could smell something on her breath. Something stronger than Bulgarian red or white.

'There's gin in the kitchen,' she whispered. 'I've had some of it. Oh, help! I'm sorry.' Stepping back to gauge the effect of her information she'd snagged her heel in a trouser turn-up and a freshly filled glass of Balkan Cabernet had splashed Alan Randall, the newsagent and confectioner. Randall gave a short angry cry. He was a dapper middle-aged bachelor who looked younger than he was, thanks to hard work and a sun-bed. Appearances were important to him and, though the well-pressed navy blue blazer took the brunt of the spill, a small wine slick was spreading visibly across the dove-grey Terylene on his left thigh.

'I'll fetch a cloth.'

'Salt!' hissed Randall.

Elaine made for the kitchen, hot with embarrassment.

Martin was aware of a throat loudly cleared, followed by a general hushing and shushing. As usually happens in the presence of a large unruly crowd, the message took a while to reach the peripheries of the room. By that time the current Mayor, a builder called Ken Stopping, had heaved back his broad shoulders, adjusted a pair of horn-rimmed glasses and embarked, with the help of an ominous stack of index cards, on a thorough and ponderous eulogy.

'. . . for many years . . .'

'Sssh!' Someone hissed loudly in at the door of the kitchen from which fragments of Elaine's plangent account of the wine incident emerged to vie with Stopping's barely audible bass rumble.

'. . . and I dare say Padge would agree . . .'

'Hear! Hear!' from those who heard, and a little later from those who didn't.

As Stopping carefully picked his way through the career of the retiring Postmaster, a certain restlessness could be observed around the room. No one was really listening. Stopping's remarks were so judicious that he might well have been speaking of anyone over the age of sixty who had lived in Theston all their life. Even Mrs Padgett looked bored. Dr Cardwell, young, keen and once a runner-up in the Suffolk Wine-Taster of the Year competition, yawned shamelessly. Barry Burrell, the vicar, equally young and keen, found himself staring quite hard at the long, well-displayed thighs of Maureen Rawlings, a novelist, recently arrived in the town, as she in turn rose on tiptoe for a better view of the clean-limbed pertness of the youngest of the men from Post Office Headquarters.

Maureen's husband, Quentin, an occasional journalist, tugged at his wildly disordered hair and stared about him sourly. Cuthbert Habershon, the solicitor and district coroner, head thrown back, seemed utterly absorbed in the ceiling, as if seeking divine assurance that his own retirement, now only fourteen weeks away, would not involve a speech from Ken Stopping. At last Martin caught the eye of one of the suits from Head Office, and smiled at him as comfortably and conspiratorially as he thought was appropriate. He certainly didn't want to appear to be assuming anything. He would be ready when the time came. The man, whose hair was greying, smiled back warmly and Martin looked quickly away. He felt the heat and eased himself towards the bar.

Mr Meredith was there, shakily refilling his wine glass.

'I knew his father,' he said, for no particular reason.

At that point there was another outbreak of shushing, and a renewal of interest among those closest to the Mayor.

'. . . garden shed . . . green fingers . . . all of us . . .'

The group broke to one side. Stopping looked anxiously at the door and after a moment that seemed like an eternity, Norman Brownjohn from the hardware store wheeled in the present from the people of Theston – a gleaming new Arcrop Major lightweight alloy barrow containing a hundred pounds worth of garden tools. Not Martin's idea, for he knew Padgett to be a lot less fit than he ever let on. A Zimmer frame might have been more use.

But there was undeniable warmth in the chorus of 'For he's a jolly good fellow', and by the time Padge had been persuaded to speak there were, at last, a few handkerchiefs out.

Padge fought to focus. He breathed in cautiously, didn't cough and felt relieved.

'Well, I don't know what to say . . .' he began.

'First time in your life, Padge!' a woman shouted from the back.

'Ssh!'

'I've been looking forward to this day for forty-eight years, and now it's here I wish it had never happened.'

It seemed as if Padge had surprised himself with that one, and those close to him could see his eyes fill. A low hum of 'aah's suggested appreciation but an implied preference for the jokes.

'Not that I shall be short of things to do. I've got roses –'

'And Rosie's got yours!' came loudly from one of the off-licence crowd. Groans and laughter.

'And I've got my vegetables . . . and I've got Brenda.'

'And in that order!' Brenda Padgett shouted lustily, as the

place dissolved into waves of grateful laughter.

Padge stopped, took a deep breath and went on. 'But there'll be nothing to replace the warmth and friendliness I've met at the post office. On both sides of the counter.'

'Hear! Hear!'

'We get called all sorts of names, especially closing at lunchtime on a Saturday, but I couldn't have had a more hardworking and cheerful staff.'

Martin felt his face burning as heads turned to seek him out. He fiddled with the tablecloth. Padge went on. 'It's been a pleasure and a privilege to be your Postmaster and I wish my successor all the very best.'

The applause seemed to go on and on. Eventually Martin looked up, tentatively, like a soldier after a bombardment, and he caught the eye of the grey-haired man from Head Office who was clapping as enthusiastically as the rest and smiling in his direction.

'Brenda and I will still look forward to seeing you at the post office, only this time we'll be in the queue with the rest of you. Thank you very much!'

After the applause had died down the man who had caught Martin's eye stepped forward. He was of average height and the pinstripe on his well cut suit seemed to suggest a man more at home with executive decisions than retirement parties. He was about Martin's age, mid thirties, but with hair swept back and already greying, he looked older. Martin noted with concern that he had a lazy left eye which didn't appear to focus on anyone. In Martin's delicately anxious state this cast some doubt on the accuracy of the warm smile he'd received earlier. Perhaps it had not been meant for him at all. The man cleared his throat and began.

'Ladies and gentlemen, before we all get on with this wonderful dinner I would like to say a few words on behalf of Post Office Counter Services Limited, and how proud we are to have been Ernie Padgett's employers for so long.'

Martin snorted sarcastically – Padge would have joined the Post Office almost before the man was born. 'My name is Maurice Vickers and I'm the Development Officer for the South-East Region, and I'm sure many of you will be familiar with John Devereux, the Area Co-ordinator.'

Devereux was an older man, built like a tank, with thinning dark hair and crafty little eyes. Not a man to be familiar with, thought Martin, as polite applause trickled away. Hard and uncommunicative in Martin's experience, given the inspections he was wont to spring, unannounced, on the staff at North Square.

'We would like to add our own thanks to those already expressed today,' Maurice Vickers continued. 'Ernest has been a tower of strength here in Theston, and we would like to present him with a token of our appreciation. It's not a gold watch, because that's not the way we do things nowadays, and who wants to watch time pass anyway?'

He motioned to the youngest of his party. He was in his late twenties, blond, lean, agile, well kept. Maureen Rawlings thought him the most beautiful man she'd seen in Theston for a long time. A box was handed over and Vickers continued talking as he removed the top and pulled aside protective tissue paper.

'This is a solid silver replica of our brand new Post Office Counter Services logo, designed in Peterborough, custom moulded in Sweden, and I'm delighted today to be able to present it to you, Ernest Padgett, in recognition of forty-eight years' unbroken service for Theston and the Post Office.'

Devereux and the boy applauded enthusiastically. Ernie Padgett gazed uncertainly at the heavy object, an interesting, if ultimately unsuccessful, attempt to fashion a symbol of power, energy and momentum from the letters POCS.

'Melt it down, Padge!' shouted a voice from the off-licence crowd, for once totally in tune with the feeling of the meeting. A roar of laughter filled the hall. Vickers gave a show of a smile.

There wasn't much else he could do. Martin felt a touch sorry for him. Eventually they calmed down and Vickers adopted a serious manner.

'Now many of you, I know, are worried about the future. You're worried about whether your post office will still have a role to play in a changing world . . .'

Martin moistened his lips. His mouth was very dry.

'Well, I can assure you, the new-look Post Office will certainly not be turning its back on Theston. In fact I can tell you all today that we have plans for Theston, big plans. Plans to create a brighter, faster, more efficient operation, giving all our customers the best in modern communications as we approach the millennium.'

'Half these people won't live to see the millennium,' Mrs Harvey-Wardrell observed piercingly from the back.

'Quite simply we want our customers in Theston to have the best.'

Martin felt a giddy surge of elation arise, unbidden.

'And to show we mean what we say, we are transferring to Theston one of our ablest young men, Nick Marshall.' He indicated the young Adonis beside him. Martin experienced total collapse of the stomach. The words seemed to drift away from him, as if he were watching the whole thing from an enormous distance.

'As your new Manager he will oversee the task of setting up and administering the new office, working closely of course with . . .' and here he consulted his notes for the first time, 'the present Assistant Manager, Martin Sproale, to provide continuity during these exciting times. Believe me, Theston will truly have its part to play in the fast developing future of our network. Thank you.'

Four

The next day was a Saturday and the post office closed at one o'clock. Martin needed not to feel sorry for himself, and after locking up he opted out of the usual lunchtime drink and cycled six miles inland to Arnold Julian's second-hand bookshop in the town of Atcham. Since the announcement he had endured a hell of sympathy, all of it well intentioned, and most of it doing little more than smooth the rough edges of his resentment. Protestations of eternal loyalty had flowed across the post office counter, whilst all that had flowed from area headquarters was a series of faxed instructions advising him of the arrangements for Mr Marshall's arrival on October the first. There was really nothing he could do other than accept the tide of commiseration and prepare for what he was quite certain would be the worst. It was like winning the pools on the day of your execution.

From a distance the familiar two-storey façade of the bookshop looked attractive as ever. The creeper on the walls had turned a blazing scarlet, and a thin plume of smoke spread from one of the chimneys. On closer inspection the premises were less welcoming. The sun-blistered green door was firmly shut. The separate handwritten cards stuck all over the window read like an epic of inhospitality:

Closed
Do Not Lean Bicycles Against the Window
No Free Papers
Stiff Door
Opening Hours: Thursday, Friday, Saturday only
Closed on certain Thursdays

24

Those daunted by such admonitions would not know that the door was almost always unlocked, and that all it required to open it was a shove. A thin bell sounded as it jerked open and, once inside, intrepid customers would invariably find themselves alone for quite some time, surrounded by tall and silent stacks and a slight smell of mould. Two table lamps and a weak bulb on the ceiling augmented what natural light was able to fight its way through windows overgrown with creeper. Arnold Julian would appear minutes later as if from nowhere, a tall, dark, wraith-like presence, whose age could have been anything from fifty-five to a hundred and three. He moved softly and in the gloom it was not always easy to tell what he was wearing besides the habitual black sweater that hung long and low on him like a shroud. Mr Julian never felt the need to initiate a conversation. More often than not he would stand silently by, as if daring the customer to stay in the shop.

The layout was equally unfriendly. Books were not to be found in alphabetical order, and although there had once been a rough attempt to display them by subject matter, it was no longer effective and copies of *Lorna Doone* and *The Battle for Stalingrad* clustered side by side with cookery books in the 'Modern Plays' section.

All this was quite deliberate. It was Arnold Julian's way of screening out poseurs, pseuds and other frivolous dilettantes. Once it had been proved to his satisfaction that he was dealing with a genuine enthusiast all things became possible.

Arnold Julian used to put a selection of his less esoteric books on racks outside the shop, and it was here, years ago when he was beginning to build up his Hemingway collection, that Martin had found a stained and dog-eared copy of *The Green Hills of Africa* which he was able to identify as being one of Scribner's cut-price wartime editions, rare in England. Mr Julian had been so impressed that he had taken Martin to the back of the shop and ferreted out three more titles from the same series.

This morning Mr Julian was apologetic. Nothing much on the book front but a couple of curiosities had come his way: a copy of the *Toronto Daily Star* for 27th January 1923, containing Hemingway's account of his interview with Mussolini, and the autumn 1933 edition of *Esquire* magazine containing Hemingway's piece 'Marlin off the Morro'. Martin was excited. 'Written while he was staying at the Ambos Mundos Hotel.'

Arnold Julian's long, elegant fingers turned the pages carefully. 'That would appear to be the case.'

Martin nodded. 'His first article for *Esquire*, in the first issue of the magazine.'

Julian gazed gravely at the cover. '*Esquire*,' he murmured slowly, as if it was the first time he'd ever said the word. 'Oh well, I suppose he needed the money.'

'He hooked a 750-pounder off Morro Castle. Held it for one and a half hours across eight miles of sea, but it got away. They say it was the inspiration for *The Old Man and the Sea*.' Martin tapped the paper and shook his head admiringly. 'That's quite a rarity.'

'It's not cheap, sadly.'

'Twenty-five?' asked Martin.

'Seventy, I'm afraid. And that's only what I paid for it.'

Martin flushed. The bookseller nodded sympathetically and smoothed down a corner of the magazine. He enjoyed the young man's passion and he knew the limitations of a post office salary.

'I have to look hard for surprises for you. And there aren't any bargains at that level.' He reached up with his left hand and eased a protruding early Victorian edition of *Tristram Shandy* back into place.

'And the *Star*. . . ?'

'Fifty.'

Martin whistled.

Arnold Julian spoke softly without looking at Martin. 'The two of them for a hundred?'

'Well . . . I'll see what I can do. I'll have to think of a way. I'd hoped to have a bit more money to spare, but it looks as if I shall have to wait. Will you hang on to them?'

'I'll do my best.'

Martin nodded his thanks and made quite quickly for the door, to cover his disappointment.

'There is another collector interested.'

Martin stopped, hand on the latch. 'There's someone else?'

'Enquiries have been made. I doubled the price and they went away.'

'What was he after?'

'She. A lady. American. Anything Hemingway.'

'American?'

Julian nodded. 'Unmistakably.'

'Was she going to come back?'

'It was implied.'

'Right. Well. Thank you.'

There wasn't much more he could say. He'd never had a rival, not in this part of the world. Not for Hemingway. Dealers crossed the country for Hardy and Wordsworth and George Orwell and even A. A. Milne, but not the Master. Trust the Americans. As he pedalled home clouds swept in from nowhere and it was raining well before he reached the house.

Papa called them his 'black ass' moods. Deep depressions into which he sank at many times in his life. Martin empathised as best he could but the sad truth was that even on the worst days at the post office, even when he had pensioners queuing out into the street, or even the time he had discovered that the books were two hundred and fifty-three pounds short on balance day, he had never felt a glimmer of 'that gigantic bloody emptiness' that Hemingway had once described in a letter to his fellow writer John Dos Passos. But on this particular Saturday, as the rain blew against his window and the clouds sank lower and greyer over the fields, he was

27

ruefully surprised to find that a feeling of 'black ass'-ness was not far off.

It didn't seem at all fair when he thought about it. His life was unspectacular, he knew that, but he was careful and thorough and conscientious and demanded little of others. Now, suddenly, this was judged not to be enough. He loved Theston post office and he loved Hemingway and now it seemed he had a rival for both of them.

Martin pulled open the door of the old wardrobe that had once stood in his parents' room. He selected one of his two thick American sports shirts, bought direct mail from L. L. Bean of Maine two summers ago. He pulled it on over his vest. It was big and woollen with tortoise-shell buttons and studs at the pocket tops. He tucked as much of it as he could into the top of his trousers, then walked across to the cabinet with the red cross on the front and took out a half-bottle of vodka and, from a cupboard below, a glass and some tonic water. Moving his chair across to the field-table, acquired from a sale of 1950s African safari equipment, he sat down at the Corona Portable Number 3 to write about what he felt. These were the best moments, these moments at the typewriter. With a blank sheet of foolscap and a glass of something strong he knew he was just the way the Master had been, so often.

Martin's hands hovered over the dark, round-headed keys, but his mind was paralysed. Outside he heard the soft croaking call of brent-geese heading for the estuary. He glanced at his watch. Four forty-five. At any moment his mother would call up and tell him tea was ready. As far as his mother was concerned, the day was made up of a series of closely observed times. Breakfast time, lunchtime, teatime, time for a biscuit, time for a bath, time for bed. Perhaps it came from having been a teacher. Or having been married to a postman.

Martin made a superhuman effort to concentrate, closing his eyes and thinking himself on to the hot, breezy porch of the Finca Vigia, Hemingway's home in Cuba, or the grand sitting room of a suite in the Palace Hotel, Madrid, or in a corner of Harry's Bar at the Gritti in Venice, but nothing came into his mind besides the rain on the windows of a warm, sweaty bedroom in Suffolk. He drank some vodka and felt better. Then he concentrated on the typewriter once more and set his mind to recording just how things were with him, clear and spare. The way a writer should.

But now there were voices downstairs, blurred and distracting. He drained the vodka and readjusted the paper in the typewriter and tried again. Nothing happened. There was a fundamental problem. He didn't feel bad any more, because the more he considered how bad he felt, the closer he felt to Papa. The closer he felt, the better he felt, and the less there was to write. He tried once more, but this time he was interrupted by a tentative knock on the door, followed by an equally tentative voice, calling his name.

'Martin? Martin . . . are you there?'

'Who is it?'

'Elaine.'

There had been a time, after she and Martin had become more than just fellow postal officers, that Elaine visited Marsh Cottage regularly. Often she would do no more than sit in the kitchen and drink a coffee with Martin and Kathleen. But sometimes when his mother had settled down to watch television in the front room they would have the kitchen to themselves. Martin would rummage around and produce an ageing bottle of sweet sherry and they'd drink, a little formally at first, and start talking at the same time and then apologising and talking again in odd dislocated phrases until Kathleen came in to make herself a nightcap and it was time for Elaine to go.

It had really begun about eighteen months ago. Jack Blyth, the estate agent's son, had passed his law exams and decided that Elaine Rudge, adoring as she was, wasn't enough to keep him in a place like Theston. He was offered a job at his uncle's law firm in Chester and took the first train out. After a year with one man, Elaine found herself once again looking around. On dull days at the post office she had always felt Martin's presence, but she now began to experience quite a strong physical attraction when he reached across her for a date stamp or a game licence. She was pretty sure he'd never been with a woman. Some of her girlfriends used to giggle about him, as if being thirty-five and still living with his mother could only mean one thing, but Elaine felt there was more to him than that. As soon as she began to show him she was interested she caught him taking sidelong glances at her and accidentally on purpose brushing the tips of her fingers when she handed over her bags of change. He took to reading her their horoscopes in the morning paper. One day he came in with an astrology book which said that people born under their two stars, Capricorn and Libra, were completely incompatible and he'd gone very pink and that had been the first time they had really laughed together.

Nothing happened between them until the evening she was first invited up into his room. It was Easter Monday and they'd spent the day walking the coast path almost as far as Hopton. He'd always maintained that his room was far too much of a mess to take a lady anywhere near but, as they neared Marsh Cottage on the way back, he'd admitted that the real reason was more complicated and that she'd probably laugh at him if he told her. She didn't laugh when she saw the room. She was just relieved he wasn't a train-spotter or a serial killer. What struck her most was that it was the room of a different man from the one she knew. Not someone shy and quiet and hesitant but a man of worldliness and display. He must have had well over a hundred books, many in beautiful hardback editions. Elsewhere there was a harpoon, a stack of jazz records, a typewriter, ashtrays from Parisian cafés, boxing gloves, African masks. On one wall was a huge scarlet and gold bullfight poster. On another was the biggest photograph she'd ever seen of anybody. She had asked him why anyone would want to live in a room with such a sad picture.

Martin had been shy at first, stumblingly trying to explain, but then, to her ever-increasing surprise, he'd brought out a bottle of vodka and poured them both a drink. That calmed him down. He told her who the man was and what he felt about him. She'd never heard Martin talk like that before. They drank more vodka and she slipped off her shoes and curled up on the low sofa, beneath the brooding gaze and swirling cape of the bullfighter, and Martin insisted they drink a toast to every one of the man's novels – all ten of them. This had seemed a pleasantly silly thing to do, but they'd only got through a couple when, without much warning, he came over to her and knelt beside her and smiled and ran his fingers across her face. Then he kissed her, directly on the lips, but with his own lips pressed firmly together. She had opened her mouth to let him in but he seemed uncertain how to proceed.

Nothing daunted, she had pulled herself up to allow room for his arms to go around her but in so doing caught him off balance and he fell to one side, knocking her drink with his hand and spilling vodka across her handbag.

Martin had been mortified and the next day at work the incident wasn't mentioned. Elaine was sad because she would have been perfectly happy for Martin to make love to her, but there seemed no way to say it without sounding cheap and for a while things had been distinctly awkward between them.

A few months after that, at the end of a long summer day of too much sunshine and beer, they'd ended up back again beneath the bullfighter and this time Martin had been attentive and loving, but her pleasure had only increased his pleasure and it was all over before he had his clothes off and he'd gone out of the room, leaving her gazing up into the flashing dark eyes of El Cordobes, and the hot, cruel promise of the Spanish sun. She had driven home soon afterwards.

So their affair remained on the runway, grounded by fog. Elaine let things take their course. She knew he was still attracted to her and sooner or later it would work out. But last night he had left Padge's leaving party without a word and this morning when she'd put a sympathetic hand on his arm, he'd pulled away from her.

'Can I come in?' she asked from the other side of the door.

Martin looked quickly around. There was no time to change anything, but he put away the vodka bottle before answering.

Elaine looked in cautiously.

Martin, so erect and trim at work, seemed to be sagging under the weight of a monstrous grey and red check shirt, which bulged into his trousers. His face was flushed, and he stood awkwardly in front of his old typewriter as if trying to conceal something.

'Were you writing?'

Martin shrugged. 'Nothing much.'

There was a glass beside the typewriter. The sight of it brought back uncomfortable memories. Indeed the whole room seemed oppressive.

'D'you want to go for a drive?' Elaine asked him, as nonchalantly as she could.

'A drive?' he repeated.

'The rain's stopped. Looks like a nice evening.'

She drove them north along the coast, in her old and fast-corroding Fiat Uno. The heavy rain had emptied the usual beauty spots and when they parked up at the Point, midway between Theston and Hopton, they were entirely alone. They sat in the car in silence.

The slate grey clouds had drifted out to sea leaving a jagged, messy, storm-streaked sky. Elaine watched it for a while until she felt it impossible not to say something.

'I had to get you on your own. Just to know what you were thinking.'

Martin was glad he'd taken vodka, rather than scotch or tequila. There was no trace on the breath.

Elaine didn't hurry him. She knew he'd been drinking. Probably vodka as there was no trace on his breath.

'Why didn't you let me talk to you?' she asked.

Martin stared at the sea. He reached forward and flicked open the glove compartment. There were some very old Opal Fruits in there. So old that Elaine didn't offer him one. Eventually Martin spoke, gruffly and reluctantly. 'Nothing to say. I should have got the job. I didn't get the job. It's not the end of the world.'

'It's a rotten thing for them to do.'

'It's happening,' he said. 'It's part of a process, you see. We've got to move with the new technology. All of us, not just me.'

'But this man Marshall. They say he's good.'

'He's probably bloody good. As an undertaker.'

'Meaning what?'

'Oh, come on, Elaine, you know what they're doing all over the country. Licensing off post offices, closing post offices, getting out of expensive premises. Slimming down for privatisation. All that talk about new eras. They're selling out. The days are over when the post office had to have the best place in town. Look at Atcham, they've got an insurance company in the old post office building and the post office franchised out to a sports shop.'

Martin snapped the door of the glove compartment open and shut as he spoke. 'Perhaps we'd better start thinking where *we*'d like to be for the rest of our working lives. How about the back of Brownjohn's, they could squeeze us in between the fertiliser and the plastic buckets? Or maybe round at Omar's. Cod, chips and child benefits.'

'You know . . .' Elaine, pleased to hear him angry, chose her moment carefully. 'There is an alternative.'

Martin grunted scornfully. 'Street cleaning?'

A car sped past, tyres hissing on the shiny wet road.

'You know that Dad wants to retire,' she said.

'Good for him. I'm thinking about it myself.'

A pair of seagulls screeched low over the car, landed on the railings and started to set about each other.

'The point is,' Elaine persisted, 'that he wants the business to stay in the family and, as I'm the only child . . .'

Martin nodded and stayed looking forward, through the rain-spotted windscreen, to the colourless sea.

'The point is . . .' Elaine turned to him and took his hand firmly, as one might take that of an elderly relative, in need of reassurance.

'The point is that his business is mine for the asking. It's not worth a fortune but it's a lot better than working in a post office and . . . and I *would* like to run it, but . . .' Elaine turned to look out of the side window, away from Martin. '. . . it really needs a couple.'

There was a silence.

'Well?' She waited.

'Well . . .'

'It could be a . . . sort of . . . answer to a lot of problems. I mean we'd have to relearn a bit but, you and me, we're good with people. People like us because we talk to them. There'd be no shortage of customers.'

'You mean, give up the post office?'

'Why not? If it's giving you up.'

Martin frowned and flicked again at the door to the glove compartment.

'I can't walk away. I can't have people saying I've no loyalty.'

Elaine was incredulous. 'After what they've done to you?'

Martin nodded. 'I can't let them down, can I?'

Elaine took a deep breath. It had taken a lot out of her to say what she said. She tried to sound unconcerned at the outcome.

'Well, think about it, that's all I say. Think about it. And leave that bloody glove compartment alone!'

Five

October the first came, as it had to, and the staff of Theston post office – Martin, Elaine, Arthur Gillis, John Parr and Shirley Barker the part-time helper – all assembled in the cavernous, empty room that had been a postal sorting office until the Royal Mail separated from Counter Services. Now it was a staff room. There was a kitchen and a lavatory, and a table to eat lunch from. It was here they were to meet their new Manager. It was half past eight on a Monday morning. The office was due to open at nine.

At fifty-five years old, Arthur Gillis was the oldest among them. He was well-built and a little overweight besides, with a big square head, a florid complexion and tight wavy dark hair that was now turned mostly grey. He had joined the Post Office straight from twenty-five years' service in the Ordnance Corps. He'd travelled and let you know it, and his abrupt manner with the public had taken some getting used to, but he was conscientious, efficient and had never been known to have a day's illness. John Parr, on the other hand, was a quick, nervous young man who wore his long fair hair tied in a ponytail. He had a severe and uncontrollable blink. In order, perhaps, to cope with this he had developed an unrelentingly flippant persona. A constant stream of stories, jokes and fantasies poured forth, mostly concerning his huge and long-suffering wife, Cheryl, famous also for being Theston's first traffic warden. Parr's presence was a considerable strain on all of them, but particularly on Shirley Barker, a prim and humourless woman in her early fifties, who appeared to draw all the satisfaction she needed out of life from looking after a dog and two elderly parents. She came in only on Saturday mornings and busy days at Christmas and in the summer.

On this particular morning Elaine had just made coffee and the sound of stirring spoons tinkled softly in the high, empty room.

'*Do* you know . . .' began Parr, but no one ever did, for at that moment Nick Marshall bounded in, like an over-eager family pet that had just learnt to open doors on its own. His face had a ruddy glow, his neatly brushed thatch of rich blond hair bore tell-tale traces of a recent washing. His face was a little too broad to be classically handsome but his features were well shaped and pleasing. Nose straight and strong, mouth wide and purposeful, big round cornflower blue eyes set just too close to each other. He groaned in mock horror and flicked a hand up into his hair.

'*So* sorry, everyone, so sorry. Late on my first day!'

Martin glanced up at the clock. It was less than a minute after half past.

Marshall rubbed his hands together as if it were cold, which it wasn't. 'Have I missed the coffee?'

Elaine, to her own intense surprise, felt herself colouring. She pushed herself quickly away from the table she was leaning on, giving an unintentional impression of brusqueness. 'I'll do another one.'

'Lost my way on the heath,' Marshall explained as Elaine passed him.

'Cycling?' asked Martin.

'Running.'

So that was it. He was a runner. Martin knew there was some reason why he had experienced more than just routine resentment on seeing him. Martin had been a runner too but in the cold winter four years ago he gave it up and never went back. A small defeat, but it still rankled. Cycling was now the only exercise he took.

'Every morning?' he asked Marshall.

Marshall grinned. His teeth were long and regular, if a little too pointed to be perfect. 'Try to,' he said.

'Brave man.'

'I have the runs every morning,' Parr snorted. 'Not your sort though!'

Marshall ignored him, and went on chummily. 'Got to keep the waistline down, you know.' He pulled off an ingenuous smile, as five pairs of eyes swung simultaneously to the firm, flat line of stomach that conspicuously failed to trouble a well-tailored waistband.

He took the mug of coffee from Elaine. 'Thank you –'

'– Elaine,' added Elaine, feeling him hesitate over the name.

'Yes, I know it's Elaine . . .' He held out his hand. 'Elaine Rudge . . . isn't it?'

She took his hand and shook it, feeling a little foolish. It was soft and warm. He moved on.

'And you're Arthur Gillis.'

'Mr Gillis. Yes,' said Arthur. He was a bit of a stickler in these matters, but shook Marshall's hand firmly nonetheless.

There was a spring in Marshall's step, as he moved from one member of staff to the other, that was almost a lope. It lent his movements a vaguely feral quality, so that even in the seemingly innocent ritual of handshakes and eye contacts there lurked a hint of the predatory. He went round all of them, deftly saving Martin for last.

'And Martin, whose reputation I already know.'

Martin smiled warily.

Marshall took a sip of coffee and turned to them.

'I'm Nick Marshall and I'm privileged to be your new Manager. I trained at Bletchley and I was previously Assistant Branch Office Manager in Luton, so you can understand just how happy I am to be here.'

'Do you mind? My probation officer comes from Luton.' John Parr got no help from his colleagues and Marshall barely broke stride.

'This week I just want to get to know you, so if you don't mind, I'm going to be a fly on the wall . . .'

'My wife tried that but the wall fell down.'

'. . . watching how you work, meeting the customers, getting to know the ropes, evaluating the resources we have here. What I would also like to do before Friday is meet with each of you on a one-to-one basis and I'll organise that accordingly.'

Aware that this last piece of information had sown more suspicion than goodwill, he essayed a wide and winning smile that embraced them all. He set down the mug of coffee with the air of one who was not going to pick it up again, and rubbed his hands together once more.

'I can see there is great team spirit here, and I'm proud to be a part of it. Now, let's go to work!' This was followed by another round of firmly clasped handshakes. Then Elaine collected the coffee cups and Martin folded away his newspaper and went through into the main office and began the familiar preparations.

He took out his till and checked it carefully before arranging small change into the hopper beside him. He checked his stock of TV licences and fishing licences and game licences and telephone savings cards and air mail stickers and road tax discs and milk tokens and postal orders and recorded delivery forms and visitors' passports. He put in place next to him his portfolio – the indexed black ledger, its cover layered with the deposits of five years' fingering, in which he kept his own supply of stamps, savings stamps and details of charges. He glanced at the latest Operations Bulletin and made sure his stop-list of missing giro-cheques was up to date. He noted that, as from that morning, the withdrawal period for National Savings Bonds worth over two hundred pounds had been extended to twenty-eight days, and he checked that there was a mailbag ready for parcels in the frame behind him. He reset his date stamp to 1st October and, having checked his watch against the old Newmark electric wall clock, he made his way through to the public area and slid back the bolts on the main door.

Monday was one of their 'queue days'. It was the day for family allowances and there was a steady stream of claimants ranging from harassed single mothers off the twice-daily bus to the brisk and bustling wives of local businessmen. Leading them, as usual, was Harold Meredith, who on this particular morning had come in on the pretext of some query about his disability pension.

As Martin searched for the relevant information, Mr Meredith leaned close and confidingly towards him.

'Here's one you didn't know, Martin. Old Mellor, the Postmaster before Padge, had his own private toilet out the back. I bet you weren't aware of that, old boy. He even had different toilet paper from the rest of the staff. Much softer.'

'I've had a look, Mr Meredith,' said Martin, who sometimes surprised himself with his own patience. 'It's only payable on Wednesdays. All right?'

'Those were the days when they *were* Postmasters. What are they now . . . eh?'

'Managers, Mr Meredith.'

The queue was shifting restlessly.

'Are you a Manager?' Mr Meredith asked him.

'No, I'm not a Manager.'

'Good for you.'

'Mr Marshall is the new Manager.'

'Who?'

'Mr Marshall from Luton.'

'They're calling them marshals now are they?'

'No, he's the Manager. His *name* is Marshall.'

Mr Meredith turned to the queue behind him, as if appealing for sanity.

'It's getting like the Wild West in here.'

At that moment John Parr, wreathed in smoke from a last-minute cigarette, opened his position. There was a wholesale defection from Martin's queue.

John Parr blinked wildly and held up his hands.

'All right! All right! I know I'm beautiful . . . Who's first?'

A slim, striking woman with a dark, vulpine look, a small black cashmere beret and a cigarette, had beaten the rest of the field. She pushed a heavy envelope forward.

'How much is America?' she asked in a voice that was surprisingly deep, almost masculine. And American.

'More than you could afford, darling.'

Parr laughed, uninfectiously. A quick, perplexed smile crossed the woman's face.

He blinked at her. 'Put it on the scales, my love.' Her smile turned to a frown.

Harold Meredith, having lost the bulk of his audience, heaved a sigh at Martin, folded his pension book and tucked it with equal care inside a plastic cover which he then transferred carefully to the inside pocket of his tweed jacket.

'Well, I can't stay here all morning. I've got a job now you know.'

John Parr leaned across. 'Don't tell me. Night club bouncer.'

'Very close, Mr Parr. I'm going to be a church bouncer.'

'I thought they were trying to throw people *into* church, not out of it.'

Harold Meredith shook his head gravely. 'They've had things pilfered, you know. Reverend Burrell's asked me to sit at the back, two hours a day, and keep an eye out.'

The unmistakable tones of Pamela Harvey-Wardrell rose above the general mutterings. 'I only hope this news hasn't reached the criminal fraternity. They'll be bussing them in.'

Mr Meredith knew his time was up. He reached for his walking stick and the tweed cap which he had laid upside down on the counter when talking to Martin.

'Well, I'll be off.'

In the momentary lull following Mr Meredith's departure and the next document being slid across the counter, Martin briefly registered the dark woman at John Parr's position. She was smoking. Very few women smoked at the counter these days and he found himself watching with fascination as she drew heavily on the cigarette, retaining the smoke with effortless confidence. Her concentration was total and, as she waited to be given her change, Martin, too, found himself waiting, riveted, for the moment of exhalation. When at last it came it was a triumph. An imperious flick of the head and the smoke was cast out high and wide, away towards the parcel counter. Martin stared, willing her to take the cigarette up to her mouth again, so he could once more see that long neck turn and elegantly lengthen.

'It's open at the page,' said a quavering voice.

Martin smiled quickly at a tiny headscarved lady staring in at him. 'Sorry, Miss Loyle.' Hettie Loyle was one of a pair of identical twins, both still alive in their eighties. They were like a double act. Their humour was sharp and rather dangerous and they had few real friends in the town.

'Looking at the ladies again, Martin?' she said.

He gave a dismissive grunt of laughter, but coloured all the same.

'You know what we used to say when *I* was young?'

Martin shook his head. 'I wouldn't know, Hettie.'

She flashed a row of perfect teeth. 'Your eyes were popping out like bulldogs' bollocks!'

Martin shook his head. Hettie Loyle laughed happily.

Martin had stamped the counterfoil, handed back the book and was counting out the money when John Parr slid a large brown envelope along the counter.

'Sling it in the bag could you, Mart. Cheryl came over romantic last night and I can't move my back any more.'

'American?' Martin nodded in the direction of the departing customer.

'Yeah, looked like a witch.'

Martin winced. He reached for the packet, and was about to send it swiftly into the grey prison-made polypropylene sack behind him when he caught sight of a printed heading on the address label. In incongruous Gothic script it read, 'The Hemingway Society of New Jersey'.

He turned it over and there, in bold capitals and purple ink, was the name and address of the sender. 'Ruth Kohler, Everend Farm.'

A voice came from behind him. 'Problem, Martin?'

Martin looked up. Nick Marshall was standing there. Martin couldn't be sure how long he'd been there. He had something in his hand that looked suspiciously like a mobile phone.

'Mmm?'

'Problem with the packet? You seemed to be spending a long time with it.'

Martin lobbed the parcel quickly into the sack.

'No, it was . . . American, you know. Don't get many Americans in here.'

'So you thought you'd better check the spelling.'

Marshall smiled and Martin thought it best to laugh.

'Your queue awaits,' Marshall said and patted him professionally on the shoulder.

The next evening Martin was still working at half past six. Tuesday was balance day when post offices across the country checked their stock and their tills at close of business. There was only one personal computer at Theston and Martin and Elaine were the only two qualified to work it. Martin was on his own tonight, apart from Marshall who hovered, checking figures, examining returns and asking a lot of questions. At the end, when the last figures had been fed through, and everything tallied, Martin felt relieved. It hadn't been easy having his new boss there and he'd been all fingers and thumbs on the keyboard. Now suddenly he felt the younger man's hand rest lightly on his shoulder. There was a hint of something like lemon on his skin.

'Martin. . . ?'

'Yes, Mr Marshall.'

'Oh, Nick, please. How's Thursday evening looking for you?'

'Thursday?' Thursday had come to mean only one thing. Elaine at the Pheasant after work.

'Thursday?' Martin repeated lamely.

'For a little chat.'

'Well –'

'I'll pick you up after work. We'll go somewhere for a beer or two. D'you know the Pheasant Inn? I'm told it's the nearest thing round here to a decent country pub. We can sit outside. Enjoy the Indian summer.'

'Well, why did you have to say yes?' asked Elaine.

'It was *his* suggestion.'

The next day, Wednesday, Elaine had persuaded Martin to take a walk with her in the lunch hour. There was a quick, licking wind as they crossed the square. The heavy grey storm clouds had passed over and the sunbeams fell from behind them like bands of rain.

'You could have said you were doing something on Thursday,' she said reprovingly.

'He doesn't give you time to explain.'

They turned and walked in the direction of the church.

'And why can't he talk to you at work, like he does the rest of us?'

This was news to Martin. 'Has he talked to you, then?'

'Yes. And he's nothing to say. Afternoon, Miss Loyle.'

Viv Loyle was, marginally, the more eccentric of the Loyle twins. She was a regular churchgoer, but didn't mind which church she went to. One week she would turn up among the Methodists, the next the Catholics. She had even been known to go by Super-Saver to the mosque at Bedford, to make her simple point that God was not petty-minded.

'And how is the most handsome couple in Theston?' she enquired, playfully.

'Just good friends, Miss Loyle.' It was Elaine's regular riposte and was more than usually curt today. Viv Loyle gave a shriek of laughter, wagged a finger and stepped off the pavement into the path of a delivery lorry. There was a screech of brakes, nothing new in Theston. Lettuces scattered across the road.

'When did he talk to you then ?' Martin asked Elaine.

'Yesterday afternoon some time.'

'You never told me that.'

'I was going to tell you tomorrow night,' she said. 'When we went to the Pheasant.'

'Well, I'm sorry.'

Elaine seemed about to say something, but she stopped and shook her head. A largish middle-aged woman, her Puffa jacket inflated to Michelin size by the wind, blew along the pavement towards them.

'Hello, Elaine! Hello, Martin!' she trilled.

'Hello, May,' called Elaine. 'How's *Mr* Pimlott?'

'No better. He has to be turned twice a night.'

'Oh, poor man.'

'Poor man! *We*'ll be in the grave before him. Bye!'

The wind blew harder by the church and Elaine held the hair out of her eyes as she stopped and turned.

'Martin?' she said. 'Can I ask you something?'

Martin dug his hands deep in his anorak pockets.

'Do you love me?' she asked.

He kicked out. A small stone shot across the road.

'There's so much going on at the moment, Elaine.'

'Not between you and me there isn't.'

'Look . . .'

She interrupted him. 'There's no future at that post office, Martin. Marshall's only interested in himself. He doesn't care for people like us. We're dispensable. He just wants to get the most out of us and if he doesn't get what he wants he'll find someone else. Mark my words.'

They were out of the wind now but her eyes were still watering. She turned away from him and, reaching in her bag, drew out a purple tissue and blew her nose into it. She took a deep breath and turned to face him.

'Just remember what I said to you the other day, Martin. In the car.'

Six

It was Thursday. Martin had felt uncomfortable all day. Even physically uncomfortable. He couldn't face his sandwiches, which was quite unlike him. Women were beyond him. He'd combed the Master's works to try and find some clue to Elaine's behaviour. But none of Hemingway's women fitted Elaine.

He had to admit that Papa could be strange and brusque and bullying with women (as he could be with men). He liked them either mysterious and witty or loyal and submissive, and Elaine would have failed on both counts.

'Ready?'

It was a quarter to six. The day's work was done and Nick Marshall was holding open the back door of the post office whilst Martin fiddled around with his briefcase.

'You won't need that,' Nick assured him.

'Can you drop me back here? For the bike?'

'Of course, I've got to get back for a meeting anyway.'

'Oh?'

Marshall grinned quickly and pulled back his shoulders. 'Trying to drum up more business.'

As he settled nervously into the figure-hugging front seat of Marshall's Toyota Carina, Martin had to admit to a certain buzz of excitement. On a Manager's salary, which he knew well enough to be sixteen thousand one hundred and fifty pounds a year, the man seemed to live like a king. There was even a car telephone. In addition to his mobile. A bottle of champagne was adrift on the back seat.

Martin slowly relaxed and watched the seaside boarding

houses give way to the new estates and then to the farms and then to the close, dark woods. He was struck by a new and quite unfamiliar sensation. He felt important.

'Where d'you like to sit?'

'Anywhere'll do,' said Martin. It was too cold to sit outside.

Marshall, two pints in hand, led him to a corner table in what was the old snug bar, which Ron Oakes had now carpeted, curtained, hung with stuffed birds and renamed the Hatchery. Martin had often shared this same table with Elaine.

'You and Elaine are an item, then?'

Martin frowned for a moment, then blushed in surprise. 'Oh . . . well, yes we . . . er . . .'

Nick Marshall tugged his neck muscles tight. 'I clocked you at lunchtime. Yesterday, taking a walk. You're well in there, Martin. I could think of worse people to sit next to all day. Cheers!'

He smiled appreciatively and raised his glass. Martin did too, wondering, as he did so, where Marshall had seen them from and, more to the point, what he had seen.

Nick Marshall set down his glass and looked squarely at Martin. 'Are you happy with the way things are?'

Martin shifted uncomfortably. He made a noise which he hoped would suggest he was thinking hard.

'At the post office.' Marshall went on.

'At the post office?'

'Where you work,' Marshall added helpfully. 'Are there any things you'd like to change?'

Martin experienced intimations of panic. He couldn't at that moment think of how to reply to the question. Or indeed why he'd been asked it in the first place. He recovered a little and opted for caution. 'Well, I think possibly we're a little traditional.'

Marshall looked pleased. He pulled his chair closer, leaning forward expectantly, one arm upright on the table, elbow bent

48

at a right angle. With his head thrust forward, Martin thought he resembled one of the gargoyles on Theston church. 'Martin,' he asked, 'why did you join the Post Office?'

The truth was that Martin had joined because he felt he owed it to his mother to stay in the area after his father died. And there had been no other jobs. 'Because it had a future,' he said, hoping it would sound convincing.

To his relief Marshall nodded enthusiastically. 'Exactly! You joined because you could see the potential. You didn't join to sit selling stamps in the back of someone else's shop.'

Martin was happy to hear this. 'It's happening a lot round here. Franchising,' he said.

'Well, it's going to be different at Theston. This is where the Post Office is going to show what it can do.'

'I'm glad to hear that, Mr Marshall,' said Martin.

'Nick,' replied Nick Marshall, expansively.

'I'm glad to hear that, Nick,' repeated Martin.

'I mean, what are we talking about here?' enthused Nick Marshall. 'The Post Office is part of national life. Part of our national identity. It's our legacy and I'm damned if I'll sit back and see it kicked around like the railways, the coalmines and shipbuilding.'

Martin had rarely, if ever, felt excited about his work. It wasn't one of those emotions you associated with working at a post office. But now he could actually feel his heart beating a tiny touch faster. Like everyone at the Theston office, and as far as he could tell everyone else in the union too, he had sat there like a rabbit in car headlights as the split-up of the Post Office had gone on. The telephone service hived off. Royal Mail split from Parcels, then Royal Mail and Parcels split from Counter Services, and they'd all meekly accepted it. Franchises and rural closures had followed and they'd meekly accepted them too. They'd lived off everyone else's bad news, shutting their eyes to the fact that it could one day be theirs as well.

Martin took a long mouthful of beer and set down his glass. 'A man can be destroyed but never defeated,' he declared.

Nick Marshall looked mystified.

'Ernest Hemingway,' explained Martin. '*The Old Man and the Sea.*'

Marshall's eyes narrowed, then lit up. 'Ah! Humphrey Bogart?'

Martin shook his head. 'Spencer Tracy.'

'That's the one. It was on television. About a month ago. That line wasn't in it.'

Martin bought himself another pint. Marshall refused on the grounds that he was driving, but Martin concluded that he didn't much like beer, and he'd taken the trouble to come all the way out to Braddenham to put Martin at his ease.

They drove back along the narrow lanes. At one point a pheasant clattered, panic-stricken and screeching, from the hedgerow ahead of them. Marshall put his foot down but the bird flapped out of danger and away over into the field.

'Damn!' said Marshall. 'Missed a good supper.'

It was almost half past seven when they pulled up in North Square. Nick Marshall switched off his headlights, but kept the engine running.

He turned to Martin who sat awkwardly in the front seat, his anorak trapped in the door. Nick flexed his slim, powerful shoulders. 'I've enjoyed our talk. There's a lot of similarities between us, you know. We're keen, we're young still. We want to get things done.'

Martin plucked helplessly at the hem of his coat.

Marshall nodded across at the brick and stone bulk of the post office, turned back and confronted Martin. 'Let's face it. We both bloody know that should be the centre of the town. That's why they put it there in the first place. We've got to make sure it stays that way, eh?' As Marshall spoke, a minor series of convulsions seemed to affect the right-hand corner of his mouth as if there were some fundamental tension between his thoughts and his words.

'I'll go along with that. Oh yes,' Martin replied, not liking to stare.

Marshall put his hand out. He appeared to have the mouth problem under control. Martin shook his hand, awkwardly.

'Good man. I can't do much without your help.'

Martin felt his self-confidence growing. 'Count on it,' he said. The perfect parting line, he thought, except that when he went for the door handle he stuck his fingers in an ashtray.

'It's the one underneath.'

'Oh! Right. Thank you. And thanks for the drink.' Martin squeezed the door handle.

'No, pull it down.'

'Ah!' Martin laughed desperately. He tugged at the door.

'You've got your elbow on the window lock. Now try.'

Martin was hot, but the air was cool when he eventually got out of the car. When Marshall had driven off he stood and looked across at the building in which he'd spent half his life. Marsh Cottage, windswept and isolated, was a place he would always associate with his father's illness and death. North Square was home.

Seven

Ruth Kohler curled her feet around the leg of the old kitchen table, its surface lightly corrugated by decades of washing and scrubbing, and read what she had written.

Dear Beth and Suzy,

    The countryside here is very beautiful, though large swathes of it lie in my log basket (my English is coming on, don't you think?) waiting to keep me alive. It's only October but I have already consumed two small woods. You might have thought central heating, like family planning, was pretty much a universal item in the First World, but I assure you it has not reached Everend Farm Cottage. Indeed the twentieth century as a whole has not made much impact on Everend Farm Cottage. Electricity is coaxed nervously in through a hole in the wall, a 'Calor-gas' boiler explodes with atomic force, brighter than a thousand suns one minute, a black hole the next. There is a telephone up at the farm, and I guess the nearest fax machine is in Paris. How romantic, I hear you say, and you're probably right. Hemingway would doubtless have written his best work here, and the bird life is wonderful. Duck, partridge, pheasant. Everything he liked to kill.

    I have spent most of the last three weeks on a title. *The Hemingway Project* is a good name for a grant application, but a bummer for a book. I finally came up with one I like. *Admiring Ernest*. It's from Dashiell Hammett's line about him, you know the one – 'Ernest has never been able to write a woman. He only puts them in books to admire him.'

    It may sound a tad playful for a university press so I'll have to attach some suitably dry subtitle: *Admiring Ernest: Contradictions, Correlations and Gender Roles in the Life and*

Work of E. H., that sort of thing.

What do you think? I like it. It has fashionable irony and hopefully will lull those macho reviewers into a false sense of security. Reviewers? Who am I kidding?!

I bought a car! Nothing exotic. It's called a Cherry (no wonder they don't sell them in Trenton!) despite being bright yellow. It's perky and has a funny little thing called a gear-stick! The countryside is very gentle and not at all impressive until you get to the sea which, I'm told, is eating up the land at the rate of a foot a year. Nice to know that, by the time I leave, England will be a foot shorter! There are villages hidden away all over the place, and the nearest town is Theston. Untidy but everyone very friendly. The church is *beautiful* and ancient and has a rood-screen that's older than Atlantis and I'm quite seriously thinking of believing in God again. Well, at least for a year.

What more can I tell you ? My little laptop sits in the alcove (south-facing) winking at me greenly. There are cats up at the farm, and one fat marmalade fellow has been eyeing me up with a view to making friends. I am trying to encourage things to grow inside the house as fast as they grow outside but my green fingers have turned blue in the cold and I may have to lure in a hawthorn hedge or the corner of a sugar-beet field. As to human contact, well, not a lot yet. Mr Wellbeing (sic!) the farmer is pure Thomas Hardy and barely comprehensible. His wife a bit of a dragon. I shall have to make an effort to MIX, won't I?

> Missing you, and everyone.
> Never-ending Love from Everend,
> Ruthie.

She took a sip of coffee. It was lukewarm. She didn't like it lukewarm and she didn't like drinking it on her own. Coffee break at the English faculty was when everyone got together and grumbled about funds and gossiped about absent colleagues. It was a noisy sociable time, as opposed to classes, which were just noisy. Here she drank in silence, which was beginning to be much less attractive than she had expected. A cottage in England had always featured in her dreams of contentment but at this precise moment she would have exchanged all the green fields and oak-fringed lanes of Suffolk for an hour in Quakerbridge Shopping Mall.

Ruth shared a house in uptown Trenton with Suzy Weiss and Beth Lucas, one a fellow Assistant Professor, the other a TV weather-girl. Her apartment was known affectionately as the Jungle, on account of Ruth's propensity for plants that crawled, climbed, entwined and otherwise romped about the place.

When she was in it, it seemed quite ordinary. Convenient for the faculty but close to the city. The generous expanse of stripped pine floor and tall south-facing windows only just made up for the dust and noise from the traffic below.

Still, it was hers now. And hers alone. No longer rented. Why then had she left so soon after buying it? Because she prided herself on being a free spirit, belonging to no one, and the idea of a sabbatical year in Europe was a way of proving it?

She stood up purposefully, hummed to herself, and went out of the small, brick-floored kitchen and into the leathery low-beamed parlour. She hadn't lit a fire, and the room, with its barely detectable, omnipresent whiff of damp, was not yet welcoming. She crossed to the desk at which she worked, a scrubbed pine bargain which she had bought at a local antique shop, and switched on the radio. Some gloomy piece of Mahler droned into the room. She tried the talk radio, but it was a phone-in about death. She switched the radio off, reached for an envelope, addressed it, stamped it, sealed her letter inside and reached for a cigarette.

Besides these occasional bouts of homesickness there was another reason why she felt so irritatingly out of sorts. It was to do with her work. Hemingway's women, her chosen field of study, did not seem particularly relevant to rural England. Hemingway, Anglophile though he might have been, liked to meet his English friends as far away from England as possible.

Though he had created many memorable English characters, they were always to be found in France or Italy or Spain or Africa. The England of winding lanes and pubs and tea-shops was too cosy for Mr H. As she lit up, inhaled gratefully and flicked out the match, she could not help thinking that perhaps this whole adventure had been a mistake and that she should have taken her year off in Paris or Venice or even Havana. Anywhere but this pretty, passionless place.

Eight

'I don't like all this,' complained Harold Meredith. He tapped on the double-strength shatter-proof glass of the anti-bandit screen. 'Can you hear me in there?'

' 'fraid so, Mr Meredith,' Martin assured him.

In less than a month since Nick Marshall's appointment the first signs of change had appeared at Theston post office. Already the old-style weighing machines had gone, replaced by digital scales which gave exact weight and cost almost instantly. Bar-codes were appearing on everything from recorded delivery forms to pension books, and Marshall had introduced decoders, speeding up transactions and saving time at the stock-taking end of the day. Now a brand new counter-to-ceiling security screen had replaced its scratched and yellowing predecessor.

Martin was cautiously approving. For all his initial reservations, he was flattered that Marshall saw him as an ally in his fight to improve Theston's status. It was a refreshing change from the years with Padge who moaned and grumbled but had stoutly refused to join the union or reply to any of the questionnaires they sent out.

All Martin wanted was for those at the top to stop fiddling around with a system that worked perfectly well, to stop treating the Post Office as a political football and to accept that it was, as Marshall had said, 'part of national life' and would stay that way for a long, long time.

'How am I going to give you the book?' asked Harold Meredith.

'Just drop it down in the tray.'

'I can't, there's something over it.'

'I'm going to move that for you.' Martin slid back the protective cover. 'There you are.'

Reluctantly, as if parting from a loved one for the last time, Mr Meredith let his pension book slip down into the stainless-steel retainer. Martin slid back the cover, almost catching Meredith's still-outstretched hand.

'Is this because of Aids?' Meredith stared enquiringly up at him.

Martin swiftly passed his checker over the bar-code. It pinged appreciatively.

'No, no, it's just to make us feel a little bit safer.'

'Who from?'

'Blood-crazed pensioners, Mr Meredith,' called out John Parr, leaning over. 'People with a score to settle.'

Martin cast his eye over the docket for date and signature. Harold Meredith watched suspiciously.

'It's this new man, isn't it?'

Martin reached for his wooden-handled date stamp and thumped it down, first on the docket and then on the counterfoil. Since Marshall had told him of digital scanners that could read a pension card, check details on a database, mark the transaction and automatically count out the sum to be paid, Martin had been unusually sensitive to the laboriousness of the process.

'Armed raids on post offices increased twenty-five per cent last year, Mr Meredith.'

He tore the docket from the counterfoil and, sliding open the till at his right-hand side, began to count out the money.

'How many armed raids did you have in Theston?' asked Mr Meredith.

'That's not the point.' Martin laid a fifty-pound note, three five-pound notes and ninety pence into the tray together with the book. 'It could happen any time.' He slid the cover back.

'What do I do now?' asked Meredith.

'Take the money.'

'Is it electrocuted?'

'Only the fifty-pound note.'

'I don't want a fifty-pound note. What am I going to do with a fifty-pound note?'

Martin withdrew the note wearily. 'It makes it easier for us, that's all.'

Martin replaced the note with a twenty, two tens and two fives.

'What would I do with a fifty-pound note, old boy? I'm too old to buy wedding rings.' He chortled with laughter. 'Eh?'

Martin gave a weak smile. 'My mind was elsewhere.'

'What? I can't hear you through this thing.'

John Parr watched him go. He grinned. Martin clipped the fifty-pound note back with the others and slid his till shut. John Parr sniffed, twitched, blinked and leaned across to him. 'Now you know why they put those screens up, Mart. It's to stop *us* shooting the customers.'

Nine

After much persistence Ruth had felt the first flickerings of a friendship with Mrs Wellbeing. It turned out her name was Rose. She'd married Ted Wellbeing quite late in life after nursing him through a long illness. Ruth had begun by regarding her as prudish and censorious and Rose, as it turned out, had jumped to the conclusion that Ruth must have been a scarlet woman, hiding out from some scandalous love affair. The shared relief in finding each other wrong helped them to a sort of friendship. Rose Wellbeing determined that Ruth should meet someone. She didn't think it was right that an attractive thirty-five-year-old should still be unattached. She began by bringing her the local paper with interesting events ringed. These included folk evenings and dressmaking classes and even Mothers' Union meetings: 'You could *say* you were a mother.' Ruth resisted, as politely as she could.

Theston Fair seemed the perfect answer. By ancient tradition the first Saturday in November was set aside for this annual festival which celebrated Queen Victoria's granting of a borough charter in November 1893. As this year was centenary year it was to be celebrated with even greater enthusiasm than usual. It was, Rose assured her, an occasion not to be missed, one that would offer Ruth a chance to observe the locals without being too conspicuous. Even so, she woke up on the appointed day feeling apprehensive. As she selected an outfit she realised that although she had many friends back in America, she hadn't had to make them. They mostly came with the job. And they were nearly all women. She was not entirely comfortable with men. They were so unpredictable. Friends, pals and buddies one minute and urgent, demanding appetites the next. Her analyst told her this was as much to do with her as them, that her equally demanding appetites led her unerringly to the wrong men.

She smiled at this thought as she checked herself in the bathroom mirror. Dark, olive skin (mother's side), hair black and thick, bunched back over her ears and desperately needing attention, eyes deep green and staring back at her with a disturbing intensity, nose narrow and rugged like a headland running down into the sea, mouth wide, lips thin, chin rather fine (father's side). Neck average and unremarkable, shoulders carrying on where the face left off, angular and rocky, breasts slim and neat and even. Sometimes it excited her, this dark and secretive body, but most of the time she saw it as something to be covered quickly. To be unloaded away from bright light, like exposed film.

A couple of hours later, she was in Theston. Wearing her black beret and black boots and a baseball jacket over freshly ironed black Levi's, she locked up the yellow Cherry in the temporary car park on Victoria Hill, and made her way towards the festivities.

Everyone in Theston, or so it seemed, either visited or worked at the Fair. Stalls selling everything from railway signs to organic cheeses sprouted along the pavements of High Street and Market Street. There were sideshows along the sea front. There was a fairground in Jubilee Park and kite-flying competitions on Victoria Hill.

Quentin Rawlings, who had once been a Reuter's man in Paris, and whose published work was now confined to short, angry pieces in the *East Suffolk Advertiser*, could be seen in the garden of his overgrown Victorian house, clad in beret and Breton fisherman's sweater, running the *boulodrome* and celebrating what he called a day of Gallic Xenophobia.

Alan Randall, purveyor, by his own admission, of the last remaining hand-made chocolates in Theston, provided the Punch and Judy show. This year he was engaged in a fierce wrangle with the Blood Transfusion Service, who had seen fit to park their trailer in the school playground, which he regarded as his own private auditorium.

The Sea Scouts gave resuscitation displays in the church hall and there was an Army recruiting caravan in the British Home Stores car park.

At the church of St Michael and All Angels, Barry Burrell, the vicar, left Harold Meredith to guard its priceless collection of fourteenth-century treasures (plate, chalice, both mentioned in Pevsner along with the rood-screen), whilst he threw himself into organising the Cricketing Christians, who traditionally played forty overs of beach cricket come rain or shine, with trusties from the local prison.

But North Square remained the nucleus of the day's activities. Here were located the prime sites occupied by the most celebrated businesses – the Rudges' nearly-new clothes stall; Dr and Mrs Cardwell's home-made wine kiosk; and Maureen Rawlings's Spice Bazaar.

A stage had been set up at the bottom of the post office steps where a jazz band played during the day and the Keith Stackpole Experience played by night. It was towards this throbbing centre that Ruth Kohler was remorselessly drawn.

What was happening around her seemed most un-English. Everyone appeared to be talking to each other. Despite the cold, grey weather, the atmosphere of jollity and involvement was pervasive and yet she had no idea how to connect with it all. She would have given anything for a quick Bloody Mary, but the pubs she passed were full of noisy male laughter and didn't seem welcoming, so she settled for a coffee instead. She was looking hesitantly in at the door of the Theston Tea Shoppe, when she heard a voice.

'Are you going in?'

She turned to see who had spoken and found herself face to face with a youngish man, pale-skinned, with soft reddish hair and a round, unmemorable face. He was breathless and quite pink. She apologised and moved to one side.

'I'm sorry. I can't seem to make up my mind.'

His pinkness deepened, alarmingly, leaving Ruth to assume some unintentional gaffe on her part.

'You were in the post office?' he blurted out.

'Yes, I . . . er . . . I've been to the post office,' she admitted.

'I work there.'

'Oh really.'

'Yes . . . Behind the counter.'

'Ah.'

This was a conversation he seemed to need more than she did, but it was the only one on offer so Ruth stayed with it as best she could.

'I like English post offices, they're kind of relaxed.'

'They certainly are in a town like this. We get to know everyone. They all know us.'

There was a pause. Unlike an English post office, the man who had accosted her seemed far from relaxed. He ran his tongue over his lips, wrinkled his nose and threw darting glances off into the crowd. He gave off a sense of thwarted intimacy and it occurred to her that he might have mistaken her for someone else.

'Are you looking for somebody?'

'Me? Oh . . . er . . . no, I just have to take something to those friends over there.'

'Well, look, don't let me hold you up.'

Ruth smiled, broke eye contact and turned away. This seemed to precipitate him into some sort of decision. He took a deep breath.

'I saw an address on your envelope.'

Ruth turned. She felt a rising of the defences.

'I couldn't help noticing the name,' he explained.

'The name?'

'I know it's unprofessional and all that, but it caught my eye.'

'Well, it may be an odd name in England, but it's pretty common in America.'

'No . . . no . . . not *your* name.'

At that moment a short, wiry man wearing an old woollen cap approached from across the square, calling out as he came, 'How about that coffee, Martin? I've been out here since eight.'

The younger man leapt as if stung. 'Coming, Frank.' He darted away into the shop. The older man eyed Ruth with unapologetic interest and held out his hand.

'Frank Rudge.'

His hand was powerful. His fingers were thick and his skin was rough and hard as the bark of a tree.

'Ruth Kohler,' she said.

'American?'

She nodded.

'On holiday?'

'Working over here for a year.'

'In *Theston*?'

'Not far away. I've taken a cottage at Everend Farm.'

'Whatever for?'

'I've a book to write.' She smiled. 'Don't want any distractions.'

'What sort of book is it?'

'It's about Ernest Hemingway.'

Rudge frowned.

'The writer,' she added. 'And the women in his life.'

A sudden, wide grin broke across Frank Rudge's face, sending his lined and leathery skin in a mass of directions.

'Should write about me next.' He laughed, though there was a hint of seriousness in there somewhere.

At that moment the man Ruth had been talking to emerged from the crowded café clutching two polystyrene cups.

'Sorry, Frank.'

Frank smiled benevolently. 'You needn't have hurried.'

He nodded towards Ruth. 'Ruth's living at Everend for a year. Come over here to write a book about Hemingway and his women. I'll take the coffees.'

Despite her protest Martin also bought a coffee for Ruth. As she seemed lost, he took her across North Square to see the Rudges' stall and he introduced her to the family.

The friendship between the Sproales and the Rudges had begun nineteen years ago when Martin's father died. At that time Frank Rudge was running the Theston branch of the Suffolk Eagles, a charitable organisation which raised money for local projects. They had been generous with help and support for the family and Frank still saw it as his business to keep an eye on Kathleen and Martin. He'd always had a soft spot for Martin's mother. He had tried to persuade her to move back into Theston, but now he knew her better he respected her wish to be left alone.

Elaine had known Martin since she was eleven and, though he would never admit it, Frank took quiet pleasure in the fact that they were now seeing each other.

Martin introduced Ruth, a little awkwardly. Joan Rudge was the way she was with everybody – direct and blunt and unconcealed. She said she'd never heard of Ernest Hemingway, and asked if he was a golfer. She then embarked on the story of her best friend's holiday in Florida, which Frank interrupted with brutal swiftness. He pointed out that the last thing Ruth wanted to hear about was the country she'd just left, and what she needed to know a little more about was Britain's glorious heritage.

The inside of a typical English pub seemed to him the perfect place to start learning. Leaving his wife and daughter to mind the stall, he led Ruth and Martin down Market Street in the direction of the Codrington Arms.

It was midday by now and the carnival procession had begun

to wend its way through the town. To cross the road Frank, Ruth and Martin were obliged to dodge in and out of slowly moving floats upon which shaky tableaux portrayed the great moments of Theston's history.

These had been remarkably few and, though Theston High School's headmaster had creatively embellished the record with bogus sea-battles, fires, plagues, murders and visits from Winston Churchill, much of the historical slack had been taken up by the big companies. Miss NatWest Bank and the Prudential Story gratefully plugged any gaps in the historical imagination.

All the set pieces were greeted with equal enthusiasm. Proud mothers waved at children dressed as pirates and embarrassed younger brothers wolf-whistled at sisters in fishnet tights pretending to be mermaids. It was noisy, chaotic, bizarre and somehow all very innocent.

Frank elbowed his way through the crowd to the door of the Codrington Arms. Here his way was barred by Gordon Parrish, a long- serving waiter at the Market Hotel. He was dressed in a long white satin dress, gold sling-backs, false nose and a shoulder- length wig of sleek black hair.

'My God, who have we here?' asked Frank as he pushed by.

'Barbara Streisand,' Gordon said icily. 'The diva.' He produced a collecting tin.

'Not the word I'd have used,' muttered Frank, but he searched in his pocket and dropped a pound piece into Gordon's tin.

'It's for the sailors,' said Gordon with a fluttering of eye-lashes.

'He used to be a merchant seaman,' Frank called to Ruth as they passed on in.

The main saloon bar was packed. There were men dressed as carrots and policewomen in miniskirts and Father Neptune and his six watery cohorts, downing final pints before climbing aboard the P & O Ferries display.

'The English pub is one of the glories of this country,' Frank Rudge intoned as a body slumped to Ruth's feet at the end of the bar, but no one could hear him anyway and he moved them through the crowd into a back bar which was quieter.

The first person they saw there was John Parr. He seemed to be the only person in Theston who was drinking alone. On seeing them he nodded quickly and drained his glass.

'Well, well, half the bloody post office is in here,' Frank observed, adding mischievously, 'I haven't seen Mr Marshall, but I think he prefers the wine bar. You seen your pal today, Martin?'

Martin spread his arms. 'New boss,' he explained to Ruth. 'Doesn't drink beer.'

Frank Rudge turned to her. 'Should have heard the fuss when he was appointed.' He winked at Martin. 'Now they're bosom pals.'

'He could have been worse.' Martin turned to John Parr. 'Isn't that true, John?'

Parr stubbed out his cigarette. 'I'm off,' he mumbled.

'Oh come on, John!' Martin took him firmly by the arm and led him back to the bar. 'Day off tomorrow.'

John Parr shook his arm free. He blinked fiercely and rapidly. 'I'm not going to be short of days off, thanks, Martin.'

There was venom in the delivery and Frank and Ruth both turned.

Martin looked hurt, but mainly mystified. 'What's the matter, John?'

John Parr snorted derisively. 'You trying to pretend you don't know?'

'Know what?'

John Parr looked at Martin, narrowing his eyes then laughing grimly. He headed for the door.

'The Boy Wonder thinks we're overstaffed.' John Parr pulled the door open. The sound of loud cheers and raucous laughter swept in from the saloon. He reached into his jacket and produced a letter which bore a familiar heading. He waved it at Martin.

'At least they used the Royal Mail to tell me.'

Ten

The streets of Theston were swept clean. The carnival floats stood in car parks and back yards waiting to be dismantled. Only the strands of coloured lights in North Square remained to be taken down. The town was weary and mostly still asleep. There were scattered signs of life, early-morning dog walkers, sea-anglers packing up after the night's vigil, a visitor or two collecting the Sunday papers. They were rewarded with an unusually appealing early winter's morning. The sun shone low through a veil of high cloud, mist drifted off the marsh and the air was still and cool.

Martin Sproale had also risen early. He had business to do in Theston and despite it being a Sunday he had set off from Marsh Cottage not much later than on a normal working day. He was standing now in Jubilee Park, watching a tennis match.

Only two of the half-dozen courts were occupied. On one of them a young couple warmed up with desultory shots and frequent apologies, but at another a full-blooded battle was nearing its conclusion. Nick Marshall was serving to a young woman wearing a light grey tracksuit. Despite being considerably smaller than him, five foot two or three, she could have been mistaken for a sister. Her face was a little plumper and her nose short and tilted slightly upwards. But she had the same fair hair, cut short and dampened now with sweat. She was playing with quiet, watchful energy. Marshall, all in white save for a blue and yellow shoulder flash on his tennis shirt, served, making himself grunt with the effort. The first serve was low and deep and the ball kicked and spun away, unreturned.

'Fifteen love,' he called. The next serve his opponent

returned well. Her shot skimmed the net but Marshall was up there and waiting and he volleyed it away to the far side of the court.

'Thirty love!' called Marshall, with the increasing relish of one who liked to hear the score, especially at times like this.

On the third point he served into the net, bitterly reproached himself and delivered a second serve that was hard down the centre line.

'Forty love! Match point . . .'

His opponent settled herself on the line, then crouched forward and waited with admirable patience as Marshall bent low, leg outstretched like a ballet dancer. He paused interminably then slowly uncoiled himself, tossed up the ball, twisted with whippet-like grace and struck a third and final ace.

He clenched his fist, punched the air and made for the door of the court, bobbing up the two remaining balls with his racquet as he went.

Martin watched all this from the shelter which people used as a makeshift changing room. As Marshall came off the court, Martin took a deep breath, removed his bobble hat and stepped forward.

'Nick?'

Marshall turned, looking surprised. 'Martin. Are you a tennis player?'

'No, I'm not. But I know you play on Sundays.' He cleared his throat. 'And I er . . .'

Marshall must have noticed him looking uncertainly at his partner.

'This is Geraldine. Geraldine Cotton, Martin Sproale. He works with me at the post office.'

Geraldine mussed up her hair and smiled, screwing up her face against the low sunshine.

'How d'you do,' she said, in a neutral accent, with possibly a hint of Home Counties cockney. Martin shook her hand. It felt remarkably cool considering what she'd been through.

'Could I . . . could I talk to you a moment, Nick?' asked Martin.

Marshall rubbed an arm across his brow and grinned at his partner. 'You see, I told you my staff were keen.' He peeled a sweat-band from his head and looked across to Martin. 'Sure. See you later, Gerry.'

Geraldine seemed unconcerned and with a wave at the two of them, walked towards one of three cars already parked beneath the last few faded yellow leaves of a chestnut tree. Martin followed Nick towards his Toyota. He cleared his throat again.

'Didn't see you at the fair yesterday, Nick.'

'No, I couldn't make it. Had to be in London. Relations, you know. Besides, I don't like crowds.' He pursed his lips quickly.

'It's one of the big days in Theston's year. A lot of customers there,' said Martin.

Marshall's eyes flicked on to him.

'Well, it's just as well you were there, Mart. My man on the spot.' He unlocked the back door of his car and reached inside for a black and silver tracksuit. Martin took the bull by the horns.

'I certainly *was* on the spot, Nick, when I met John Parr.'

'Oh?'

'He was looking very sorry for himself.'

'Well, that's a change.'

Marshall began to ease on his tracksuit top.

'Why didn't you tell me?' Martin asked him.

The right-hand side of Marshall's mouth began to tremble ever so slightly. He stretched his cheek muscles to cope with it, but when he spoke it still wasn't entirely under control.

'Look, if you're talking about what I think you're talking about, it's true that I told Devereux that in my opinion there were economies to be made. The next move was up to him, Martin. I make recommendations, but *I* don't have the authority to fire people, you know that.'

'Well, whoever did it, John Parr's been told he's out of a job.'

'He can always go somewhere else.'

'He's born and bred here. His family are here.'

'So? I was born and bred in Bristol.' Marshall slipped the tracksuit top down over his broad shoulders and adjusted it carefully. 'I worked in London, I worked in Luton and now I'm here.'

Martin felt a sudden chill breeze. It reminded him that in his rush to cycle over to the courts he'd forgotten his gloves. Marshall put his hands against the car, extended his arms, and stretched out his right leg until the veins stood out on his temple. He relaxed and took a deep breath before changing to the other leg.

'Look Mart, I'm sorry if that's the way they've chosen to go with Parr, but I never said we could pull this off without a few . . . ugh! . . . sacrifices. I ask them for investment, I try to squeeze my case to the top of the list. I have to . . . ugh! . . . give something in return. I have to impress them that we are doing things right here.'

He changed feet again, once more holding his position until it was obviously uncomfortable.

'That security screen is an . . . ugh! . . . expensive item. The waiting list for the digital scales is months long. We got them in three weeks because they have . . . ugh! . . . confidence in my plan for Theston. A plan which I need you and . . . ugh! . . . everyone else to help me with.'

'But not John Parr.'

Another car was approaching up the long driveway. Both of them turned to look at it. Marshall reached into the back of his car and fetched out a small red towel. He dabbed at his brow as he talked.

'Martin, I've been watching the way you all work. To be honest, you, me and Elaine could run that place between us.'

He raised his hand as Martin made to protest.

'I'm not saying we should, but we *could*, with two or three others on part-time contracts. That would mean big savings, which everybody wants, no matter who's behind the counter.'

Martin tightened his grip on his bobble hat. 'That's where you're wrong, Nick,' he protested. 'People here like to see the regular faces, they like to see local people. They might not want to take a holiday with John Parr, but he is one of them and they like him being there. You lose that goodwill and we're done for.'

Marshall blew out his lips, and rubbed his hair with the towel.

'Martin, nothing is ever gained by standing still. We're talking about a very special post office, in a very special town. Eight thousand people, on the coast, less than a hundred miles from the busiest ports in Europe. That's quite a potential. Unrealised at present, because people are frightened, that's all. They need some leadership, Mart, someone to say, "Look, don't worry, it's not all over, it's just beginning".'

He jabbed an arm out towards the unexceptional sprawl of red brick and brown roofs which lay below them to the east.

'I want to do things here that make outsiders take notice of the place. I want people to say, "Hey, Theston did it, why can't we?" There are a very few people here who can rise to that sort of challenge, Mart. You're one of them. John Parr isn't.'

Martin made to reply but Marshall went on. 'You have the potential. You can make things happen. And I think you should start to behave as if *you* believe that the way I do.'

Martin shifted out of the way as a car approached. He was confused. He had set out that morning to tackle Nick Marshall over a perfectly simple matter. Now Nick Marshall had changed the agenda and Martin had quite lost track of his original purpose.

An ancient Volvo drew up beside them. Inside was a heavily built man in early middle-age with a worried frown, curly dark hair, one or two chins and, low and long on his upper lip, a George Orwell moustache. It was Quentin Rawlings. After leaving Reuter's Rawlings had moved himself and his family from

London to Theston. Since then he had devoted himself almost exclusively to the completion of his autobiography *Someone Answer That*. This had not sold at all well. Besides local journalism, he sent occasional environmental pieces to the *Independent*, who invariably sent them back. His wife, Maureen, who under the *nom de plume* Beverley Bull, wrote highly lucrative bodice rippers for the Middle Eastern market, lingered in the car a moment, transfixed by a last tantalising glimpse of Nick Marshall's thighs as he slid the tracksuit leggings up across his slender buttocks and tightened them around his waist.

Quentin Rawlings caught Martin's eye and shouted across. 'Are you a tennis player, Martin?'

Martin shook his head brusquely. It was bad enough trying to hang on to Marshall's drift without having to answer footling questions about tennis. All right. He couldn't play tennis. It wasn't an international crime for God's sake.

'One day perhaps,' he shouted.

'Bloody marvellous game!' Rawlings called back, before turning, reluctantly, to his two teenage sons who climbed sulkily out of the Volvo. 'Come on!'

There was much slamming of car doors, and Martin watched them walk towards the court.

'I feel really ill, Dad,' said one of his sons.

'You're pathetic,' said the other.

The voices trailed away. Marshall, fully suited now, towelled his face vigorously and finally pushed his car door shut.

'Martin, I'm sorry about Parr. I'll make sure it doesn't happen like that again. I promise.'

He got into his car and had it going pretty quickly. He raised a hand, but it was against the sun and Martin couldn't tell if he was waving farewell or adjusting the mirror. Marshall turned the car briskly and scrunched down the gravel drive, heaving his seat-belt on as he went. Martin's eyes followed him down to the gate, where he turned left and headed away from the town.

As it happened life was only lightly disrupted at the post office. Nick Marshall put in longer hours at the counter and was concerned to keep the staff happy. A new part-timer called Mary Perrick was recruited to help in the run-up to Christmas. She was in her late fifties, a large, maternal ex-teacher. It was the busiest time of year and no one had much time for regrets except on green giro day when John Parr came in to collect his dole money.

But something had changed. The lazy coffee breaks and gossipy lunch hours of Padge's day were replaced by a more formal and businesslike routine. Marshall could barely conceal his impatience for what he called 'non-productive' time. He made it clear that a ten-minute break was a ten-minute break and a rota had been posted on the staff-room wall with twenty-four-hour timings attached. But without John Parr there was no one prepared to laugh at the absurdity of the Individualised Leisure Rota with its terse, inhospitable injunction: 'M. Sproale. Afternoon Period November 9th–17th. Break commencement: 15.20 hours, conclusion: 15.30 hours.'

Then, one morning in early December, before the office opened, Marshall called them all together. He was wearing a sweater in preference to his usual suit. His hair was freshly cut and he looked like a schoolboy. He stretched his hands tightly together. 'Good news,' he began. 'I've had a promise from HQ that the P50 Advance system will be installed first thing after Christmas.' He smiled and looked around him expectantly.

'What does that mean to a simpleton like me?' asked Arthur Gillis.

'It means that as from 27th December all Theston cashiers will have their own on-counter computer terminal.'

Arthur Gillis glanced at Martin and raised his eyes heavenwards.

'All computerised transactions are connected to a modem –

you get the information faster, the customer spends half as much time hanging around, and balancing up takes ten minutes instead of two hours. It's standard issue in Crown offices now.'

'Are these things easy to work?'

'Well, I'm not expecting you to learn it between eight thirty and nine, Arthur.'

'Thank God for that.'

'They're delivering a couple of them at the end of the week and I'm proposing that we have a session together after closing time on Saturday to iron out any problems.' He caught Arthur Gillis's eye. 'Don't look like that, Arthur. They're not monsters.'

'No, but my wife is and there'll be hell to pay when I tell her I'm working Saturday afternoon. It's only two weeks till Christmas.'

A curious expression appeared on Marshall's face, a quick puckering of the corners of the mouth as if he'd swallowed something unpleasant. 'I'll tell you what, Arthur, why don't I bring someone in on Saturday to cover for you, and you can have all the morning for your shopping?'

Gillis looked unexpectedly grateful. 'Well . . . Well, if you could do that, Nick. I'd very much appreciate it.'

Elaine raised a hand. 'Excuse me, Nick, but who comes in instead?'

Marshall looked up at the rota on the wall. 'Well, let me see now.'

He nodded thoughtfully before turning to her. 'Have *you* done your Christmas shopping?'

Elaine shook her head emphatically. '*I*'m not coming in. It's my first Saturday off in a month. You must be joking.'

Arthur Gillis intervened. 'Look, forget it. I'll ask Pat to do the shopping.' He tried to make the best of it. 'She doesn't mind so long as I give her the money!'

But Elaine was indignant now, and wasn't going to let the

matter drop. 'All we need to do is to have the training session another time,' she said. 'I mean why not Monday?'

Marshall held up his hand and looked from Elaine to Arthur. The side of his mouth had gone into mild spasm.

'There's no need to worry. You both need your Saturday. I'll get a part-timer in. Okay?'

'Another one?' asked Elaine suspiciously. 'Where from?'

He tensed his jaw and flicked quickly at his hair. 'Leave it to me.'

Later that day, Martin and Elaine were alone together in the small, cluttered sitting room of the Rudge's two-storey terrace house. It was one of a modest, attractive row of Victorian fisherman's cottages set in a cul-de-sac between the sea front and the main street, close by the handsome fourteenth-century church. Frank and Joan Rudge were both out, Frank at an extraordinary session of the Town Council and Joan over at Marsh Cottage collecting some chair-covers from Kathleen Sproale.

Martin and Elaine were eating TV dinners and watching *Inspector Morse*. Martin was glad they made programmes as good as that because it meant they could be in each other's company without the need to talk. Talking wasn't comfortable between them any more. Elaine wouldn't let Nick Marshall be mentioned, indeed any talk of work produced a bitter response.

Martin looked over at her. Elaine's attention was rapt. She was leaning forward, frowning at the television. He found her concentration appealing. She clutched herself at the elbows and her back was now so straight and long that it would not have taken much for him to free her sweater from the trouser band and feel the smooth soft skin and run his fingers round the line of her waist.

Then the music came and the commercials began and she stood up, holding the remains of a sticky lasagne. 'I can't eat all this, d'you want it?'

'No thanks. I think I'd better be getting back.'

Martin got up. In the kitchen Elaine scraped the contents of the foil container on to a saucer and dropped the container into the waste bin. 'Back to your Mr Hemingway,' she said.

Martin said nothing. He picked up his tray and carried it through.

'What's it like having a rival for his affections?' she said as he came into the kitchen.

'What d'you mean?'

'That Ruth woman. She was all over you at the fair.'

Martin stamped the waste bin open with his foot and dropped his cartons in. He shrugged. 'She's too high-powered for me. She's one of those scholars. Probably writing a five-volume thesis on his left toenail.'

'She's writing about his women isn't she? That's what she told Dad.' Elaine lifted the kettle, found it empty and ran some water into it.

'Did he have a lot of women?' she asked.

'Papa?'

'No, clever Dick, Hemingway.'

Martin laughed. 'I *meant* Hemingway. That's what he liked to be called. Papa. He hated his name. Hated Ernest.'

Elaine wasn't amused. 'Well, did he?'

'Did he what?'

'Have all these women?' She looked up challengingly.

'Oh yes. No shortage. They used to fall at his feet. Ingrid Bergman, Marlene Dietrich, Ava Gardner. He was married four times. Mind you, a lot of it was talk. He used to say he'd slept with Mata Hari the first time he came to Europe. Then someone pointed out that she'd already have been dead a year.' Martin smiled affectionately at the thought. 'He did like to exaggerate.'

Elaine unhooked a mug which she'd bought on last year's holiday. It demonstrated the difficulties of capturing Ventnor on a small curved piece of china.

'You know a lot about him.'

Martin nodded. 'That's true.'

Elaine unscrewed the top from a jar of coffee and dug a spoon in. 'That American could use your help to write her book.'

Martin shook his head. 'She won't need me.'

Elaine snapped the lid back on. 'Why not? You know all there is to know about him. Excuse me.' She squeezed past him to switch on the kettle. He felt the brush of her breasts against his back. 'Maybe it's what you need. Someone with a shared interest. Someone who isn't always moaning at you.'

The kettle began to hiss and rumble.

'I don't want anyone else.'

Elaine turned her large, bright hazel eyes on him.

'Then prove it.'

Eleven

The letter lay open on top of a stack of scribbled notes Ruth had been making on Pauline Pfeiffer, the second Mrs Hemingway.

> Marsh Cottage, North Theston
> Saturday
>
> Dear Ruth,
> I hope you don't mind being addressed this way but I never really caught your second name. I was probably bowled over by the fact that I had met another Hemingway aficionado! Though I am by no means a scholar I have acquired quite a bit of information about our mutual friend and someone suggested that this might be of use to you in compiling your book. I enjoyed meeting you and if you would care to meet up again and discuss it, I would be more than happy. The Market Hotel does tea. Four o'clock on 10th December would be very good for me. Drop me a line at the above address (*not* at the post office).
> Yours sincerely,
> Martin J. Sproale.

She had received the letter almost a month ago and, feeling guilty that she had treated him curtly at the fair, Ruth had accepted. Four o'clock on 10th December had then seemed a long way off. Now it was only an hour away.

She rubbed her eyes and stared at the little blue and silver screen. She had been working hard these past few weeks and had grown more used to the cold east winds. The lack of company had also bothered her less as, having completed the difficult early chapters on Ernest's relationship with his mother, she had taken on the company of Hadley and Ezra and Scott and Zelda and Gertrude Stein and James Joyce and Sylvia Beach and all that crowd that seemed to have had such an effortlessly exciting time in Paris in the early 1920s. And now a new, attractive, immensely eligible and thoroughly dangerous addition had arrived on the scene in the shape of the young, well-to-do fashion journalist Pauline Pfeiffer.

Finding out how, when and why Pauline proved irresistible to Hemingway, a married man with a baby son, was now Ruth's task. Armed with letters, hotel registers, newspaper cuttings, street maps and her own intuition she had been pursuing the pair across Paris for several days, along boulevards and into gardens and through galleries. She had trailed them from salons to bars and restaurants to night clubs like a hired investigator in a divorce suit. What she was discovering was sad, because she liked Hadley, the current Mrs Hemingway, and had grown fond of their little son Bumby. But it was exciting too, for the ways in which a woman attracted and held on to a man was an endless source of fascination for Ruth.

But right now she had to leave Pauline waiting for Ernest in a bedroom in the Venetia Hotel in Montparnasse, and make her way to the Market Hotel in Theston to meet a barely articulate post office clerk who hero-worshipped the old bastard. She switched off her laptop. Hemingway had a lot to answer for.

Though she was on time her host was already there. He looked better dressed than she remembered. He was wearing grey flannel trousers and a brown tweed jacket with strange suede pads across the shoulders. His hair was short and neatly brushed. His face shone in the light of an ornate table lamp that reared up beside him in a corner of the residents' lounge. It occurred to her, with an twinge of irritation, that he must have made an effort for her.

He stood quickly as she came in. She apologised for being on time, and he apologised for being early.

'I came straight from work,' he explained.

'You work Saturdays?' she asked.

'Only in the morning. But today we had some extra training to do.'

'You've been working out?'

'Not that sort of training. Computer training.'

'You're keen.'

Martin gave a short laugh. 'We had no option.'

'How'd it go?'

'Well, you know, it's not so bad for me. It's harder for the older ones, learning from scratch. But . . . well, you've got to move with the times.'

Ruth, settling herself in an armchair, looked quickly around. 'Unlike this place.'

Martin grinned uncomfortably. Most of the tables were occupied. A lot of tea was being taken. There were some loud voices. He tugged at the knot of his tie. He was very hot.

'I hope this place is okay with you,' said Martin, knowing he'd made a mistake.

'I like it here,' she lied. 'It's busy.'

Martin nodded. Busy with the wrong people. It was an expensive place, much patronised by the County set. He himself had already been patronised by Mrs Harvey-Wardrell. He had been in the foyer as she arrived. Hearing her voice approaching from the street outside, he had swiftly turned his attention to an illuminated display of Doulton china which occupied the corner furthest from the door.

'I've a disabled person in the car,' she announced to the hotel in general. 'I shall require some assistance.'

There was a pause. Her entrance seemed to have created much the same effect as that of a lone gunman. All the staff had taken cover.

'Hello?'

Martin had shrunk closer to the cabinet. He had stared with extraordinary intensity at the china display, hoping that by some epic feat of concentration he might actually be able to translocate himself into one of the soup tureens. But it was no good.

'I say! You . . . You over there!'

Martin knew there was no escape.

'You,' she called. 'Porter!' He turned to see the towering, all-too-familiar figure swathed in cascades of fur and leather.

When she recognised him there had been a momentary apology, but he had still ended up having to grasp the front end of a wheelchair and carry a corpulent banker up the two or three steps to the front door. The man, who had a kindly smile concealed inside a strawberry-red face, had pressed a pound upon him. Martin had slipped it quickly into the box for the blind.

Mrs Harvey-Wardrell and her party were now sitting at a window table being fussed over by Gordon Parrish the waiter. Martin knew all about Gordon Parrish. He was something of a legend with the below-stairs people. He was a fully paid-up anarchist and loathed just about everybody he served. He was forever boasting of peeing in the soup and putting sheep droppings in the muesli. He'd been had up several times for exposure and once, it was rumoured, for interfering with cattle, but he fawned so successfully on rich guests at the Market Hotel that many of them regarded him as the family retainer they never had and rewarded him generously.

'Now, Gordon,' he could hear Mrs Harvey-Wardrell confiding from four tables away, 'these are two of my absolutely oldest friends – Freddie was with Hambros for many years, and there is *no one* in the art world Diana does not know – so we don't want any of your ghastly trippers' teas. Could you find us something a little special?'

Gordon, who had once slipped a condom in a cassoulet, bowed and scraped and rubbed his hands and promised that he would find them something very special and Martin didn't doubt that he would.

'Do you know all these people?' Ruth asked Martin.

He nodded. 'Most of them. They all have to come in the post office.'

Ruth stole another look at the roomful of tweedy men and ample-bosomed matrons. 'It's like a scene out of *The Lady Vanishes*.'

'It's city money, a lot of it. They all want to play country squires for the weekend. Then on Mondays they go back to selling futures.'

Ruth leaned down and picked up her voluminous black leather bag with silver studs. A present from a Moroccan she'd once known fleetingly. She reached inside for her cigarettes. 'Mind if I smoke?'

A look of alarm appeared on Martin's face. He swivelled himself round in his chair. 'I think there's some sort of rule in here.'

Ruth smiled as sweetly as she could manage and put the pack back in her bag. 'Forget it,' she said. 'We are a cursed breed.'

Martin smiled uncomfortably.

Sarah, the new waitress, came across to them. She was pink-cheeked and unhurried, with bright, wandering eyes and a black dress drawn tight across her bottom. 'Tea for two?' she asked.

Martin nodded and looked across to Ruth. 'Tea?'

'Could I have coffee?' Ruth asked.

Sarah scribbled 'coffee' on her pad and asked, 'D'you still want the tea?'

Ruth looked confused.

Sarah heaved a sigh and repeated her question. 'D'you want your coffee *with* the tea?'

'I would like my coffee with the coffee, if that's possible.'

Now Sarah looked confused.

Ruth turned helplessly to Martin. 'Is drinking tea a legal requirement here?'

Martin stepped in, explained the differences between tea you drink and tea you eat and Ruth was grateful and Sarah went away.

A gleeful cry wafted across from the Harvey-Wardrell table: 'Smoked salmon, how perfect!'

'Scottish?' asked Freddie from his wheelchair.

'Loch Tay, southern end,' confirmed Gordon.

It could have been from Mogadishu for all he knew, but in twenty years he'd learnt to say what they wanted to hear.

Soon Ruth and Martin found themselves engaged on a major logistical exercise. Balancing the array of cups and saucers, plates, jugs, cake-stands and pots of hot water on the table was difficult enough. Quite another skill was required to transfer the profusion of delicacies from hand to mouth without leaving a trail of debris along the way.

All this concentrated their minds and offered a convenient distraction from the real reason for their meeting. Then Sarah brought the bill, which lay a little too long on the table before Martin claimed it, and it seemed as if they would just get up and go and that would be that. Martin was beginning to feel a touch of panic.

Ruth wasn't sure what was going on either, or who was supposed to make the first move. All she knew was that she desperately needed a cigarette. She leaned across to Martin. 'Is there a bar in here?'

'The spirit of Hemingway cannot be invoked in an English tea-room,' pronounced Ruth as a double vodka began to take effect. 'I think we can now confirm that with some authority.'

'Have you . . . have you been an admirer of his . . . for long?' Martin asked her, tentatively.

Ruth exhaled copiously. Though she might not admit it, his eager awkwardness was calming her down. 'Put it this way, Martin, I'm not a fan. I just know an awful lot about him. And the more you know about Ernest Hemingway, the less of a fan you become.' She allowed herself a thick, smoky laugh.

Martin decided it was time to stand up and be counted. 'I can't agree with that,' he said.

'Well, good for you.'

'I think he was a great man,' said Martin.

'Men usually do.' She reached for the ashtray. 'I think he wrote some good books and even better stories. I think at his best he was a great writer, but he could also be cruel, boorish and inconsiderate. I don't go along with the adoration and the sycophancy.'

'Nor me,' Martin agreed. 'I know his faults. But if I could write stories one-tenth as good as "The Snows of Kilimanjaro" or "The Short, Happy Life" . . .'

Ruth puckered her nose. 'Why those two?'

'Well, I think they're just about perfect. There's not a word I would change.'

'And *The Old Man and the Sea*?'

'Extraordinary.'

'*A Farewell to Arms*?'

'Superb.'

Ruth laughed and drained her glass. 'You *are* a fan.'

'You didn't ask me about *Across the River and into the Trees*. That was the one everyone hated.'

'Okay. What about *Across the River and into the Trees*?'

'Outstanding!'

This time they both laughed. Ruth leaned forward and picked out a dressed olive from a bowl on the bar. 'I have to admit that if a lot of other people didn't feel the way you do, I wouldn't be writing a book about the guy,' she said.

Neither of them spoke for a moment.

'What's your book about?' asked Martin.

Ruth pulled the ashtray towards her. 'Well, it's about Ernest Hemingway.' She saw Martin was about to speak and she went quickly on. 'And Grace and Hadley and Pauline and Martha and Mary Hemingway. And Agnes Von Kurowsky and Duff Twysden and Gertrude Stein and Jane Mason and Adriana Ivancich and all the other women without whom he would not have written the way he did.'

85

Ruth stubbed out her cigarette and picked a tiny tobacco strand from the end of her tongue.

Martin was disappointed. Since the time he left school he had dreamt of the chance to talk about his hero with someone else who knew as much about him as he did. He had never once entertained the possibility of meeting someone who knew him and hated him.

'Same again?' The barman was pointing at Martin's glass.

Martin looked to Ruth. She looked unsure. 'I have my car.'

Martin looked sympathetic. 'I have my bike.'

'Oh, what the hell,' she said. 'It's Christmas. I'll take a small one.'

The barman poured two more vodkas. Martin raised his glass. 'To Ernest. And his women.'

Ruth grinned ruefully. 'Tell me,' she said. 'How many times did *he* crash his car?'

Martin barely took breath. 'Once in 1930, twice in the Second World War, once in 1953 and once in 1959. July. Burgos. Spain.'

Ruth rolled her eyes. 'You *are* a fan,' she said again.

Martin had rather understated the hopelessness of the computer training session that had been held earlier in the day. It had been embarrassing from the start. Nick Marshall had asked not one, but three part-timers along. Shirley Barker had been expected. She had been part-time almost as long as Elaine had been full-time. Mary Perrick, Parr's replacement, was efficient and sensible, but Martin was surprised to see the new employee brought in only that morning. It was Geraldine, the same girl Martin had last seen damp and dishevelled from the tennis court. Today she was in a tight little light grey suit which revealed a little more of her compact, muscular body than he had been aware of on the tennis court. Her honey-blonde hair, fairer than he remembered, was brushed back quite severely from the temples.

Marshall had announced her briskly. 'This is Geraldine Cotton. She will be coming in when necessary to fill any gaps over the next few weeks.'

And that was that. Martin found himself feeling embarrassed, compromised. Geraldine met his eye with a quick smile and then looked away. She seemed to him serious, efficient, over-qualified. Something was not quite right.

The training itself had been equally uncomfortable. Nick Marshall was not a natural teacher, preferring exhortation to instruction. From the outset he assumed a basic standard of computer literacy and an unquestioning devotion to the new technology. This soon split the class into two, those over fifty and the rest. But at least Shirley Barker knew what a cursor was. Soon it was Arthur Gillis versus the rest. Gillis, who had once been taught to strip down a machine gun blindfold, was lost at the keyboard. He tried to laugh it off.

'At least I got it switched on. It would have taken Padge three weeks to learn that.'

But Marshall kept the pressure up, ignoring the jokes. Elaine sat beside Gillis and guided him through. The atmosphere was tight and uncongenial and at the end Marshall's thanks for their time had rung pretty hollow.

Twelve

On the last Wednesday before Christmas, not long after his tea with Ruth, Martin found himself once more at the Market Hotel, this time for dinner at the invitation of Nick Marshall. Marshall had sprung it on him only that morning. Martin had barely time to cycle home, wash the ink off his hands, change into his dark grey suit and cycle back into town again. Nick was there already. As he watched Martin standing by the cloak-room being helped out of his anorak he allowed himself a little pity. Martin was a decent man. He knew the job backwards. But he was chronically passive, irretrievably agreeable, pain-fully inept, one of those obliging individuals who would go out of his way to help anyone but himself. The salt of the earth, some would call him and Nick, being seriously concerned with fitness, knew that too much salt was bad for you.

Martin came towards him, one hand smoothing down his hair, the other tugging at his collar. 'Sorry I'm late. Foul night!'

'You've still got your clips on.'

'Oh, God!'

Martin bent down, and looking quickly round as he did so, took off his bicycle clips and dropped them into his jacket pocket.

He laughed nervously.

'Shall we have a pint first?' Martin said, remembering how much he'd preferred the bar last time.

'No, let's go in,' said Nick. 'They've got the table ready.'

Martin followed him obediently into the restaurant. He found himself wondering, not for the first time, how Nick Marshall could live like this on a post office manager's salary.

They sat down near the window. Gordon Parrish obligingly, and in the case of Nick, lingeringly, draped napkins over their crotches.

Nick looked across at Martin. 'I expect you're wondering how I can live like this on a post office manager's salary?' He winked. 'Don't.'

They ordered. Nick chose fish, Martin steak and kidney pie. Nick selected a bottle of white wine, and as soon as it came he insisted on pouring it himself.

'I hate other people telling me how fast I should drink my wine, don't you?'

Martin had always assumed that the pouring of the wine by the waiter was the way things were done, and clearly the wine-waiter did too, for he took his redundancy badly and stood across by the sideboard arranging bottles sulkily.

'I hate Christmas,' said Nick. 'How about you?'

Martin knew by now that such enquiries were intended less as expressions of interest than rhetorical springboards for whatever Nick had to say, and he treated them as such.

'Well, I always like a day off,' Martin ventured.

'What are you going to do with it?'

'I shall get up late,' Martin shrugged. 'We usually go to dinner at the Rudges'.'

Nick raised an eyebrow. 'Christmas dinner at the Rudges'. Must be fun.'

'Frank tends to run the show. No one else gets a word in.'

Nick Marshall took a mouthful of Saint-Véran and thrust his lips forward like a goldfish as he drew the air in over it. Martin was pleasantly relieved to see that he could look quite ugly. Marshall swallowed the wine, nodded to himself and poured them each a glass.

'Cheers!' he said. 'To you and Elaine.'

Martin's mouthful disappeared down some passage at the back of his throat he'd not known about before. He choked helplessly and dabbed at his mouth with a napkin. Nick

Marshall watched him like a fox might watch a chicken laying an egg.

'You *are* going to get married?' Marshall asked.

Martin could only muster a non-committal grunt, but this didn't seem to be enough.

Nick leaned forward as if he might have missed something. 'Mmm?'

'I think when we're both ready,' Martin began, uneasily.

'You must have been waiting to see what happened at the post office.'

Martin, once again, felt himself back on a conversational roller coaster.

Nick went smoothly on. 'I do understand, you know. Your expectations and everything. You must have hated my guts when I took over.'

Martin forced a laugh.

'It's true isn't it?'

'I never hated your guts,' Martin lied. 'I was upset for a while, yes. Promotion would have made a difference to my life. A bit more money wouldn't have gone amiss.'

Nick nodded agreement. 'But you resigned yourself to it.'

'What else could I do,' Martin said, guardedly.

'Elaine didn't, did she?'

Martin bristled at this. 'Well, you sound as if you know all about it, Nick.'

'She makes it obvious, Mart. And I don't blame her. But I'd rather she saw me as a friend, not a devil. I can actually make things very nice for us all.'

The last thought hung pregnant in the air as the food arrived and there was much fussing around with knives and forks and plates and serving dishes. Nothing more of significance was said until Gordon Parrish had finally wheeled his trolley away. Nick took barely a mouthful of Dover sole before leaning forwards. 'I suppose you're following the privatisation debate . . .'

90

Martin, engaged in disentangling a stray piece of meat which had appeared inadvertently amongst the gristle, tried his best to convey his strong feelings on the issue.

'The way I see it,' Nick went on, 'is that the Government's committed to change – it's just a question of how fast it'll happen. The Post Office is big, but it won't stay big if it has to pay two hundred million pounds back to the Government every year. My guess is they'll fudge it. Half public, half private. What do you think?'

Martin swallowed hard and raised his head from his plate. 'I'm against it,' he said firmly. 'I don't want to see some Arab millionaire end up with half the British Post Office.'

Nick set his fork to one side, as if the business of eating was a tiresome distraction. He picked up his wine glass and looked across at Martin. 'If an Arab millionaire *wanted* to own half the British Post Office wouldn't that help everybody working in it?'

'You must be joking. It wouldn't be British for a start.'

'Look at what the Arabs own already, Mart. Harrods, the Dorchester Hotel. You can't get much more British than that.'

'But not the Post Office. That's different.'

'Why? Why is it different? It supplies a service. Harrods supplies cheese and chairs, the Dorchester supplies hotel rooms, the Post Office supplies deliveries, stamps and driving licences.'

Across the restaurant Martin caught sight of Cuthbert Habershon, the coroner. This must be the day he retired. He and his friends crowded, jovially, round a corner table. Champagne was already in the bucket. Martin found himself envious of their easy familiarity. He swung his attention back to Nick Marshall, who was still talking. 'There would, if the privatisation bill was passed, be nothing to stop a post office selling a lot more.' Marshall paused to weigh up the effect of his words. 'What's wrong with them selling insurance, holidays, goldfish . . .'

Martin couldn't answer straight away. Another glob of fat had wedged itself in a crevice in his upper jaw not due for filling until the New Year. His tongue worked frantically to dislodge it.

'Mmm?'

Martin worked the pinguid morsel to the front of his mouth, bent low over the plate and deposited it, alongside several others. 'Why?' he said eventually. 'What's the point?'

'They've a guaranteed, built-in customer base that any other shop would be crying out for. They're right at the heart of domestic finances already. They would have a head start on all communications-related merchandise. Mobile phones, home computers, fax machines.'

'Isn't that going a bit far?' Martin protested.

Nick Marshall shook his head vigorously. 'The problem, Mart,' he said, 'is not going far enough.'

They finished the meal and as swiftly as the bill arrived Nick sent it back accompanied by a Visa card. Martin reached inside his coat. 'How much do I owe you?'

'Business expense, Mart.'

'You're not self-employed.'

'Well, put it this way,' Marshall added mysteriously. 'I do the odd piece of consultancy.'

'Thank you,' said Martin. 'You didn't need to do that.'

'Well, Mart, I feel I owe you a lot of thanks. An outsider taking over a well-loved local office. It wasn't easy, and I didn't always get it right. Especially over that business with John Parr. I did that badly.'

Martin toyed with an empty wine glass. It was his turn to be magnanimous. 'We all make mistakes.'

'Exactly,' said Nick. He patted the side of his mouth with the linen napkin, then rubbed his hands and stretched them back against each other. 'That's why I'd like you to be the one to tell Arthur Gillis.'

'Tell Arthur Gillis what?'

Nick put down the napkin. He sorted the credit card and counterfoil carefully into his wallet and looked up. 'I've recommended him for early retirement. I don't think Head Office will put up much of a fight.'

He pursed his lips very tightly. Martin sat and stared.

Nick stood, abruptly. 'Shall we go?'

Martin didn't move.

'I'm sorry, Mart, but the man's computer illiterate. He won't survive.'

'He's hardly had a chance.'

'Mart, there are people who get it slowly and people who get it fast and people who will never get it. Arthur Gillis will never get it. He knows it too. He'll be offered decent terms. He's only five years off retirement age.'

'But I've worked with Arthur for ten years. Everyone knows him.'

This time Nick made no attempt to conceal his irritation. He felt unduly conspicuous standing there with Martin gazing up at him, dumbstruck. It was all unnecessary and overdramatic, and any moment his mouth might start giving him trouble. Resting his hands on the table, he leaned down and spoke briskly. 'He's not going to disappear off the planet, Mart. People can still *know* him. He just won't have to sit behind a post office counter any more. Lucky man, some would say.'

Martin remained obstinately seated. 'Well, you tell him that yourself.'

Nick Marshall leaned closer. 'Look, Mart. You gave me stick over the way I dealt with Parr. You were right. I should have told you what I was doing and let you handle it. It's what you do best. Well, this time I shan't make that mistake.' He reached into the inside pocket of his grey flannel suit and held out an envelope.

Martin flicked his eyes sideways. He saw the name of Arthur Gillis on the front, swallowed hard and then looked up.

'And if I say no?'
'I'll just put a stamp on it and he'll hear about it in the normal way.'

Thirteen

On the Thursday evening before Christmas the Gillises were watching television when the doorbell sounded. Pat Gillis looked across to her husband and was about to get up when he motioned her back. 'Let them sing something first. You're always up like a jack-in-the-box. Let them sing something.'

Pat Gillis squeezed the handkerchief she was holding. She was a small, nervous Yorkshirewoman, with dark, centre-parted hair and prominent green eyes. 'I don't like to have them hanging around. They sing these long carols just to give them time to have a look at the house.'

'Who've you been talking to?'

'It's common knowledge. One of them sings and the others look in the window to see where your video is.'

'Well, they've sung nothing yet and anyway, we haven't got a video.'

'We've had the television on. They might have sung already for all you know.'

They sat there, listening.

The doorbell sounded again. Two chirpy notes, as if announcing a cartoon character.

'Maybe it's not them,' said Pat. She got up from her chair.

'Who could it be? It's half past eight.'

Outside the door Martin shifted uneasily from foot to foot. He didn't like the new estates. They looked as though they had been assembled from kits, freshly unpacked and set down, arbitrarily, on what were once attractive fields. The little roads bore bogus off-the-shelf names like Lakeside Crescent and Farmview, though the only view the houses had was of other houses. He didn't like what he was doing here either. He'd had a pint at the King's Head after work and a large whisky back at home but his mouth was still dry and his stomach still tight. For the umpteenth time he checked that the envelope was in the right pocket. Not in his anorak which he might hang up, but in his old brown corduroy jacket, and not in the side, but the inside pocket. There must be no prior hint that he had it. When the time came to deliver it, it must be swift and sweet.

He pressed the bell a third time. Perhaps they weren't in. Perhaps he'd got into this dreadful state for nothing. Then he started. A light had gone on in the hall. He took a deep breath. The door, still on a chain, was cautiously opened. Mrs Gillis peered out.

'It's me, Pat. Martin Sproale.'

'Oh, Martin! Whatever time do you call this?'

'I'm sorry. I've been working late . . . What with Christmas and everything. I was on my way home.'

There was a pause and then the sound of the chain sliding back.

'Well, I'm glad it's you. I was sat there thinking all sorts of awful things.' She held the door open. 'Come in, love.'

She fussed around offering him cups of tea and slices of freshly made parkin and telling him how much they missed their son who was working in Germany as a builder and who sent money home and photographs too but that wasn't the point, they'd rather see him in the flesh.

Then Martin said that he had to talk to Arthur about a business matter and she apologised for going on and took the cups away to wash them up.

Throughout all this Arthur had hardly said a word and when his wife had shut the door and left them alone he unnerved Martin by fixing him with a smile.

Then he spoke. 'Well, it's not good news, is it?'

Martin looked away. He frowned and scratched his head.

'How long have we known each other, Martin?'

Martin felt himself reddening. 'Ten, twelve years.'

'Have we ever had a bad word for each other?'

'Not that I can remember.'

'No, well, let's not start now. I know what you're going to say. It's been written on your face all day. I knew it'd come sooner or later. I'm not stupid. I can see the way it's going with Marshall. He's young. He wants to change the world. But mark my words, Martin, once your computers and your electronics run the Post Office there'll be no talk of 'loyalty' or 'service'. You'll either be in or out. Well, I'm fifty-five and it doesn't matter much to me. But you were brought up on loyalty and service too, Martin, and you're going to miss all that. So don't worry about me. You worry about yourself.'

Martin found himself halfway down Elmdene Way before he remembered that he still had the letter. He cycled back, miserably, and slipped it through Arthur's letter-box.

The news of Arthur Gillis's departure broke on the Saturday, the day before Christmas Eve. With two and a half days' holiday ahead Nick Marshall congratulated himself on the timing. He sweetened the pill by announcing that he had successfully persuaded John Devereux, at Head Office, to bring forward plans to renovate and upgrade North Square Post Office by six months – from late summer to early in the New Year.

The customary exchange of staff Christmas presents took place in a peculiar atmosphere of glum jollity. Boxes of chocolate, bars of soap, tins of nuts, books and bottles were passed about peremptorily, as if everything had to be done before the music stopped.

Martin watched Arthur Gillis slip the present he'd given him from its blue wrapping paper. Arthur smiled and Martin wished the ground would open up beneath him.

Arthur held up the bottle. 'That'll go down well.'

Martin nodded speechlessly.

'We like a drop of Bailey's.'

Martin saw only a poisoned chalice.

By two o'clock everyone had gone except for the Manager and his Assistant. As he locked up and set the alarms, Martin heard Marshall whistling as he completed the stock check. He heard the safe click shut. As Martin threw the last bolt on the main door he became aware of Nick Marshall behind him.

'I think I've spoiled someone's Christmas.'

Martin corrected him bitterly. '*I* was the one who spoilt it for him.'

Marshall shook his head. 'No, I mean Elaine's. She didn't even say goodbye.' He seemed less hurt than puzzled.

Martin locked the door and pocketed the heavy key. Marshall gathered up his papers. He stopped and examined one of them.

'Do you want to know how much we've saved on staffing in the last three months?' he asked Martin.

Martin shook his head firmly. It was the last thing he wanted to know.

'Four and a half thousand pounds. And do you know what we'll save in the next three months? *Six* and a half thousand. That's twenty-four thousand pounds this branch will save Post Office Counter Services in a full year. That's why I was able to get next year's renovation put forward.'

Outside in the yard a car horn sounded. Marshall bent to look out of the window. 'All right! I'm coming!' he muttered. He turned back to Martin and patted him on the arm.

'Mart. I know it's been tough, but you wait. You won't recognise this place in a year's time. That's a promise.'

At the door to the counters Nick Marshall waved, shouted 'Happy Christmas!' and was gone.

Martin stood with his back to the main door and looked around him. He saw a cracked linoleum floor worn thin below the positions and a solid wooden counter with its once high varnish cuffed and scratched by shopping baskets and pushchairs and the heels of fidgeting children. He saw the new security screen rear incongruously up to the ceiling, its anodised aluminium frame gleaming, its extra-toughened glass naked of all the posters, stickers and exhortations to customers to check their change which had covered its predecessor like moss on stones. He saw the wooden writing shelf that ran the length of the opposite wall with sheaves of forms sprouting from blue plastic boxes and biros chained to the wall.

Above the shelf he saw the wooden calendar box which Padge had insisted on changing personally each morning, using the stout round knobs that protruded from the side to change date, day and month. He saw the Newmark electric wall clock, arbiter of coffee- and lunch-breaks for as long as Martin could remember. He caught the familiar, comforting smell of ink and old money. He set the master alarm and, dangling keys like a prison warder, let himself through the door to the counters, locked it behind him and flicked off the lights.

Martin was going to go straight home but on an impulse he turned right out of North Square and cycled down the High Street where the shop windows were already illuminated against the December gloom, desperately flaunting themselves one last time before Christmas. He rode on down to the sea front. He could see Elaine striding purposefully along the pebble-strewn promenade. A dog was running backwards and forwards in front of her, occasionally barking, eyes flicking, beseechingly, from her face to the well-chewed tennis ball in her hand. Martin wheeled his bicycle down the cliff path.

'Elaine!' he called and she looked up, startled. The dog saw Martin too and, with a joyous yelp, peeled off and scampered towards him.

'Hello, Scruff, boy.' Martin tugged at the dog's ears, fighting to keep its nose away from his crotch.

'Scruff!' shrieked Elaine. 'Come here!'

The dog turned as she flung his tennis ball towards the sea.

He raced away over the beach, barking at each bounce and skidding into the sand.

'Well I never,' said Elaine, glancing quickly at Martin before moving on. 'All the dogs are out today. Even Mr Marshall's.'

Martin followed her, as Scruff came hurtling back. 'I wanted to explain,' he said.

Scruff stood, panting heavily, his tail thumping Martin's leg.

'Don't bother,' Elaine said, stooping to extract the ball from his slobbery grip. 'Everything's quite clear,' she said, hurling it away again. 'Marshall throws the ball and you fetch it for him.'

'I only did the decent thing and warned Arthur what was going to happen.'

Elaine gave a short cry of protest. 'Martin, the only decent thing you had to do was to stop that bastard from sacking a perfectly good employee.'

'Early retirement. That's all it is. It's not the end of the world.'

'Martin, no one ever asked him if he wanted early retirement. He wasn't allowed to choose, was he? Did *he* want it? Did Pat want it? Did anyone ever ask *them?*'

She turned and walked on. Martin skirted a neatly piled dog-turd and wheeled his bicycle after her. 'Listen, it's stupid to keep on being angry.'

Scruff raced back from the sea. Martin held back to avoid the shower of spray as he shook himself down. Elaine turned. Her eyes were blazing. 'The only stupid thing I ever did was fall for you. I must have been bloody mad!'

Scruff dropped the ball and barked back, delighted at the shouting. Martin stopped. There seemed to be no further point in trailing after her. 'Look,' he called. 'I'll see you on Christmas Day. Let's talk about it after that. When we're both a bit . . . calmer.'

Elaine turned and shook her head. 'No you won't,' she said.

'Won't what?'

'You won't see me on Christmas Day. There's no point,

Martin. I . . .' She seemed to struggle to find the word. 'I don't trust you any more.'

'What?'

'You run the Post Office the way you and the Wonder Boy want to run it. I'll collect my salary for as long as I'm allowed to and I promise not to interfere. Good luck and goodbye.' She felt tears welling and fought hard against them. 'You're not wanted, Martin. You're redundant. You've been laid off. You don't fit in with my plans.'

Then the tears did come and she was angry with herself and turned sharply away towards the cliff path.

Scruff laid the ball at Martin's feet instead and eyed him, imploringly.

Fourteen

When Martin arrived back at Marsh Cottage it was almost dark. He was about to swing in to the doorway when his bicycle lamp picked out a badly parked yellow Datsun blocking the gateway. He dismounted and squeezed his bicycle alongside. It was most likely someone for his mother. Some of these Theston women parked like schoolchildren. Left their cars wherever they felt like it. To avoid whoever it might be he went around to the back door. That didn't work. His mother was there in the kitchen and, opposite her, was a visitor he recognised. Sitting, with her hands tight around one of the big white coffee mugs, was Ruth Kohler.

Martin was suddenly conscious of being damp and wind-swept, and his nose was running. He sniffed hard and pushed the door open.

'How d'you do,' he said formally and laid his briefcase on the chair.

'You look exhausted,' said his mother.

'It's just drizzle. It's not cold.'

'This lady –'

'Ruth,' Ruth reminded her again.

'Ruth and me are just having some coffee. D'you want a cup?'

Martin nodded and unzipped his anorak. Ruth looked at home in the kitchen. He was surprised. She had a cigarette in her hand and his mother had found her an ashtray. 'A present from the Vatican' was inscribed on its rim. A friend had brought it back.

'I didn't think you knew where I lived,' he said, ducking into the back porch and hanging up his things.

Ruth gave a quick, short cough and tapped the ash from her cigarette. 'The most discreet man in the world told me, but only after I threatened him.'

Martin bent down, pulled off his bicycle clips and tucked them into the pocket of his anorak. 'I'm not with you.'

'Our mutual friend in the book trade. Mr Julian.'

'Ah, yes,' Martin crossed to the sink and ran his hands under the hot tap. He caught sight of his scraggy red-brown hair in the mirror and wished he could have had time to comb it.

'I must go and see him. He's got some magazines for me.'

Ruth expelled two long columns of smoke. 'Not any more, I'm afraid.'

Martin reached for the towel. 'Have they gone?'

Ruth nodded. Martin's face creased momentarily. 'Well, that's the way it goes,' he said, and dried his hands briskly.

'It's my fault,' said Ruth.

Martin turned. 'Your fault?'

'I was the one who bought them. He didn't tell me until after I'd paid. Said he felt quite sad about selling them, but he'd waited a couple of months. I thought I should come by and explain.'

Martin smiled ruefully. 'I don't have the money anyway.'

Ruth reached down to the chair beside her and produced a silver-ribboned parcel wrapped in Christmas paper. She pushed it across the table towards him. 'I hope this'll make up for it.'

Kathleen Sproale poured the hot water on to the coffee. 'He's got quite enough bits and pieces anyway,' she said appeasingly. She turned to Ruth. 'He's got his own bookshop up there. And I have to clean it.'

'No, you don't,' retorted Martin. 'You clean it because you like to have a snoop.'

Now it was Ruth's turn to be the appeaser. 'I love books. Any chance I can see it?'

Martin smoothed his hair down as best he could, shot a

fierce glance at his mother and cleared his throat. 'You can see it if you want.'

Martin led Ruth upstairs, across the landing, and pushed open the door. Once inside she looked around, shyly at first, occasionally shaking her head and exclaiming. She peered closely and wonderingly at his first editions and asked if she might take them down. She ran her hands over the Corona typewriter and stared hard at the photographs he had stuck on the wall. She ignored the hats that hung behind the door and was not much interested in the punch bag, the billhook (possibly Cuban), or the bullfight poster. She made a face at the kudu horns and smiled and shook her head at the *Wehrmacht* belt.

Then her eye was taken by the medical cabinet and she asked him about it and he told her it was from a hospital in Milan and it was of the same design and vintage as the one in the American Red Cross Hospital where the nineteen-year-old Hemingway fell in love with his nurse Agnes Von Kurowsky.

She whistled at this and asked if it still had period bandages and eighty-year-old iodine inside. Before he could stop her she had pulled at the enamel catch. As the door swung open she stood back, visibly impressed. 'Now that's one hell of a bar.'

More than two dozen bottles, some with old, faded, unfamiliar labels, were clustered inside.

'All his favourite drinks,' said Martin, sheepishly. 'I've sort of collected them over the years. All except applejack brandy. The off-licence in Theston keep saying they'll get me some but they don't know if anyone makes it any more. Oh, and absinthe. That's a tricky one. It's illegal in most countries.'

'I don't see any Bollinger Brut, 1915.'

Martin picked up the reference eagerly. 'As bought for David Bourne by Marita.'

She nodded and smiled. 'Right. *The Garden of Eden*. The only novel I can still read.'

Martin ignored this. 'I only buy his non-fiction drinks,' he explained, pushing the door shut again.

'There's not much non-fiction in Hemingway,' Ruth smiled. 'Except in his novels.'

Martin looked vaguely troubled.

Ruth felt for her cigarettes.

'Are you going to offer me a Christmas drink?' she asked, indicating the medicine cabinet. 'I'll pass on iodine but take anything else you've got.'

She watched, amused, as he dropped to his knees and searched carefully through the ranks of bottles.

'Do you mind if I smoke?'

'Go ahead,' he called from the cupboard. After much rummaging he produced a bottle from right at the back. He held it out to her.

'Grappa,' she said approvingly.

'This is Nardini,' he said. 'There's lots of them, though.'

'Well, well,' said Ruth. 'He talks about it often enough, but I never knew what it was.'

Martin looked pleased, nodded, poured a glass and handed it to her. 'They call it the poor man's brandy. It's made of everything the wine-makers throw away. Skins, pips, stalks. They all go in. Sit down, if you can find room.'

Ruth perched herself on the edge of the bed. She waited until he had poured one for himself, then she raised her glass.

'*Salute*,' she said.

'*Salute*,' Martin replied, a little less confidently.

She took a mouthful, caught the dry, fiery flavour and made a face. 'Boy, that hurt!' Her eyes watered and she grinned painfully.

'D'you like it?' he asked.

She shook her head. 'A little strong for me.'

'You get used to it. Hemingway loved it.'

She nodded and held the glass up with mock solemnity. 'Exhibit A,' she said.

'Exhibit A?'

She glanced towards the photograph.

'This is what killed him.'

Martin shook his head vigorously. 'He killed himself because he couldn't write any more.'

'Why couldn't he write any more? Because his liver was gone and his blood pressure was sky high and he was overweight and ill. Don't tell me that wasn't because of the booze.' Ruth took another sip of the grappa. This time she caught the dry, woody flavour and it was strong, but friendly.

'Ernest Hemingway's life, Martin, is a case study in alcoholism.'

Martin was stung. 'He could have come off the booze, but he enjoyed it. Anyway he was never drunk. I mean, rolling drunk. Never incapable.'

'I'll soon be making tea,' shouted Kathleen from the bottom of the stairs. 'Are you staying, Ruth?'

Ruth glanced at her watch and set her glass down. 'No thanks,' she shouted back, and turned to Martin. 'I have to go.'

'There's no hurry. I enjoy talking about him.'

Ruth laughed and stood up. She brushed down the creases in her well-cut black trousers and Martin saw that her legs were long and slim.

'Well, I've spent the last three months unravelling his love life and I need a break.'

Martin held out the bottle towards her. 'One for the road?'

'No, really Martin.' She held her hand over the glass. 'This is just fine.'

Martin poured himself another and raised a toast again. '*Salud.*'

She raised hers back and laughed. '*Skol.*'

Martin drank most of it back in one. 'Are you on your own at Christmas, Ruth?' he was surprised to find himself asking.

Ruth shook her head emphatically. 'No, I have to go to Oxford. There's a lot of material I need to dig out of the Bodleian Library. I'm combining it with a trip to see friends. And you?'

Martin retreated. Played safe. 'Well, we usually go to the Rudges.'

'That's nice. I envy you.'

After Ruth had gone, Martin sat at the kitchen table and contemplated the parcel she had given him. Then curiosity got the better of him and he pulled the silver ribbon and ran his fingers under the flaps at both ends of the wrapping paper and folded it back. Inside there was a card. On the front was Robert Capa's photograph of Hem, his son Gregory and two rifles, leaning against a log in Sun Valley, Idaho. On the back was written, 'From Ruth Kohler and the Admirers of Ernest. Happy Christmas.'

Beneath the card was a copy of the *Toronto Daily Star* for 27th January 1923 and below it a copy of the first *Esquire* magazine ever printed.

As Martin was opening her present, Ruth was driving along a narrow road that led between wet, ploughed fields wondering if he had opened it yet and wondering why she had lied to him about spending Christmas with friends.

She wound down her window. It was warm and the easterly air was stale.

Fifteen

It was early January and the weather had turned numbingly cold. But inside the post office Harold Meredith was concerned with more than the temperature.

'What's wrong with it?'

'There's nothing wrong with it, Mr Meredith,' said Martin.

'Then why are you –' He tapped on the glass. 'Can you hear me?'

'Yes, I can hear you.'

'Then why are you closing down?'

'We're not closing down, we're going to move into another part of the building whilst the improvements are done. When you next see it it'll be a different place.'

Harold Meredith's eyes narrowed suspiciously. 'What will it be?'

'It'll be a post office, but much more comfortable and easy for you to use.'

'It's easy to use now, except for this blooming thing.'

'What's that?'

'This thing.' He jabbed a thin finger at the sliding security box. 'Jaws. You could get rid of that for a start.'

'It's for security reasons, Mr Meredith,' said Martin wearily. 'You know that.'

'If you ask me, it's the criminal that runs the country these days,' went on Mr Meredith. 'It's like that card they've given me for my meter. What was wrong with putting a coin in? Oh, no, they said, this is much more secure. Well, I said, I've got three jars full of 10 p's. What am I going to do with them? Well, they said, give them to us and we'll give you a credit. I said, you take your hands off my 10 p's.'

'That's the electricity company, Mr Meredith, you'll have to go and talk to them.'

Pamela Harvey-Wardrell, looking like some legendary Cossack general in a lovat greatcoat, knee-length leather boots and black astrakhan hat, glared into the back of Harold Meredith's head from three places away. She cleared her throat. Without turning, Mr Meredith sighed, picked up his gloves and cap, unhooked his walking-stick and made his way slowly across to the writing desk.

Mrs Harvey-Wardrell reached Martin and handed over the details of her road tax renewal. 'I don't know why all our post offices have to be fortresses these days, do you Martin? I mean take France – d'you know France at all?'

Martin shook his head. 'I'll need the test certificate,' he said.

Mrs Harvey-Wardrell rummaged in her bag. 'We're terribly fond of the Ardèche, always nipping off there if Perry can be spared from the City, and the post offices there are frightfully good. Cats on the counter, glorious smell of cooking from the back, *ragoût* simmering for the lunch hour. Everything quite wonderfully relaxed.'

A small furtive man in a tight brown suit whom Martin had not seen before came briskly up to the counter. 'Excuse me –'

Mrs Harvey-Wardrell's head flicked down. 'Excuse *me*!'

The man appealed to Martin. 'I'm looking for –' But he got no further.

'I don't care who you're looking for, it is the absolute height of bad manners to intrude upon a private transaction.'

'Can't we just get on with it,' suggested an increasingly aggressive nursing mother who had been queuing for nearly twenty minutes.

Mrs Harvey-Wardrell swivelled round to deal with the new threat, and the furtive man took his chance. He leaned towards Martin. His eyes were set well back in a narrow, pinched face. 'I'm looking for Mr Marshall, please.'

Before Martin could say anything, Nick Marshall, looking

none too pleased, came up behind him and ushered the man rapidly to the door at the end of the counter.

Martin checked the test certificate and the certificate of car insurance and wrote down the registration details of Mrs Harvey-Wardrell's nine-year-old Daimler on the new licence.

She looked around the office proprietorially. 'And when is the grand transformation to take place?'

'The end of January.'

'Well, I can't wait.'

'*We* all have to,' muttered the increasingly militant nursing mother.

Mrs Harvey-Wardrell chose to ignore this.

Elaine was in the outer office when Martin went through for his lunch. He reached up on to the shelf, took down the plastic container, peeled off the lid and removed a foil-wrapped package, wedged in beside an apple and an overripe tomato.

Elaine was reading a magazine and marking the page every now and then with a ball-point. Her wide, strong face wore a preoccupied frown.

Martin had not been alone with her since that day on the sea front. Despite what she had said to him then, he had half-expected Elaine to ring and reinstate the Christmas invitation. But she hadn't and for the first time in many years Martin and his mother had spent Christmas alone together at Marsh Cottage. They'd had a chicken from the deep freeze.

A howl of laughter came from Echo Passage. Schoolchildren used it as a short cut into the town. Martin peeled back the foil and took out a shapeless bread roll. 'How are you, then?' he asked, with unconvincing nonchalance.

'All right.'

He nodded at the paper. 'Quiz?'

'Passes the time.'

'You must know every answer in the world by now.'

Having examined his roll for optimum point of entry he bit

carefully into the combination of ham and cheddar cheese. It was predictable but comforting.

Elaine laid her biro down and rubbed her eyes.

'What is going on, Martin?'

'Mm?' Martin grunted, his mouth full.

'I wish you'd tell me. I just wish you'd tell me.'

'What do you want me to tell you?'

'Well, what's going on here? I suppose I'm meant to have got used to the fact that my workmates get sacked. Now I'm supposed to jump up in the air because we're being modernised.'

'Look, Elaine.'

'Don't "Look, Elaine" me, I'm not one of your hired today, fired tomorrow part-timers that Marshall's screwing in the evening, I am a salaried postal officer with six years' experience and I expect to be told what is going on in this office!'

'Who's he screwing in the evening?' asked Martin with genuine bewilderment.

'God, I thought *I* knew nothing. Geraldine, of course. It's obvious, isn't it. She picks him up after work you know.'

'Well, I didn't know they were –'

'You mean to say he doesn't tell you everything over your three-course dinners at the Market Hotel?'

Martin was aggrieved. 'We only talk about work.'

'Really?'

It was almost true. 'Yes, that's about it.'

Elaine looked at him and thrust out her chin. 'Well, I wish he'd invite me. I might learn a thing or two.'

Martin tried, unsuccessfully, to catch a shower of crumbs that fell as he took another mouthful. 'He told us before Christmas the work was going to be done.'

'Like he told us Arthur Gillis had been sacked.' Elaine picked up an orange drink with the straw already protruding. Then she set it down again. 'Just telling isn't enough, Martin. Padge would have had us in there and explained what was going to happen. He'd have treated us like equals. He'd have asked us what we wanted, not told us what we were going to be given. Don't you see that?'

'Padge never had to explain anything. He never did anything.'

'Well, I'm beginning to think it was better that way,' she said.

Elaine sucked fiercely on the straw of her orange drink until it gurgled dry.

'I'll keep an eye on him,' said Martin. 'I'll tell him he has to let people know what's going on. Trouble is he's too busy. He's always got some meeting or other. Trying to drum up business. He talks to people all the time.'

'Like Joe Crispin?'

'Who's Joe Crispin?'

'He's a little man with a face like a ferret. He came in this morning looking for Marshall.'

'Oh, him. I didn't much like him.'

'Nobody does. He's a builder. And he's cheap and he's crooked, and when I came out here for coffee I saw Marshall shaking hands with him as if he'd just agreed to marry his daughter. Talking of which –' She had got no further when the door to the main office swung open and Geraldine appeared. She gave a quick professional smile, as a nurse might to a couple who must eventually be given bad news.

'Martin, there's someone to see you.'

He made a face. 'I'm having lunch.'

'I told her that, but she insisted. She says,' and here Geraldine mimed the flourish of a cigarette and mimicked a familiar drawl, 'you guys *know* each other.'

'Is she American?' Martin asked.

Geraldine's eyes rose heavenwards. 'No, she's Spanish. What do you think?'

Martin threw a sidelong glance at Elaine. He cleared his throat in what he hoped would sound a businesslike way.

'I'll come through,' he said, and laid aside the remains of his cheese and ham roll. Geraldine held the door open for him. Martin went through and surveyed the customers from behind the glass. Geraldine flashed a smile at Elaine, snapped her fingers, whispered, '*Hasta la vista*,' and followed him through. The heavy door swung shut on Elaine.

Ruth Kohler was at the end of the counter, beside the parcel scales. She waved at Martin and called out his name. As he moved down the counter towards her he anxiously scanned the queues. No one was showing much interest apart from the new coroner's wife. She was a woman called Bridget Moss and she'd been eager for everyone in the post office to know that. She was sharp, alert, professionally friendly and a good fifteen years younger than her husband, Eric.

Ruth looked excited. 'Can I come round?' she asked.

Martin shook his head. 'It's not allowed.'

'Can you come out?'

Martin looked up again. Bridget Moss threw him a bright smile. He knew that sort of smile. It was the sort of smile that said, 'I'm watching everything.' Ruth was beginning to laugh. 'My God, this is like the zoo!'

Other heads were turning now. The more she tried to suppress it the more hysterical Ruth's laughter became. 'And I've caught you at feeding time!'

'I'll come round,' said Martin severely.

He found the key and let himself into the public area. Ruth was recovering but was still the focal point of interest.

'Oh, I'm sorry, I'm sorry.' She blew her nose, severely, into a crumpled tissue.

He followed her eyes down to the waistband of his trousers. A flap of cheese had somehow lodged itself there. He brushed it swiftly away and lowered his voice. 'How can I help you?' he asked, trying to sound like a bank manager.

'Other way round, Martin. I might be able to help you,' said Ruth, rather more loudly than Martin might have liked. There were half a dozen people at the writing desk, filling in forms, or licking and applying postage stamps, and Ruth squeezed into a gap in the middle and beckoned Martin over. He tugged at his tie. He felt exposed out here in the public area. Like an engine-driver would sitting with the passengers. Ruth, unfazed, took out from her bag a large brown envelope from which she carefully withdrew a black and white photograph. She laid it on one of the blotters provided for customers. 'You see that?'

Martin peered down at it. It was a photograph taken in some sort of store-room or workshop. Various pieces of furniture stood about. 'What am I meant to be looking at?'

Ruth pointed to the centre of the photograph. 'There, against the wall.'

His eye was drawn to a sturdy, wooden armchair built like a garden seat. The base was slatted onto a chunky wooden frame, at each side of which were three vertical supports topped with a wide arm-rest. The chair-back was a plain, slightly-angled arrangement of two verticals and four curved cross-pieces. Leather straps and a broad footrest were attached to it. But the remarkable feature of the chair was that it had only one leg. And that was in the centre. It appeared to be of metal, the shape and thickness of a scaffolding bar, and it protruded some two feet from the base of the chair. Leaning awkwardly against the wall, it looked pathetic, a little like Tiny Tim's crutches at the Cratchits' Christmas party.

Ruth indicated the photograph. 'Interested?'

Martin was more aware of a fast-filling post office. 'Look, maybe I should have a look another time.'

Ruth ignored this and reached into the envelope again, pausing as she did so, like a magician at a children's party. 'Here it is again.'

This time she produced a larger picture. It was in colour, taken from a magazine, and in the foreground was the same single-legged chair. This time, however, the leg was bolted firmly on to the deck of a ship, which was listing in a high sea of towering navy blue waves and smudgy white foam. An unmistakable figure – broad-shouldered, wearing a white tennis cap, a brown cotton jacket and holding a fishing rod – was sitting in it with his back to the camera.

'Hemingway,' breathed Martin.

Ruth nodded and smiled with a touch of pride. She held the black and white photograph alongside it, then turned it over. 'Now you'll understand what you're looking at,' she said.

On the back of the black and white photograph was a gummed label, which bore a description in the big, bold, slightly ornate lettering of an elderly typewriter. 'Fishing chair,' he read, 'as used by Ernest Hemingway, Cabo Blanco, Peru, April 1956, whilst shooting action footage for the feature film of *The Old Man and the Sea*.'

Martin stared at the photographs again. He felt oddly nervous. 'Where is this chair?' he asked Ruth.

'It's in London.'

Martin looked from Ruth back to the photograph. He moistened his lips.

'It's yours if you want it,' she said.

'Mine?' he asked, huskily.

'There is a catch. You'll need seven hundred and fifty pounds.'

Martin felt his heart thumping. He glanced quickly around. At the counter three of the four positions were open and occupied. At one, Nick Marshall was enmeshed with a frail elderly lady and a lot of stamps. At another, Geraldine was patiently explaining some knotty point about Benefits to an unhappy young man whom Martin vaguely recognised from the garage, and next to her Mary Perrick, holding a fistful of notes and frequently dabbing her finger in the wet sponge, was laboriously counting out a savings withdrawal. The fourth bore a 'Position Closed' sign. The queues had lengthened now and heads turned quite openly towards him. He knew from experience that no matter how friendly customers might appear none of them ever saw a 'Position Closed' sign as anything other than a deliberate act of defiance on the part of the workforce.

Martin looked back again at the photograph. At Hemingway and his broad back against the chair and his huge bare foot revealed on a makeshift rest.

'We're too busy now. Can I talk to you later?'

'Look,' Ruth slipped the photographs back in the envelope and handed it to him. 'Take it, check it out and let me know. I think it's pretty neat, don't you? It would certainly go with the typewriter.'

Martin shook his head gloomily. 'It's not the sort of thing I can afford.'

'Nor me,' she said. 'But true fans find a way.'

She smiled, waved and was gone.

As he turned to go back behind the counter Martin noticed that Elaine had taken down the 'Closed' sign at his position and was already serving a line of grateful customers. He checked the Newmark electric wall clock, ascertained that he still had fifteen minutes of his lunch break left, unlocked the door and went back into the staff room. He lifted the flap of the envelope, brushed the crumbs from his sandwiches off the table, laid the photographs out and for quite a while gazed from one to the other.

Ten minutes later, Ruth reappeared in the post office, jumped the queue and pushed a note across to Elaine.

'I'm sorry, would you mind giving that to Martin? I have a telephone now. Tell him Ruth said to call.'

Sixteen

Dearest Beth and Suzy,

It's the time of goodwill here, and life is hell. But I *am* getting used to it. England is a comfortable, dull place where the bad things aren't as bad and the good things aren't as good as they are at home. People are 'awfully kind' and very decent and I feel safe and cared for the way I would in some awfully kind and very decent private hospital.

Christmas was sweet if a little weird. I picked out a place called the Bridge House Hotel, which is in the Cotswold Hills, west of London. Unlike any other hotel in the world the Bridge House has no reception, no check-in, no name on the door, no nothing. Not even a bell to ring, just a nice Merchant-Ivory hallway which smelt of polish and dried flowers. I guess I stood there admiring the polish for upwards of five minutes. Then someone tall and silent shows me up to a nice, chintzy little room on the second floor which is called not 4 or 12 or even Presidential Suite. It's called 'Filibeg'. (To save you looking it up in Funk and Wagnall's a filibeg is another name for a kilt.) Why call a room 'Filibeg'? The answer's obvious if you think about it. The owner's father's brother lived in Aberdeen.

Come the evening other human beings appeared in the bar, but they either knew each other or ignored each other. Four couples, one party of three with an elderly relative and two single women. The women throw me quick, shy smiles and the men quick, shy smiles followed by something more appraising.

On Christmas Day about half of them went to church, but I explained I was of the Chosen and went instead for a long walk by the river with the lady from 'Tam O'Shanter' (Scottish cap with a broad, circular flat top). She was nice and polite and civilised and we discussed the metaphysical poets, but all I really wanted to do was get back to see if there had been any further developments with the couple in 'Sporran' (an ornamental pouch of leather and/or fur worn hanging in front of the kilt) whom I'd heard fighting like bantams in the middle of the night. At Christmas dinner there was a sort of institutional jollity – the sort of good time you have when you feel obliged to have a good time. I sat next to Miss Tam O'Shanter and it was all very proper and decent. Until the next evening, the evening of what they call Boxing Day. Well, I don't know if it's just that they all know they're moving on next morning, but suddenly there is electricity in the air.

A small sharp-faced barrister offered to buy me a drink seconds before his wife arrived, then withdrew the offer. A golfer with teeth out of a fashion catalogue and a room temperature IQ who had ignored me for twenty-four hours, began emitting signals that were so embarrassingly blatant that at least two of his children turned to look at me as well. Mr Sporran was particularly attentive. He insisted I join him and his wife for dinner. I insisted on bringing Miss Tam O'Shanter and we all squeezed on to a corner table. We could have moved to a bigger one, but I soon got the idea that the squeezing was quite important to him.

He was tall and rather elegant in a run-down sort of way and his wife was a square-faced, heavy-jawed, hey-ho sort, and despite the night-time noises had no bruises about her person that I could see.

Anyway – plenty of thigh contact from Mr Sporran and I couldn't move out of range without making similar thigh contact with Miss Tam O'Shanter on the other side. She became a little flushed and drank a lot of water.

Mr Sporran had little trouble swinging our conversation round to his favourite topic. That the way you ate was the way you made love. Instant effect. Miss T. stops eating altogether. Mr and Mrs Sporran romp lustily through double portions of black forest cherry cake and I take chaste nibbles at my *crème brûlée* and try to remember not to lick my lips. After dinner Miss Tam O'Shanter bolts upstairs. Outside, taking much-needed gulps of English winter, I find the golfer, alone on a garden seat, sobbing. Impossible to avoid him, so I have to listen for nearly forty minutes to how much he hates his wife.

Followed, a little brusquely, by thirty seconds of why he should have married someone like me.

Thoroughly sobered up by now I flee back to Filibeg. There is a note under the door from Tam O'Shanter apologising for her behaviour and asking me to be sure to knock on her door before going to bed as she would like to explain everything. There was a cross after her name.

I checked the closet for Sporrans, closed my window against golfers, locked the door and went to bed with Ernest and Pauline. He snored.

Next morning at breakfast glaciers once more covered the face of the earth and it was impossible to make eye contact with anyone but the waitress! Then, quite by chance, the way the English do these things, the little barrister who'd made the first move of all came up to me as I was packing up the car, and said how nice it had been to meet me. His name was Roger Morton-Smith. He lived in London, was recently divorced, and was travelling with his new lady. She was in antiques, unusual things, nothing run of the mill (Kate, her name was). She was 'used to dealing with Americans' and they would love me to come and see them and maybe stay over in London at New Year. Then they swept off in a powder-blue Mercedes leaving me basking in a glow of vicarious affluence.

I was a little wary of visiting, but after a week's work in Oxford (not enough!) I took up their offer and we had lunch and I told them what I was working on and they showed me some pretty nice stuff. Clarice Cliff art deco, oak bookcases, Japanese screens. They think all Americans are oil millionaires and I fear I was quite a disappointment. However, a couple of weeks later, in the mail, come details of something 'right up my street'. My little heart leaps only to fall in pieces to the ground when I see that what they have for me is some goddamn chair in which EH tried unsuccessfully to reduce the world's marlin population and which they would sell me for ONLY eleven hundred dollars (though the big institutions could pay a lot more!) Well, I was about to write back and say I'll buy it for firewood . . . when I remembered. My fan! Girls . . . he is absolutely hooked –

The telephone rang. It was still new enough for the sound to take her by surprise. As she got up she noticed how suddenly darkness had come. She felt carefully beneath the shade of the rickety table lamp and found the switch. With the other hand she lifted the phone.

'Hello.'

'Is that Miss Kohler?' It was a man's voice.

'Ruth Kohler, yes.'

There was a pause. Not a heavy breather, prayed Ruth. Not already.

'It's Martin Sproale.'

'I'm sorry?'

'Martin, from the post office.'

'Oh, Martin. Yes.' With one hand she pulled the phone to her, with the other she extracted the last cigarette from a pack of Camel Lights. 'I'm sorry. I've been working. My mind is still in 1928.'

'*A Farewell to Arms*.'

'That's right.'

'Father's suicide.'

'Yes, indeed.'

'Did you know that he changed the ending of the book after his father's death?'

Ruth transferred the phone to her shoulder and reached for a box of matches. 'Well, that's pretty well known. Hemingway claims he rewrote the last page thirty-nine times.'

'Catherine and the boy were not going to die. Their death was his way of coming to terms with his father's suicide.'

'Well, it depends which way you look at it, Martin. I think the women around him at that time were exerting a much stronger influence on his writing than the men.'

There was a silence at the other end of the line. She struck a match, lit her cigarette and waited. When the voice came again it sounded a little thicker.

'I'm ringing about the chair.'

Ruth laughed and apologised. 'I'm sorry about all that. Bursting into the post office like an hysteric.'

'That's okay.'

'It just struck me as funny, you know, and I knew you'd appreciate it.'

'Funny?'

'Well, to sell a thing like that for over a thousand dollars.'

Martin's voice corrected her. 'Seven hundred and fifty pounds.'

'Yeah.'

'I don't think it's funny. I think it's unbelievable. To have the chance to sit in a chair he sat in, leaned on, fished from, every day for two months.'

Ruth pulled hard on her cigarette. 'Well, for a thousand bucks I'd want himself sitting in it.'

There was a pause.

'I'm sorry,' she said. 'Just a bad joke.'

'I know you hate him,' he said.

'Martin, his life is my work, but I happen to think that there are a lot of other people in his life just as interesting as he was.'

'Yes. Well, that's up to you. I think he was . . . he was like the ocean liner.' The way he said the word 'ocean' confirmed Ruth's suspicion that her caller had taken a drink or two.

'Yes?' she said cautiously.

'He was the ocean liner and they were the little tugboats that buzzed around him.'

Ruth laughed a little nervously. 'Never underestimate tugboats. They guide the liner into port.'

At the other end she could hear a sip and a swallow. This was all getting too serious.

'You sound as if you're finishing off the grappa,' she said, brightly.

'The grappa? No, that's your drink. I'm saving that for you.'

She laughed.

'Save it for both of us,' she said.

'I'm saving for the chair. That's what I'm saving for. I may only work at the bloody post office but I'm going to have it. You see. Excuse my language.'

'Be my guest. I come from New Jersey.'

'Will you please ask your friends, or your contacts to hang on to it. Okay? Will they do that? Will they give me some time?'

'If you're serious.'

'I'm deadly serious. I want that chair.'

Ruth narrowed her eyes as the smoke stung them. She could see a light moving outside. Mr Wellbeing worked until after dark these days when the fields were wet and heavy.

'In that case I'll tell them I have a buyer.'

'Tell them that. Tell them I need a week or two, though.'

'D'you have the money?'

Martin almost shouted down the phone. 'I'll *get* the money.'

'Okay, fine.'

There was a pause. She waited.

'Tell them I want it.' There was an urgency near to desperation in his voice now. 'It may take time, but please don't let it go.'

'I get the message,' said Ruth, stretching down and reaching out for the letter from the Morton-Smiths.

A beam of light swung across the room, followed almost immediately by the sound of Mr Wellbeing's tractor changing down a gear as it turned up the track towards the farm.

'Let me know if I can be of any more help then,' she said in a winding down sort of way.

'I will.'

There was a pause. The tractor rumbled past on its way up to the farm.

After a moment Martin's voice came again, and this time she detected the sound of a smile. '*Adiós, hija.*' His Spanish wasn't bad.

'*Adiós*, Papa.'

She hung up and smoked thoughtfully for a while. The

sound of the tractor receded. Soon she heard it turn and she heard the jarring scrape of metal as the trailer was reversed into the barn, then a shudder as the engine finally died.

When everything was quiet again she could feel her heart beating. She should really finish her letter home, fix something to eat and then read for at least a couple of hours. There was plenty to do, but at this precise moment she could do nothing. She felt unsettled. She was here at Everend Farm Cottage for the sole purpose of completing a book. A book that was important to her. A book that would establish her credentials as a serious scholar and maybe even make her a little money. She needed her time to be left clear and uncluttered. Now, almost without her noticing, she had allowed a stranger into her life and she had the uncomfortable feeling that he would not easily be persuaded to leave.

Seventeen

Elaine had inherited a fighting streak from her father. Frank
Rudge was an obstinate man and he'd never been far from a
fight. He was born down the coast at Alford, third son in a
family of fishermen. His father, John Rudge, had never had
much of an opinion of his youngest son. He thought him soft
and unambitious. When Rudge Senior retired he handed over
the business and the half-dozen boats it involved to Frank's two
elder brothers.

Displaying an unexpected abundance of the family talent for
stubbornness and tenacity, Frank moved north to Theston,
took a job with the local harbour-master, married a Theston
girl and set about finding a foothold in the tightly controlled
fishery business of his newly adopted home. Theston fishing
was in the hands of two or three families who didn't take kindly
to newcomers. But, with the help of some inside information
from the coast guards, Frank outmanoeuvred them by winning
a contract from the Ministry of Defence to maintain an area of
beach south of the harbour for amphibious vehicle training.
Three years later the army pulled out but Frank had made
enough money to build a processing and refrigeration depot
which the local fishing families reluctantly agreed to use. For a
while he was one of the most successful businessmen in
Theston. He was elected councillor in 1965, the year Elaine was
born, and Mayor three years later.

Then, in the late seventies, the depot folded. Frank Rudge
claimed that deep sea factory fishing had so depleted the
lucrative herring catches that he had no option but to close.
The speed with which he pulled out and the suffering caused to

local fishermen fed rumours that there was more to the story, but nothing was ever proved. Rudge moved swiftly to invest what money he had left in a troubled local haulage business, saving a dozen jobs in the town and making him once again the local hero. A disastrous move from haulage into property in partnership with Ernie Padgett was Rudge's next attempt to prove his father's original judgement of him wrong. It cost him half a million pounds when the market collapsed a year later. After that he settled for a small greengrocery business, a small terraced house in the middle of town, a small heart attack and a small but growing role in local politics. In the last five years he had twice been elected Mayor, and he was currently the industrious and influential Chairman of the Planning Committee.

Whatever the rumours, Frank Rudge claimed never to have had any favours from anyone and it was in this spirit that Elaine had remained firmly unimpressed by Nick Marshall's invitation to a drink after work. However, Frank Rudge was also insatiably curious, and in that spirit she had accepted.

They met, at Marshall's suggestion, in the bar of the Market Hotel. In January, after Christmas and before the spring visitors arrived, it was still quiet. They sat opposite each other at a marble-topped round table beside an open fire.

'I know women don't like pubs,' Nick had said as he came back from the bar with two large orange juices and a packet of crisps. 'I thought you'd prefer it here.'

'I like pubs,' said Elaine, determined not to make things easy for him.

'Really?'

'Oh, yes. If you want to find out what's going on in Theston you have to go to the pub.'

Nick could see her trying. Trying very hard. She was tense, tight, sharp, and he knew that while she remained that way he had the advantage.

'Not to the Town Council then?' he asked as innocently as he could.

Elaine glanced up at him. 'They go to the pub as well,' she said.

Marshall smiled. 'You ever thought of following in Dad's footsteps?' he asked her, casually.

'Yes,' she lied. 'Often.'

They both drank. Elaine set her glass down first. 'D'you go to pubs?' she asked.

Marshall shook his head. 'Not if I can avoid it.'

'What do you do for a night out?'

'I don't feel the need for them,' he said, reaching for the bag of crisps.

'What does Geraldine think about that?'

His clear blue eyes flicked up to hers. Nick had never really looked at Elaine, not for long anyway. Her nose was big and her face oddly old-fashioned, like in those Second World War pictures of wives waving their husbands goodbye. But when she was on the attack her jawline hardened and her nostrils widened and her eyes sparkled attractively.

'What's Geraldine got to do with it?'

'Well, you're the one to answer that. You know her better than I do.'

Elaine took a crisp and pushed the bag towards him. He caught the smell of scent on her neck. A little too much. He smiled, shook his head and pushed the packet back.

'What's wrong, Elaine?' he asked, leaning forward, back held straight, lips slightly parted revealing almost faultless teeth.

Elaine sat back, paused, then spoke, chin thrust forward.

'Well, as you ask, quite a lot. I didn't like the way John Parr and Arthur Gillis were sacked. I think that part-timers are a cheap, easy option for the post office. They confuse the customers and they slow down business. And I personally resent being told nothing and asked nothing about a complete change to the office I've worked in for six years.'

'And Martin's not seeing you any more.'

Elaine felt herself redden. It was as much with shock as anything. She fought it angrily. 'I was talking about post office business.'

'So was I.'

She took a long draught of the orange juice. It tasted sweet and sickly.

'You asked me about Geraldine. I asked you about Martin,' said Marshall quietly. Then he moved in. With one controlled, continuous movement, he leaned forward, palms flat on the table, neck extended effortlessly forward until the strong, straight line of his nose and the smooth curve of his fine chin fixed her like gun-sights.

'I'm not a fool, Elaine. I was aware right from the word go that you and Martin regarded that post office as your own private little empire. You saw a nice little earner for Rudge and Sproale, protectors of the past, guardians of the ancient rights of the customer. Well, it's not easy for an outsider coming into a family business, you know.'

Elaine made to speak, but Marshall held up his hand.

'Unfortunately I'm not the sort to sit and file my nails waiting for the next customer. I saw another future for Theston. I saw a wider picture than wedding bells and baby socks and cosy Christmas dinners.'

Elaine's jaw set. She could hardly bear to look at him, but he wouldn't let her look away.

'I saw the business that paid for all these little dreams slipping quietly back into the Stone Age. I saw it waving goodbye to E-Mail and fibre-optics and video telephones. I saw Telecom and Mercury and anyone else with money and nous knocking Postman Pat off his bicycle and making off with his jolly old sack of letters.'

Nick Marshall kept his eyes on Elaine. She began to feel like she used to at school when the headmaster had her in. She had to remind herself that this man was younger than she was. Then Nick Marshall suddenly smiled.

'You're aggressive, Elaine. I like that. I am too. But don't fight *me*. Fight them. Fight everyone out there who wants to keep the Post Office small and cosy and cuddly.' His face came, almost imperceptibly, closer to hers. 'The business is changing. The only way to preserve what we've got, Elaine, is to go forward. And by the way, Geraldine and I don't live together.'

He suddenly stood up. 'Shall we go?'

Elaine looked around. She was too shaken to move. When she found her voice it sounded thin and unconvincing. 'Go where?' she asked.

Nick Marshall leaned down and took her elbow. 'For dinner. I've booked us a table in the restaurant.'

Elaine had no gloves or scarf with her as she left the Market Hotel that night, but she was only two streets away from home and warmth. She walked briskly along the High Street then slowed and stopped. She turned down towards the sea, then changed her mind and walked back in the direction of the church. The skies had cleared during the evening and a cold north wind gripped the town tight. With Elaine it had been the reverse. She had gone into the evening cool and clear and she had come out of it hot and confused. She stopped outside Mountjoy's Fashions and stared in at the vacant faces of the mannequins. Down one side of the lighted display was an enfilade of plaster bosoms. Some were black and some were white. At least half a dozen were quite badly chipped. The brassieres they carried were all different but the busts were the same. That's wrong for a start, she thought. No two busts are the same. She looked at them more closely and tried to imagine what it was men saw in busts, what it was that made them want to stare and touch and fondle. Jack Blyth had once told her that she had perfect breasts, and when she asked him how he was so sure he told her it was because he'd seen a great many.

Suddenly she missed Martin. She missed his moodiness. She

missed his uncertainty and his indecision and the pain in his expression as he tried to work out what was for the best. She realised that whatever they had or hadn't done together, she felt she knew him better than any man she'd ever met.

She walked on a few steps until she could see the church clock. It stood out clear and sharp tonight. It was fifteen minutes to ten.

Without any more debate she walked home, took a scarf and a pair of gloves from the basket inside the hall, took her car keys down from the hook and, shouting as nonchalantly as possible that she was going for a drive, she left the house again and climbed into her car.

She had been repelled by Nick Marshall. Repelled by his mocking, self-regarding arrogance. His presumption that she would want to do whatever he suggested made her breathless with indignation. She switched on the car radio. A lonely man was phoning in. She switched it off. There was frost about and she had to keep clearing a space on the inside of the windscreen in order to see the road ahead. She was excited at the thought of taking Martin by surprise. She would tell him as much as she could of the evening. It would be easy to tell him what Marshall had said about them and their relationship. It would be easy to tell him about Marshall's health obsession and how he had asked for the sauce to be removed from the salmon and the potatoes to be boiled without salt, and it would be easy to tell him how angry he'd been with the new waiter when he poured the wine, but it would be less easy to talk about the rest. Because it wasn't really what he had said, so much as how he'd said it, and how he'd looked at her when he was saying it.

She hit the brake pedal hard as the road shook and a massive truck cannoned past her heading south. The heavy lorries that used to have to crawl through Theston stopping for school-children were happier now they had the bypass. They thundered down it with relish, avenging thirty years of delays.

She pulled across into the turning lane then over the road, up a short landscaped rise and down along past the ragged silhouettes of gorse and hawthorn until after a mile or so she could see, with some relief, the lights of Marsh Cottage.

As she got out of the car the intense cold took her breath away. The wind was hard and grating out here. Straight from Siberia they were saying in the post office that day. The winds they talked about always came from places like that. Siberia, the North Pole, the Sahara. They never seemed to start in Middlesbrough or Falmouth or Preston. As she approached the house she could see the flickering blue glow of a television on the curtains. When she rang the doorbell, there was a long pause, and she was about to ring again when she heard Kathleen call out from the other side of the door.

'Who's there?'

'It's Elaine!'

A key turned and the door opened. 'Elaine? What a lovely surprise.'

'I'm sorry it's so late.'

'Come in, girl. You'll be freezing.'

Kathleen Sproale switched a light on and fussed her into the sitting room. Martin wasn't in there. On the television there was some unhappiness. Rows of gaunt, expressionless faces, gathered at a border crossing. In the bay window was Kathleen's work-table, from which hung a length of curtain, and a folded square of lining. 'I was doing some stitching,' she said. 'But I can't see so well at this time of night. Wait while I switch that off.'

Mrs Sproale felt around in an armchair and produced a remote control. On the screen a camera zoomed in. An amorphous crowd of people became a young boy's face. The zoom continued until only a pair of listless eyes filled the screen. Mrs Sproale pointed the control at the face and it disappeared.

'Tea, Elaine?'

'Well, I've really come to see Martin. Is it too late?'

Mrs Sproale shook her head apologetically. 'I'm afraid you're too early. He's still with his American lady.'

Eighteen

'Hemingway's nickname for Mary?'

'Kitten.'

Martin nodded. 'Correct. Her name for him?'

'Lamb?'

'Name of his dog at the Finca Vigia?'

'Black Dog.'

'Name of his cat?'

'Which one? There were fifty-two of them.'

'His favourite.'

'Christopher Columbus.'

The first frost of the winter was making its mark around the metal frames on the windows of Everend Farm Cottage, but it was still just possible to catch a glimpse of two figures sitting close by the red and gold glow of an open fire. It burned beneath a copper hood which drew the air and the smoke up an ageing brick chimney stack. The cottage itself was one of those modest, unambitious constructions which have a knack of surviving longer than their more palatial counterparts. Parts of the building were a hundred and fifty years old. A tiled roof had replaced thatch, metal frames had replaced wood on the windows and the lavatory had been brought indoors. Otherwise it remained much as it was built. Single storey, with a latch door that gave straight on to a parlour. An alcove window faced out to the west and on either side of the fireplace two smaller windows faced due south.

From the parlour a doorway led through to a low-ceilinged bedroom from which two other doors led off, one to a tiny space into which Ted Wellbeing had managed to squeeze a lavatory, a wash basin and a shower and the other to the kitchen.

Martin sat to one side of the fireplace, in a fat, low, well-worn leather armchair. There was a matching sofa at an angle to the fire but Ruth preferred to sit on the floor. All the floors in the cottage were uneven and, apart from the kitchen, cheaply carpeted. Her knees were drawn up tight to her chin and the firelight accentuated her angular, pointed features.

Martin had become daily more obsessed with the thought of owning the fishing chair. Every other evening since Ruth had first shown him the photograph he had rung her to make sure that it did exist, that she knew where it was and that it would not be sold to anyone else. His waking hours had become filled with visions of riding it high over the ocean swell, creaking and twisting this way and that, strapped in as if for execution, grappling to wrench some mighty aquatic adversary from the balmy waters of the Pacific Ocean.

Meanwhile he agonised over the finances. On eleven and a half thousand pounds a year, with his mother to help and their mortgage to pay, there was not a lot left over. He had already begun to put some by, but he reckoned it would be six months at the very least before he might have enough.

It was in the hope of heading off some of the constant phone calls that Ruth had invited him round. At the start of the evening Martin had been the painfully shy, polite and tongue-tied young man she first met, but she had poured liberal Scotches and talked about Hemingway rather than real life and the combination had opened him up.

One of them, she couldn't now remember which it had been, had suggested making up a sort of Hemingway *Trivial Pursuit*. Several Scotches later the idea had given way to a fiercely fought version of *Mastermind* in which they took turns to ask the questions. Ruth was having to work hard to keep up.

'You want to go on?' Martin asked her.

Ruth sighed doubtfully. 'Sure,' she said.

Martin laid his head back against the faintly discoloured top of the armchair, frowned in concentration, and began again. 'Hemingway's favourite bar in Havana?'

'Florida?'

'Wrong. Floridita. Name of the cabin cruiser he bought in 1936?'

'Pilar.'

'Horsepower?'

Ruth shook her head. 'I have no idea.'

'One hundred and fifteen. How did he pay for it?'

'Loan from Pauline?'

'No, loan from Arnold Gingrich, editor of *Esquire*, against future contributions.'

Ruth shook her head impatiently and reached for another cigarette. She shook the box but it was empty.

'Adriana Ivancich was the model for which story?'

'*Across the River and Into the Trees*.'

'What was her brother's name?'

'Older or younger?'

'Older.'

'Gianfranco.'

'In 1934 the Hemingways came back from Africa to Europe. On which ship and to what port?'

'The *Gripsholm* was the ship, yes? And the port was . . . Marseilles?'

'Villefranche.'

'Ah!' Ruth reproved herself angrily. She got up and walked across to the alcove where she had taken to working.

Martin leaned back. His head was beginning to ache. 'Shall we stop?' he asked.

Ruth searched about among her books and papers for the packet of cigarettes she knew was there. 'Keep going,' she said tersely.

Ruth found her cigarettes, lit one and resumed her concentration.

Martin began again. 'In which town did he marry Martha Gellhorn?'

Ruth muttered the question back to herself, then answered 'Cheyenne, Wyoming.'

'Year?'

'1939?'

'No, 1940.'

'Shit! Yes . . .'

'What sort of pistol did Lieutenant Henry carry in *A Farewell to Arms*?'

Ruth shook her head irritably. 'Guns. I don't know about guns.'

'Astra 7.65, short barrel.'

She held up her hands theatrically. 'Okay, that's boys' talk. No more guns, right?'

'Which of his wives left all his manuscripts on a train?'

'Hadley.'

'Where?'

'Gare de Lyon, Paris.'

'*Life* magazine ran *The Old Man and the Sea* in its entirety. How many copies did it sell in its first two days of publication?'

Again Ruth bit her lip and shook her head. 'I've no idea.'

'Five and a half million,' said Martin emphatically. He usually asked the questions without looking at her, but this time he watched her reaction to the answer. She didn't appear to have one, other than looking a little cross. Martin went on.

'Which year did Hemingway win the Nobel Prize for Literature?'

'1953.'

'1954.'

Ruth cursed herself roundly. She leaned back and closed her eyes. 'I've had it.'

Martin looked up at the clock with a small smile of satisfaction. It was almost midnight. They'd begun nearly two hours ago, with decorous, generous questions about titles of books and wives' names, but now it was a matter of pride and persistence.

'Is this stuff good or bad for the memory?' asked Ruth as she reached for the Scotch.

'Probably both,' said Martin.

She poured herself a generous measure.

'We'll see,' said Ruth. 'Your turn.'

'We going on then?'

'Sure. It's time you took a bit of punishment.'

Martin made a half-hearted attempt to pull himself out of the armchair. 'I've got to be at work at half past eight.'

She stood and moved across to the kitchen. He heard the tap running as she watered the whisky. She returned, stood in the doorway and took a drink. 'One more round then we're done. Okay?'

Martin nodded. 'What's the score?' he asked thickly.

'God knows.'

Ruth drank again. She was a little unsteady by now, but with a deep breath she summoned up all her energy.

'Okay,' she decided with a final flourish. 'Welcome to the last, deciding round of *Hemingway Challenge*.'

'It *is* midnight,' Martin added edgily.

'Mr Sproale is anxious and who wouldn't be with so much at stake. So, here goes. How old was Ernest when he stopped wearing dresses?'

'What?'

'I'll repeat the question. How old was Ernest when he stopped wearing dresses?'

'Three months?'

'Three and a half years. For how long after his birth did Mrs Hemingway keep Ernest in her bed?'

'Pass.'

'Six months.'

'Well, that's not the kind of thing –'

136

'Just answer the questions, please. How did he commonly refer to his mother in later life?'

'Grace?'

'No. "That bitch".'

'What sort of question's that?'

'Which letter did he have trouble pronouncing?'

'L,' said Martin, reluctantly.

'Good!' Ruth went on, eyes half-shut, her body tense with concentration. 'Which of his books was described as "lapsing repeatedly into lachrymose sentimentality and containing crucifixion symbolism of the most appalling crudity"?'

Martin pulled himself up on to the edge of his chair and shook his head. 'Look, I'm not answering that. That was in Kenneth Lynn's biography which was a load of tripe.'

'Answer the question please, Mr Sproale. Which was the book referred to?'

'*The Old Man and the Sea*,' Martin muttered, making another effort to get to his feet.

'Thank you. How did Max Eastman title his review of *Death in the Afternoon*?'

'Pass.'

'*Bull in the Afternoon*.'

Martin protested. 'Lots of critics were jealous. They couldn't afford to say they liked him.'

'Why do *you* like him?'

There was a silence between them. Then Martin pushed back his chair and stood up. 'I like him because. I like him because he wouldn't have got himself involved in a stupid game like this.'

Ruth sounded a mock fanfare. 'The winner!'

As he was leaving she leaned one arm against the wall by the door and bowed her head contritely. 'I had too much Scotch . . . I'm sorry . . .'

Martin shrugged. He pulled on his anorak. She raised her

head and watched him for a moment. He took the cycle clips from his pocket and attached them to his trousers. Then he felt in the pockets again and produced a pair of blue knitted gloves.

'That was incredible,' she said. 'Have you ever thought of going on a game show?'

Martin didn't smile. He pulled on the gloves. 'Of course not. Have you?'

Ruth spread her arms again. 'There I go again. Big feet.'

Martin nodded goodbye. He took off a glove and held out his hand. Ruth shook it with mock formality. He pulled open the door and was about to leave when she stopped him. 'Look, will you do something for me?'

'So long as it's not another quiz.'

'Well, it's sort of a quiz, but I don't want to play it with you.'

'Who do you want to play it with?'

'Hemingway.'

'I'm not with you.' Martin was tired now. He'd had enough of games, but Ruth was suddenly animated.

'Please,' she said, beckoning him back in and pushing the door shut. 'Five minutes, that's all.'

She walked a little way into the room, picked a cigarette out of the pack and turned back to him. 'I spend my days writing about all the women who knew Hemingway. Right?'

Martin nodded wearily and watched her light the cigarette. She blew the smoke out urgently and began to pace the room again. 'I read their letters, their laundry lists, their diaries, their notebooks, whatever, and I feel I know them better than they know themselves. But Ernest I have a real problem with. I just don't like the guy very much.'

Martin managed a weak smile. 'You don't have to tell me,' he said, but she didn't seem to hear.

'I can respect his work, some of it, and I can admire his . . . his physical strength, his courage. But I cannot see much that would explain why so many of these very intelligent, attractive,

138

sensible women would want to spend more than a couple of days with him, let alone a lifetime.'

She walked across to the fire and flicked off the ash from her cigarette.

'The trouble is I'm getting all one-sided about it. I need to project myself into that great big, bull-necked head. I need to get in there and look around. And I can't.'

She looked across at Martin. His sky-blue anorak was zipped to the throat. His trousers were clipped. His blue knitted gloves were in place. Soon he would slip a royal blue bobble hat over his thatch of light red hair. He was an unlikely Hemingway.

'You know him, Martin. You know him better than I ever will. You just said that yourself.'

Martin shifted uncomfortably. It was the way she had used his name. She hadn't used it often.

'No, I'm not playing games,' she said. 'I'm not being a clever American bitch trying to score points. I'm serious.'

Martin was embarrassed. 'Well I'm a thick Englishman because I don't understand what you want.'

'Here's an example.'

Martin frowned.

'Just real quick. Please?' She indicated the armchair. 'Just sit down a minute, somewhere comfortable.'

Martin shook his head, moved reluctantly to the chair and perched himself on one of the arms. Ruth reached for the bottle, found his glass on the table, recharged it and handed it to him. Her lean, light olive skin seemed to shine. Her eyes were darker than ever. Her long, rangy body seemed light and alert.

'Now, if I were your wife Pauline and less than three weeks ago I had just delivered you, Ernest, a son by Caesarean section after a seventeen-hour labour which I thought I would never survive, and you, Ernest, had just planned a fishing trip to Wyoming, how would you tell me about it?'

'Well, he might say –'

'No. What would *you* say, Ernest?'

Martin sat quite still for a moment. He raised the whisky glass to his lips and drank. Then a curious thing happened. First it was a sort of physical transformation. Martin lowered his head and when he raised it again it seemed heavier and his narrow shoulders rose, went back and widened to accommodate it. But even more extraordinary than this sudden illusion of bulk and substance was the way he looked at her. Keeping the head rolled a little forward, Martin jutted out his jaw and fixed her with a scowl which, as she was to describe it later, did not belong to him.

He stood up and took a step towards her. Ruth instinctively retreated.

'Listen to me for Christ's sake.' His voice had dropped an octave. The accent was robust, if not entirely accurate. The point was that whoever this was, it wasn't Martin.

'I ain't gonna apologise for a crime I didn't commit. You do your job, I do mine. Right?'

Then the scowl vanished as swiftly as it had come and a smile spread across the face like sun emerging from a cloud. He straightened his shoulders and raised his head until he was looking down on Ruth the way she remembered her father used to.

'I'm a writer, baby, and I love you very much, Mrs P. and I love the boy. Wyoming at this time of the year is the only thing in the world that's more beautiful than you are.'

A slow smile spread over Ruth's face. She shook her head slowly. The man opposite her stopped, relaxed, smiled quickly and awkwardly, and became Martin Sproale again. He cleared his throat and made for the door.

'That's bullshit,' Ruth said admiringly. 'That's *very good* bullshit.'

Nineteen

The refurbishment of Theston post office was taking longer than was expected. Meanwhile pensions, licences, benefits, packets, parcels, recorded deliveries, visitors' passports and the rest all had to be dealt with in the cramped confines of a temporary area, half the size of the old one.

One Thursday, with February approaching and still no escape from plaster board and unshaded light bulbs, Martin felt disgruntled enough to confront Nick Marshall at close of business.

Marshall was defensive. He pulled out the aerial of his mobile phone, then pushed it in again, with what would have passed, in a lesser man, for nervousness. 'The improvement programme is a lot more complicated than we thought, Martin. There's a problem with the roof.'

'The *roof*? I thought we were just putting up a few new partitions.'

'Well, that's what I thought, but they've found a serious weakness. With the beams.' Nick Marshall felt the onset of the twitch and Martin saw it too. Marshall clenched his jaw and looked purposeful, but the right side of his mouth still fluttered. 'This is an old building, Mart.'

'1934?'

'Well, that's old. That's nearly sixty years old. Padgett should have reported all these problems a long time ago.'

'So, how much longer do we have to put up with this?'

'I've got Crispin to do a full report on the state of the place.'

'Crispin?'

'The builder,' added Marshall, quickly.

'Ah, yes.' Martin remembered where he'd heard the name now. Elaine had called him a crook.

'If it's as bad as it sounds we may have to move to a TSA.'

'What's that?'

Nick Marshall drew his lips right back, as if someone had very suddenly inserted something into his bottom. 'Temporary Secure Alternative.'

'Like what?'

'Well,' his jaw was still clenched, as if in considerable pain. 'There's space at the back of Randall's.'

He walked away from Martin, along the counter, checking drawers, locks, computer keyboards. Martin followed him. 'Randall's?' he asked incredulously. 'The sweetshop?'

'And newsagent,' Marshall added, with a touch of asperity. 'There's a back area which they use for storage. I've had a look and that could be up and running in a couple of weeks.'

'Are you serious?'

Marshall peered closely at the latest edition of *Counter News*. 'If you'd like to remain here while the roof caves in, Martin, maybe you could explain the reason to our customers.'

'So we're ending up in a sweetshop after all.'

'It'll only be a month or two, assuming there's no real problem here.'

Martin felt weak and suddenly quite short of breath. He wished, for once, that Marshall would turn and look at him.

'How is it going to work?' Martin asked.

Marshall tapped his finger on the copy of *Counter News*. 'That's interesting. They want us to use PF 58 forms for compensation claims against Parcelforce, but they don't send us any. Have you seen them, Mart?'

Martin's hands were hot. He rubbed them quickly on the side of his trousers. 'How is it going to work?' he repeated. 'This temporary accommodation?'

Marshall cleared his throat. 'It'll be fine.'

'How do you turn the back room of a sweetshop into a post office? Temporarily?'

The side of Marshall's mouth jerked as if being raked by machine-gun fire. 'We use a company called Elldor.'

'Who are they?'

'Don't you read your *Counter News*? They're a private company formed to do post office conversions.'

'What about the post office engineers?' asked Martin.

'They *are* the post office engineers.'

'You mean they'll set up a post office and take it all down again?'

'If they have to.' Marshall unlocked one of the tills, tidied a piece of paper off the counter into it and pushed it shut again.

'They *will* have to,' said Martin.

Marshall nodded. 'Then they will,' he said quietly. He moved towards the door, anxious to keep his back to Martin. 'I certainly think the customers deserve better than this,' he said, raising his hand to avoid a cluster of wires hanging down from the ceiling.

'I think the customers need their post office back,' said Martin angrily. 'I think most of them are getting a little bit fed up with all this. A move and then another move. It's not good for business.'

Marshall turned from the door. He smiled. It was a controlled smile, wide enough both to prevent his mouth from moving involuntarily and to reveal his long, regular, largely unfilled, ever-so-slightly pointed alabaster-white teeth. He took a step towards Martin. 'You know, the trouble with you, Martin, is you're a short-term man. Maybe you should start to take the longer view.'

'I think of my customers, that's all, Nick.'

'I'm thinking of you, Martin.' He revealed his teeth again, more generously this time. 'I've been watching you. You're getting restless.'

Martin nodded at the makeshift counters. 'It's working in the middle of a bloody building site.'

Marshall looked at him appraisingly. 'No, it's deeper than that, if you ask me. What you need is a challenge.'

'Oh?'

'I think it's time to get off your bike, Mart. Take on a little more responsibility.'

'What did you have in mind?'

Marshall's left hand played again with his mobile. He put his head on one side and looked hard at Martin, as if coming to some sort of decision. Then he stretched his right hand out towards him, index finger pointing.

'If you're interested, there's someone you should meet.'

Martin looked suspicious and Marshall gave him one of his warmest, most thorough, most deliberately disarming smiles. 'Come round to the flat tonight. About seven. I'll get Geraldine to cook something up. We'll have a chat.'

Martin must have still looked dubious for he added, 'It could be worth your while.'

Twenty

Marshall's flat was small and sparsely furnished. It occupied one side of the top floor of what had once been both a family house and a country hotel on the outskirts of Atcham. A few dull prints of naval inaction relieved the blandness of avocado walls. The furniture seemed carefully chosen for its neutrality. There was a smell of new carpet about. Martin glimpsed a tidy bedroom almost entirely taken up with a large double bed covered by a paisley duvet. A pile of magazines was stacked high on one side of a dressing table. The room next to the bedroom looked more of an office. Through a crack in the door he could see shelves full of directories, at least two computers and thick clusters of wires and cables. He could detect no signs of a feminine presence, indeed it was hard to think where one might fit in.

'Why do you live right out here?' Martin asked, as Marshall handed him a pitifully small Scotch.

'Well, it suits me for now. I'm not a great one for putting down roots. Here, have a look at this.' He picked up a copy of *Business Investor* magazine, and tossed it across to him. The cover illustration featured a montage of aerials and matt-black satellite dishes beneath the heading, 'Future Perfect. The Next Revolution'.

'Page fifteen.'

Marshall disappeared into one of the rooms and a moment or two later Martin could hear him talking on the telephone. He opened the magazine and found the article, but couldn't understand much of it. It was full of terms like 'information super-highway', 'interactive services' and 'electronic cottages'. The gist seemed to be that information technology was now so sophisticated that there seemed little necessity for two human beings ever to meet again.

Martin was wading slowly through this world of endless possibilities when he heard a key in the lock and a moment later Geraldine Cotton pushed the door open and, holding it with her foot, reached outside again for two bulging carrier bags. Martin got up. 'D'you want a hand?'

She shook her head and he sat back down again. She pulled a last bag in and changed her mind. 'You could take those two through to the kitchen for me, that'd be a help.'

Martin sprang up again. He took them through and watched her as she unbuttoned an old wide-shouldered tweed coat. She slipped it off, revealing a collarless flannel shirt draped low over a navy teeshirt and a short, tight, red leather skirt. She slipped her feet unselfconsciously out of a pair of high-heeled shoes.

'He's given you a drink then,' she said.

'And a magazine.'

'You *are* honoured. People usually just get the magazine.'

Geraldine dropped the coat on a chair and quickly looked around the room. 'Not too bad,' she muttered to herself, then smiled brightly as she passed by Martin. 'Sit down. You look uncomfortable.'

Martin selected the sofa. It was imitation leather of some kind and its surface had a thin, sticky texture. It sighed unhappily as he sat down. Geraldine briskly dealt herself a Scotch and he noticed she took it neat and large and very gratefully. 'Drowning sorrows?' Martin asked.

She laughed. 'Drowning Tesco's. The whole of Suffolk was in there tonight. Don't they have any other shops round here?'

'Not many, thanks to Tesco's.'

Geraldine laughed. 'Are you a Green?' she asked, disappearing into a kitchen that gave on to one end of the room. In order to reply, Martin had to get up once again, and move closer to the kitchen. He hovered in the middle of the room.

146

'I don't save rain forests, if that's what you mean. But I care about the shops, yes.'

She gave him a faint smile, halfway between amusement and approval. 'Good for you.'

She was about to say something else when Marshall bounded back into the room. 'Sorry about that. Business call. Sit down, Mart, please.' Martin, who had only just stood up, sat down again.

'Did you read the article?'

Martin nodded equivocally. 'Interesting.'

'Yep.'

Geraldine began opening packets and crunching wrappings and clattering around in cupboards. Nick Marshall peeled off the jacket of his sage-green flannel suit, loosened his tie and settled himself into a wing-back armchair beneath a solid, unimaginative print of two First World War frigates becalmed on an unlikely pea-green sea. He was not drinking, Martin noticed. Marshall checked his watch. He glanced to the kitchen. Then he rubbed his hands together and interlocked his fingers, stretching the palms of his hands away from him.

'Mart, you remember asking me once about how I could afford hotel meals on a postal manager's salary?'

Martin didn't remember asking any such thing, but he recognised the familiar formula and he knew that it was an introduction to whatever it was that Marshall was about to tell him.

'Well, I think the time has come for me to give you an explanation.'

Martin tried to look duly grateful. Marshall indicated the magazine. 'That's what it's all about.'

Martin looked down again at the pages as if enlightenment might lie there. None was forthcoming. Meanwhile Nick Marshall cradled his hands behind his head, leaned back against the wall and launched into his explanation.

'I'm what they used to call a computer whiz-kid.

Unfortunately I never knew I had the skills until I went to work for the Post Office. I never knew I had *any* skills, which is why I went to work for the Post Office. No offence intended, but you know what I mean.' He suddenly straightened up and leaned forward. 'While I was at Luton they were installing the first counter computers and asking for our reactions. I'd become fascinated by the buggers and I got myself on a night-school course to learn as much as I could as quickly as I could and when they came round from Head Office I not only gave them my reaction, I gave them a programme which was one hell of a lot better than the one we were working on.' He stopped and from the way he flashed a look across at him Martin had the uncomfortable feeling that he expected him to understand what he was talking about.

'Well, I was thanked and patted on the head and they took my improvements and I never heard another word about it. Eighteen months later they announce their new Contour Plus system into which, surprise, surprise, half my work was incorporated. They were installing these all over the country and it would have cost them a lot of money to admit that one of their own clerks had had a hand in designing them. So they ignored me, and I protested and they threatened me with the sack. Well, by that time I'd moved on a bit and I'd become fascinated by DIANE.'

Martin grasped eagerly at this morsel of human interest. 'Diane?'

'Direct Information Access Network, Europe. I was working on a system that would be able to co-ordinate every daily post office transaction anywhere within the EC, virtually simultaneously. Unfortunately this required very powerful equipment. The Post Office had the equipment, but they'd already screwed me so I had to decide whether to stay inside and develop it with them or sell the information on.' He suddenly broke off. 'Gerry!' he called towards the kitchen. 'Did Matt call?'

Geraldine called back. 'Twice. He'll be in later.'

He switched seamlessly back to Martin. 'Thankfully there were some buggers in the Post Office who could see the advantages. Some of these people were very high up and they knew about my system and they were impressed. But they knew that the longer the legislation took the greater the uncertainty over the funding. So rather than hang around they would take a calculated risk and go into development with a European partner. That way they could hit the ground running when privatisation came along.'

'Wouldn't it have been easier just to leave the Post Office?' Martin asked.

'It's early days. We have to keep a low profile. There are two or three groups chasing the same technology, but they're not there yet. The Post Office network could beat the balls off the rest. If it's used properly.'

Martin had the distinct and uncomfortable feeling that he should not be hearing this. Geraldine was cutting and slicing and humming *Aïda* in the kitchen.

'So,' Martin had to make an effort to concentrate. 'Are you saying that you're involved with a private company –'

Marshall nodded. 'I'm a limited company, yes. I have to be for my own protection.'

'And your company is involved with an outside partner?'

'Sure. My company, Shelflife Limited, sells my services to an international communications company called Nordkom.'

'Whilst you're still an employee of the Post Office.'

'Right.'

Martin found himself glancing fearfully at the door. He started to speak then dropped his voice as Geraldine appeared from the kitchen, glanced at them both, smiled and walked down the passage towards the bedroom. Marshall nodded after her. 'She's all right. She works for Shelflife. Knows everything.'

Martin stared at him. His head swung back to Geraldine only to see a door shut behind her. He slowly turned back to

Marshall. 'Surely,' he began haltingly. 'If this is true, it's unbelievable.'

Nick flicked his hair and allowed himself a smile. 'Nicely put.'

His smugness made Martin angry as well as puzzled. 'I mean, it's absolutely wrong, isn't it? You're employed by the Post Office. It's unethical.'

'They were unethical first.'

Martin swallowed the remains of his whisky. 'Why are you telling *me* all this?'

Marshall stretched out his long legs. 'Because I have a feeling your great love for the Post Office establishment is no greater than mine. It died the day they appointed me Manager, didn't it? We're brothers under the skin, Martin. We both feel a bit thwarted. Another?' He pointed at Martin's glass.

Martin held it out tentatively. He wanted to keep a clear head so he could remember all this. 'Thanks. Small one,' he added. Unnecessarily.

Marshall stood up. He stood easily, casually, hands thrust comfortably into trouser pockets. Geraldine passed by and smiled. As Marshall spoke he moved to a trayful of bottles. 'Besides which, I need your help.'

'To do what?'

Marshall looked around. 'Seen the Scotch, Gerry?'

Geraldine's arm with a rolled-up sleeve and a bottle of Scotch appeared round the kitchen doorway.

'For various reasons – proximity to continental markets, low land values, local political stability – we, that is, we and Nordkom, see Theston as the prime location for the transmission centre of the system we're working on.' He bent forward, poured a careful quarter inch into Martin's glass and handed it to him. 'Theston will be the nerve centre of the operation. It would be nice to have someone working for us with . . . local expertise.'

Martin found his mouth was quite dry. His grip around the glass tight and warm.

Marshall replaced the bottle and walked across to the window. He pushed one of the curtains gently aside and looked out. Then he let the curtain fall back and turned again to Martin. 'And of course you would be entitled to a consultancy fee.'

'A consultancy fee?'

'Oh, yes. From the moment you came on board you'd be entitled to a fee.'

Marshall reached into his jacket and drew out an envelope. 'I didn't expect you to come here for nothing.'

He laid a long, buff envelope on the coffee table.

'What's that?'

'That's a thousand.'

'A thousand *pounds*!'

'To begin with.'

Martin stared down at the table.

He could not take his eyes from the envelope. It lay there like one of those killer plants he'd read about: innocent and deadly at the same time. Innocuous until touched, then instantly snapping shut to engulf the molester. Martin knew that whatever happened he must not touch it. He heard Marshall's crisp, classless voice, as if from a long way away. 'Think of it as an investment in your future,' it was saying. 'And the future of the town you were born and bred in. What you are becoming part of is something exciting, and groundbreaking. It's something that can only do good.'

There was a sudden hiss and a resounding clang from the kitchen. 'Shit, there goes the spinach!' Geraldine shouted.

Nick Marshall called out to her. 'What time did you tell him?'

'There's spinach all over the fucking floor.'

'What time did you tell him?'

'What? Oh, seven thirty!' Geraldine shouted back.

There was a faint noise outside. Marshall went across to the curtain and pulled it aside again. 'That'll be him,' he said.

Martin looked up quickly. An image had come powerfully into his mind. It was one of towering waves and a lone figure strapped into a chair on the stern of a pitching boat. 'Nick?' His voice was thick and barely recognisable. 'This . . . consultancy fee . . .' Nick was moving to the door.

Martin spoke rapidly. 'If I were to accept it . . . *if* I were . . . I have to be sure . . . you must *promise* me that the Post Office will never know.'

Marshall reached for the lock. 'You're safe, believe me.'

'On your honour?'

Marshall pulled the door open. Footsteps could be heard hurrying up the stairs. Marshall turned to him again. 'On my honour, Mart.'

Martin shut his eyes tight. There was a jumble of sights and sounds. The lone fisherman turned and smiled and beckoned him. Martin opened his eyes, leaned down to the table, picked up the envelope and slipped it quickly inside his jacket.

The door opened. Martin's heart froze.

The man who stood there was John Devereux, Area Co-ordinator for Post Office Counter Services, the local boss, the hard-eyed pragmatist whose official visits to the post office had been likened to night raids from the Gestapo. Martin felt a sense of searing, flooding panic.

He rose awkwardly to his feet. He was aware only of the sudden awful enormity of what he had done. The envelope in his inside pocket seemed to swell and expand. He felt it tearing through the lining, rearing up and out over his lapel, racing towards his chin like some uncontrollable erection. It must be impossible for the South East Area Co-ordinator not to see his guilt, smell his shame, feel his loathsomeness, sense his naked treachery. Devereux held out his hand.

Martin, clammy palm cupped nervously, took hold of it. Devereux's grip was strong and firm, his gaze was cool and piercing, and his South Yorkshire accent was gruff and uncompromising.

'Good to 'ave you on board, Sproale.'

Martin remained in shock for much of the subsequent meal. He hardly spoke a word, half the time listening to Marshall, the unquenchable enthusiast, and Devereux, the blunt layman, and the other half running his long fingers discreetly over the slim bulge in his jacket pocket.

Slowly, as the wine took its effect, he began to recover his confidence. He and Devereux were the only ones drinking and a tacit intimacy had grown between them as the meal went on. By the time Geraldine went out to make coffee and Marshall to make another phone call, Devereux was regarding his lowly employee with mellow benevolence.

He nodded towards the study from where the faint sound of a telephone conversation could be heard.

'Genius, that lad,' said Devereux. 'Fucking bloody genius.'

Martin, warmly full of relief and Tesco's house claret, responded with vigorous agreement.

'That's why the buggers hated him,' said Devereux.

'Who hated him?' asked Martin, not quite following.

'The fucking Post Office.' Devereux jabbed a finger in Marshall's direction. 'Just because he was a counter clerk they couldn't believe he had a brain.'

'Right.'

'I spotted him. I didn't know Jack Shit about computers but if his system could deliver what he promised I could see it was a damn sight better than the one we were about to spend ten million on.' He reached into a pocket and brought out a packet of Henry Winterman's cigars. There was one left.

'Gerry!' he shouted towards the kitchen. 'You got some matches?' Geraldine appeared round the doorway and tossed a box of Swan Vestas hard and accurately into his lap. 'Ta!'

He looked across at Martin as he lit the stubby, unimpressive cigar. It clearly pained him to be seen putting something so small in his mouth. 'Used to like 'avanas, but they didn't like me.' He inhaled with a grimace of pleasure and jabbed his head back towards the low sound of Marshall's voice in the back room.

'In six months' time, touch wood, fingers crossed, justice will have been seen to be done. And about bloody time.' He sent a wreath of cigar smoke spinning towards Martin.

Martin cleared his throat to avoid it looking as if he was coughing on the cigar smoke. It was time to make some contribution.

'Exciting times,' he said. It seemed to be enough. Devereux nodded thoughtfully.

'And we want to make sure everyone sees it that way.'

'Yes,' said Martin, uncertainly.

Another low blue cloud headed across the table.

'And that's where you come in, of course.'

Devereux looked up as Marshall returned from the telephone, muttering, shaking his head and prodding at the buttons of a calculator.

'Ah, Nick. I'm just filling Martin in on a little background.'

Marshall shook his head, set the calculator aside and took a mandarin orange from a fruit bowl on the side. He sat across the coffee table from them. Devereux watched him for a moment, almost as a father might a son, then turned his attention back to Martin.

'We see your role, Martin, as our man on the ground in Theston. The man who knows the territory. The 'uman territory. You're a local lad, Martin. People like you. People trust you. Very important that. You can keep your ear to the ground. People like me have to keep a professional distance.'

'I understand,' said Martin.

They both watched Marshall for a moment. He took out a penknife and sliced into the mandarin orange with surgical precision.

'It's also very important to us, Martin, that we maintain the best possible relations with the Town Council and in particular with the Planning Committee.'

Devereux paused. Marshall finished work on the orange and began popping the immaculately pith-stripped segments into his mouth.

'The Chairman's quite well known to you, I believe?' Devereux asked.

Martin looked uncertain.

'Frank Rudge. You're friendly with the family, I hear.'

At this Marshall looked quickly up from his orange. Martin gave a non-committal nod of the head. 'Yes. I know the family.'

Devereux put his brandy glass down on the edge of the table and, leaning forward, tugged at his socks, pulling and straightening them elaborately. 'Tell me, Martin, I've heard rumours to suggest that not everything Frank Rudge has done in his life has been altogether . . . on the level.'

'Frank? He's straight as a die.'

Martin knew the talk about Frank, but Frank had been a good friend to his mother and as far as Martin was concerned the constant repetition of the rumours only irritated him.

'Pleased to hear that,' said Devereux, immediately suspicious. He took his glass again and cradled it. 'Was it always so?'

'There's always rumours in a place the size of Theston.'

'What sort of rumours?'

'Well, a long time ago he had a fish processing plant that went of out business. People lost money. Him included. That's all.'

Devereux nodded. 'Interesting. Very interesting.' He reached for the ashtray. 'You see, the people we get involved with have to be dead straight, Martin. If they're not we have to know.' He ground the remains of his cigar into a dark, wet little mess. 'We have to know their weak points.'

There was a silence.

'Do you read me?'

Martin nodded.

'Good lad!' Devereux struck the table top and grinned.

'Sproale, if things go well your days behind the counter are definitely numbered.'

'You'll be able to buy a second bicycle,' said Nick.

'Be able to buy the fucking factory,' said Devereux.

Geraldine drove Martin home. Forcefully. She raced down the narrow lanes and revved out of the corners and it sobered him up dramatically.

'There might be something on the road,' Martin said anxiously as a particularly dark and leafy corner raced towards them.

'Did you know there's a higher risk of hitting a hedgehog at thirty than at sixty?' she shouted, as the corner unwound and the bypass loomed ahead.

'I was thinking of cyclists.'

'Shouldn't be out at this time of night,' she laughed, braking sharply and just early enough to avoid a southbound forty-foot trailer.

When they reached Marsh Cottage she turned to him. 'I'm sorry you had to go through all that.'

Martin reassured her. 'I'm all right. Not used to cars, that's all.'

'No, not the driving.' She pushed the heater up a notch and pulled up the collar of her tweed overcoat. 'The evening. It must have seemed pretty strange to you. I could see what you were going through. I could tell it wasn't your cup of poison.'

Martin had begun to open the door. Now he paused. For some reason he trusted Geraldine. 'Did I do the right thing?' he asked.

Geraldine grinned. 'Don't ask me. I'm just the maid. I do as I'm told.'

Martin nodded slowly. 'Well I did ask you. Did I do the right thing?'

'What do you think?' She reached forward to the dashboard, pulled back the heavy sleeves of her overcoat and pressed in the automatic lighter.

'How did you get involved with Nick?' Martin asked.

'Agency,' she replied. 'Employment, not dating. They advertised. I was,' she smiled to herself, 'between jobs, as we say in the theatre.'

'Who's they?'

'Nick's company. Shelflife. Nick and John Devereux are the directors. I'm the workforce.'

She flicked open the glove compartment. 'Want one of these?'

'No, I don't smoke.'

'There's not much tobacco in them.'

Martin looked again.

'Are they. . . ?'

'My life-savers,' she said and chose the longest and thickest of half a dozen carefully prepared joints. The dashboard lighter, having heated up, clicked out, and she took it and carefully applied the glowing filament to the loose paper. It smouldered and a piquant aroma filled the car. Geraldine took in the smoke unhurriedly. For a moment she was quite preoccupied. Then she let it drift slowly out again. She rolled the window open a crack. The smoke was snatched out by the cold night air.

'Just so you know the game, Martin,' she said matter-of-factly, 'Nick, Devereux and me have our salaries paid through an offshore subsidiary of Nordkom. They pay bloody well. Whatever we get from the Post Office is a bonus.'

'Oh my God,' said Martin, not bitterly or even angrily.

'Don't feel bad,' said Geraldine. 'It's the way things get done nowadays.' She offered him the joint. 'Welcome to the real world.'

Twenty-one

The sound of an alarm, emitted from a 1932 Ingersoll traveller's clock, had been drilling into Martin's consciousness for quite some time before he was awake enough to deal with it. He turned off the alarm and lay for a moment trying to think if there was any other man-made mechanism which was designed to be stopped as soon as it started working, when, quite suddenly, the extraordinary events of the night before flooded his memory like a wall of water from a newly breached dam.

He sat up sharply in bed as if to anchor himself against the torrent of names and faces and places and plans and feelings. Though draughts of cold air were squeezing in from around the window he felt a sudden flush of nervous warmth.

He thought he remembered where he'd put the money but when he looked over to the chair on which his jacket lay draped there was no sign of the buff envelope. He hadn't imagined it, surely he hadn't imagined it. Maybe it would be better if he had. He jumped out of bed and grabbed the jacket and went through every pocket. All were empty.

Then he saw the door of the medicine cupboard was open and he remembered putting it in there, behind his most precious bottles, after a long talk with Papa.

He took it out, turned it over in his hand, regarded it for a moment with fearful fascination and replaced it carefully. He locked the cupboard and, barely aware of the inhospitable darkness outside, began to dress.

He passed a restless day at work, left punctually at five and cycled furiously back to Marsh Cottage. Ten hours after he had left it he was back in his room changing swiftly and purposefully from his work clothes to his visiting clothes, which were exactly the same but newer. Van Heusen cotton shirt, Viyella sweater, creaseproof cotton and polyester trousers. When he'd finished he took the envelope in and out of the medical cabinet several times before finally removing five of the fifty-pound notes from it and replacing them behind the bottles.

Hemingway's chair had not been far from his thoughts all day long. Now the lightly bulging envelope he held in his hand began to take on a mystical significance. It was surely a sign that he had been predestined to have the chair. Could there be anyone else in the country who deserved it more than he did, who would look after it with more tender care?

Possessing the chair would be enough. He would never ask for more.

As he combed his hair he avoided Papa's eye. Today, for the first time, he had seen something in the Master's expression that he had not been aware of before. Rather than watching him, thanking him for being there, sharing the moment, there was, behind the big sad eyes, a look of pity. Well, thought Martin, if he were trying to give him some sort of moral lesson, this was not the time.

Before he left the room Martin took out a bottle of grappa, wrapped it in a scarf and laid it carefully at the bottom of his bag. There was something to celebrate.

When Ruth opened the door of Everend Farm Cottage to find Martin standing there, his breath forming visible clouds in front of him, his nose reddened like a gnome's in the bitter cold, she wisely, but with difficulty, kept from laughing.

Martin smiled nervously. She held the door open and he moved quickly inside. Ruth watched him as he dropped his bag down on the sofa, felt in his pocket and carefully laid fifteen brand new fifty-pound notes on the table.

Ruth was impressed. 'Great-grandmother's legacy? Bank raid?'

Martin was biting his lip hard. 'It's all there. You can count it.'

Ruth fingered the money. The new logs that Mr Wellbeing had cut for her hissed and spat from the fire.

'You're serious.'

'I had more money in my account than I thought.'

Martin began to hum as he pulled at the zip on his anorak. It was an odd, uneasy sound and Ruth had never heard it before. For the first time since she had met him, Ruth sensed that he might not be telling the truth and she was intrigued.

'You mean you cashed in your life savings for a one-legged chair?' Ruth did laugh then. 'I think Papa would have appreciated that.'

'Don't mock.'

'I wasn't mocking, Martin. Hemingway had a sense of humour. You must know that.'

'Not about himself. He didn't like to be laughed at.'

Ruth nodded uncomfortably. Martin's face was solemn and tense.

'He wouldn't like you to have said that.'

'No, well, look, how about a drink.'

Martin didn't move from the table. There was no trace of a smile on his face. 'I think maybe you should apologise before we drink.'

Ruth laughed nervously. 'Look, I'm sorry for what I said, Martin. It was a light-hearted remark. No big deal.'

'You goddamn well meant it though, didn't you?'

'What?'

'It's what you think about me isn't it? You think there's something perverted about a man of thirty-six who keeps Hemingway in his room.'

Ruth shrugged and laughed again. 'Everyone's entitled to live their life the way they want,' she said.

'But you want some of the action too, don't you? You want

the dirty, lousy pervert to help you to meet Mr Hemingway. That's what you said. You want to get to know him. You want some of the dirt. Isn't that right? Isn't that what you want?' Martin was advancing slowly towards her.

'Come on Martin, let's have a drink. I've made some –'

'Well if you want to meet him you have to be a little careful of what you say, because he's a difficult man sometimes. Especially with women.'

Ruth edged towards the kitchen. Martin kept on coming. 'So maybe you should apologise for being such a goddamn hypocrite.'

Ruth tried to smile, but it was hard. She knew she must stay calm. Then he lunged at her, stopping only inches from her face, right fist raised and tightly clenched. 'Okay . . . apologise . . .'

'Martin!'

'Apologise, you damn bitch!'

'Martin, I'm sorry for what I said.'

Martin stopped, beamed and pulled off his bobble-hat. 'Pretty good eh?'

'What are you doing?'

Martin tossed his hat on to the table. 'That was Ernest,' he said simply, and his face broke into an engaging, almost schoolboyish smile.

Ruth shook her head slowly. 'God, you bastard. That was good. Look at me, for Christ's sake. I'm shaking.'

Martin removed his bicycle clips, pulled open the Velcro sealing on his anorak pocket and slipped them inside.

'Don't ever do that again.'

'I thought that's what you wanted.' Martin pulled off the anorak and hung it behind the door.

Ruth leaned back against the kitchen doorway. 'Jesus, I need a drink.'

Later, when they had eaten, Ruth put the money away in a safe place and promised to ring her dealer friend in the morning. Martin remembered the grappa was at the bottom of his bag. He retrieved it and they sat beside the fire and clinked glasses. The first, sharp, eye-watering shock of the spirit took them by surprise, as usual. They sat and watched the fire until Ruth looked up.

'I think we have to make some ground rules,' she said.

'For what?'

'For the exchange of Hemingway information.'

'You sound like a schoolteacher.'

'Well, you forget, Mr Sproale, that I am a teacher. That's my job.'

'What? Pretending that Ernest Hemingway really wanted to be a woman?'

'Teaching English to the people of New Jersey.'

'Why don't you just tell them to go and read his books? Why do they need to know how long he slept with his mother or how old he was when he stopped wearing dresses?'

'We're talking about his relationship with mothers and wives here, Martin. Aren't you interested in what they were like too?'

'No. I'm interested in him. He was special. They weren't. They didn't write *A Farewell to Arms*. They didn't write *The Old Man and the Sea* or *For Whom the Bell Tolls*. They didn't fight in wars or win the Nobel Prize.'

Ruth shook her head angrily. 'Do you think Hemingway would have written *A Farewell to Arms* if he hadn't fallen in love with Agnes Kurowsky? Why did he dedicate *For Whom the Bell Tolls* to Martha Gellhorn? He shaped his life around women, Martin. You can't have one without the other.'

'Of course there were women in his life. They loved him. Women loved him. I'm not surprised. But they did what women do. They cooked for him and cleaned for him and gave him children and looked after his houses and his friends but they didn't write a single word of his books.'

'May I ask you a question as you, rather than him?'

'It's up to you. You're the one who wants the rules.'

'What do *you* think about women?'

Martin stared into the fire. 'I like women,' he said, slowly. 'But I could do without them.' He paused. 'I don't think I could do without him.'

Ruth didn't reply immediately. She leaned over to the log basket and picked out the two remaining lengths of cherry wood. She laid them on the hot but dying fire and knelt to watch them burn.

'May I suggest just one ground rule, Martin?'

'All right. I'll let you have one.'

'That both of us accept the possibility that we may be wrong.'

He chuckled. Then he held out his hand to her. 'Okay, daughter. It's a deal.'

She smiled and they shook.

That night Ruth stayed up quite late after Martin had gone, writing another letter to her friends in New Jersey.

Dearly beloved,

The book goes well and keeps me warm. (Why do I go on like this about the cold? I sound like one of those bleached Florida matrons that come north once a year to grumble about the weather. It's no worse than New Jersey. It just *feels* so fucking cold.) Anyway it's late and my Hemingway partner has just cycled off in a blaze of grappa after a kind of revealing evening. No, nothing romantic. If you saw him you'd know why, but he is interesting and a little strange. I told you that he's mad about Hemingway – has pics of him all around his room etc., all pretty much standard retarded-development high school fan stuff – except that he does know one hell of a lot about the man, has an authentic bar with all Hemingway's specialities disguised inside a medical supply cabinet from the Ospedale Croce Rossa in Milan (*Farewell to Arms*) and has this day given me ONE THOUSAND ONE HUNDRED DOLLARS in sterling to purchase on his behalf a chair (see Christmas letter) which the illustrious MCP personally sat upon while, mercifully unsuccessfully, trying to pluck innocent marlin from the Pacific Ocean. And this from a post office clerk's wage.

What is kind of fascinating, frightening and a little astral are the things he does and says and the way he behaves which are uncannily like what I imagine E H to have been like. He does this by a sort of referred experience. He hasn't been anywhere or done anything but like one of those Indian holy men who concentrate their life on the Buddha's toenail he has projected himself into Hemingway to the extent that at moments, it truly seems as if he has the potential to become him, or at least the essence of him. I know this will sound crazy but if I write it all down you can at least see that I've thought about it. I can assure you I'm not hysterical and only a little drunk, but it is weird. How can a nice, shy, screwed-up, small-town postal clerk who lives with his mother and cycles to work tell me more about the essence of Ernest Hemingway than all the reading I've done in six months?

Whatever the answer I'm going to try and push this on a little further. No, don't worry, nothing kinky. I've prepared some questions I'd like to have asked E H if he had not blown his brains out in '61. We'll see. But it is exciting and is making me think that perhaps *Admiring Ernest* could be a bit of a ground-breaker. On the other hand it may all be the onset of premature senility.

Your loving exile,
Ruthie.

Twenty-two

Theston was coming out of a dour flat winter and into brisk and businesslike March winds. Winds of change, thought Martin unhappily as he parked his bicycle against the railings beside the church and walked through to the High Street. His heart was heavy. This particular morning was not one he had been looking forward to. It was the first working Monday for sixteen and a half years that he had not cycled into North Square, turned down Echo Passage and come to rest, balletically, at the foot of the steps in Phipps' Yard. He couldn't. Over the weekend Phipps' Yard had been boarded up.

Above the doorway of Randall's, High Class Confectioner and Newsagent, a man on a ladder was fixing the red and gold lozenge-shaped sign of the Post Office. The same sign that could be seen above Wilkinson's sports goods shop in Atcham, the Koppi-Rite stationery centre in Alford and jostling for space with cigarette and soft-drinks displays outside shops all across the country. It was a vision of the beginning of the end of something, Martin was sure of that.

He felt uncomfortably self-conscious as he entered Randall's. Under his anorak he wore his old brown check shirt, green corduroy jacket and not quite matching trousers and his oldest pair of sandals, which he'd put on at the last minute, as a silent protest. He ran the gauntlet of curious shop assistants. He knew most of them, for this was where he bought Christmas, Easter and birthday presents and occasional treats for himself. He had always felt effortlessly superior in Randall's. He was Number Two man from the post office in

North Square. A man of some influence. No mere shop assistant he. But that was yesterday. Now he was nearly one of them.

Joyce, a thin, garrulous woman whose husband looked after the golf course, examined him carefully from behind the newspaper counter which occupied one side of the front of the shop. Rita, a single parent of Czech extraction, stood opposite, in front of shelves of boiled sweets and mint chews and humbugs. She had only just arrived and was still buttoning up the front of her pink nylon sales coat.

'Morning, Martin,' she said as he passed, followed by a suppressed giggle, as if the whole thing were a great new game.

Amanda, a small, defiant girl, fresh out of university with a good degree in Social Studies, was wiping the outside of a long perspex screen which curved up along the length of the confectionery counter and behind which was displayed Randall's famous selection of hand-made chocolates and toffees. The centre of the shop widened out into an area dotted with free-standing displays. Mills and Boon stories on a rack, cheap plastic toys, books about the Royal Family. Here it was that Alan Randall, the manager and grandson of the man who had founded the shop, was fussing about, attending to the construction of an Easter egg mountain. Alan Randall was dapper, artificially tanned and lived alone. He greeted Martin, who did not like him, with a professional smile.

'They're all at the back,' he said, stretching out his arm like a butler at a dinner table. 'Mind the step.'

Martin chose instead to descend the six or seven inches by means of a newly-erected wheelchair ramp. The back of the shop smelt of wet plaster and newly-laid carpet. Halogen lamplight reflected off a line of free-standing chrome posts set across the carpet. Through them ran a thick-coiled rope which led from a sign reading 'Queue Here' to a sort of no-man's-land some few feet back from the counters.

The positions lay behind shaded glass, which rose from an

expanse of grey panelling. At each one was a powder-grey computer terminal. From the side walls video monitors jutted out on stubby grey arms.

The overall effect was discreet, anonymous, characterless. He could as easily have been in a building society, an airline office or a funeral parlour. What caused his heart to sink further was that it looked anything but temporary.

'Is Marshall in yet?' he asked Mary Perrick, who was clutching a thick knitted cardigan to her and looking around in awe.

'Isn't it wonderful,' she said.

'Is Mr Marshall in?' Martin repeated more sharply.

As he heard his name Nick Marshall advanced from a corner of the room, arm outstretched. His eyes shone and his freshly washed hair glowed as it had the day Martin first met him. He had with him a short, heavy, efficient-looking woman who wore a grey suit that matched the carpet and was carrying a clipboard on which she was checking certain items. She had close-cut, tinted, blue-grey hair and a pair of half-moon glasses which she removed as Marshall introduced her.

'Martin, meet the woman responsible for this amazing transformation – Stella Holt of Elldor – the shopfitting division of Post Shops Limited. Stella, this is my trusty right-hand man, Martin Sproale. He's worked at Theston post office man and boy for fourteen years.'

'Sixteen.'

Stella Holt shook Martin's hand. She had a cool, firm grip which she withdrew quite sharply, making him aware that he had cycled to work and was still very warm. Her voice was efficient, expressionless. 'You'll know that barn in North Square pretty well,' she said to him.

'Yes, I can't wait to get back there,' said Martin. Nick, who had just noticed his sandals, looked sternly at him. Stella Holt moved on busily and Martin followed her to where the rest of the staff stood around. Elaine avoided his eye. Shirley Barker looked faintly disapproving, Geraldine faintly amused.

Marshall cleared his throat, rubbed his hands and addressed them. 'Stella and the team have done a beautiful job in an incredibly short time, and now it's up to us to make the best of it. We open at eleven, so you'll have a couple of hours together. Stella, over to you.'

Stella looked down her glasses at them. Her dead eyes were magnified as she smiled. 'Thank you, Mr Marshall, and let me say how pleased I am that thanks to your efforts Theston has had the chance to benefit from the most exciting and up-to-date developments in counter technology.'

Marshall inclined his head graciously. 'I'll leave you to it, Stella,' he said and loped gracefully away, much to Martin's irritation.

Stella turned her cold, grey professional eye upon the assembled staff. She smiled again, a rhetorical smile. Not one to be returned.

'This is the Standard Pattern Local Enterprise Office,' she began, 'and we have many hundreds operating successfully up and down the country to meet the needs of the modern consumer. Before we go on to practical matters like uniform and counter discipline, I want to start by giving you the philosophical overview of the LEO policy.'

Martin felt himself slowly suffocating, and there was no escape. He could hardly bear to think of it. Even as he stood here North Square was being vandalised by Crispin's men. In the name of what? He felt foolish and inadequate and helpless. He swallowed hard and looked up. Stella Holt was watching him, using eye contact mercilessly. He felt like a butterfly in a display case, pinned through the heart.

'We at Elldor have worked on post office conversions for the last three and a half years and during that time we have evolved, in consultation with Post Office Counter Services Limited and the Government's Customer Charter, the concept of MEC – Maximised Efficiency Control.' She held out two chubby hands, forefingers pointing upwards, like an air hostess in a safety demonstration. 'If you would care to look now at the monitors above your head.'

The monitors flickered into life, synchronised celestial music sounded from them and the initials 'MEC' appeared on the screens. Then the initials faded and merged into the likeness of Stella Holt, who now appeared in prerecorded video on screen as well as in real life. At the same time there was a cry of alarm from the front of the shop. A small child seemed hell-bent on selecting his Easter egg from the very bottom of Mr Randall's mountain.

'*The three elements of Maximised Efficiency Control are Identity, Immediacy and Impetus.*'

At that point the north face of the Easter egg mountain tilted, defied gravity for a split second and then slowly toppled to the ground.

'*Identity means enabling the customer to identify staff and facilities quickly and clearly, and to this end we have developed an in-house style with themed garments and fittings.*'

Eggs, bunny motifs and the chocolate likenesses of chirpy chickens lay scattered across the shop.

'*Staff are encouraged to wear name badges.*'

Two smiling models appeared on the screen. They attached their lapel badges. The man smilingly became '*Steve*' and the woman smilingly became '*Janet*'. Their smiles contrasted strongly with the contorted features of Alan as he surveyed the collapse of his mountain.

'*Customers will be brought forward from a single queue by the operation of a flashing number light, indicating the position available and accompanied, for the visually impaired, by a sound identification.*'

They watched a light flash and a metallic voice announce, '*Position Number Three.*'

'*The full greeting, as laid down in the Customer Charter, is "Good Morning", before twelve, and "Good Afternoon", after twelve,*' *followed by personal identification and the Assistance Information Request.'*

Obligingly Steve said, *'Good Morning, my name is Steve. How may I help you?'* and a moment later Janet said, *'Good Afternoon, my name is Janet. How may I help you?'*

Confused sounds of accusation and counter-accusation rose from the fallen egg display. Stella glared and turned up the volume on the monitor.

'Immediacy involves a clear, accurate evaluation and fulfilment of customer requirement in the minimum possible time.'

To illustrate this point Janet was joined by an elderly man, whose eyes shone with health and decency. He asked for a postal order and three stamps. Janet asked him what value of stamps he required. *'Three first class,'* he replied. *'Wouldn't you rather have a book of ten?'* asked Janet. The old man might have been offered a round the world cruise, so pathetically grateful was his response. Stella Holt reappeared on screen.

'You will note there Janet's use of the Proactive Selling Technique to maximise customer potential. And not just with stamps. A twenty-pound phonecard will often fit the bill much better than a ten-pound phonecard. Remember that your customers, whilst in a queue situation, will have been able to watch a video display of all the Post Office products and it is well worth reminding them of selected benefits.'

At this point the real Stella Holt strode across to the front of the shop to add her contribution to the egg mountain incident. Mr Randall had inadvertently trodden on one of the exhibits and the offending child, who can only have been three or four, had compounded his already incandescent rage by laughing.

'If your business also comprises a Post Office Gift Shop –' the video went on.

'Which this one doesn't,' muttered the returning Stella and switched herself off. 'Now, any questions?'

Stella Holt had assured them that it was part of her job to stay for the first few hours of opening time to see if there were any teething troubles. This meant there was no question of Martin not wearing his grey and yellow spotted sweater and identification. Unfortunately Stella had brought the wrong lapel badge and she asked if Martin wouldn't mind being called Derek until Tuesday.

His first customer was a stranger, which was an enormous relief. He was a big, thick-set young man, with an earring and short-cropped hair. He looked around suspiciously, with a wary loose-limbed aggression, as if he feared some sort of trap.

'Am I on television?' he asked Stella Holt.

She shook her head dismissively. 'This is a post office,' she said.

The man didn't seem convinced and narrowed his eyes as he approached Martin's position.

'Good morning, my name is Martin,' Martin muttered quickly. 'What can I do for you?'

'It says you're Derek,' the customer pointed out.

Stella Holt moved swiftly in. 'Don't worry, it's his first day.'

The second customer to arrive was Harold Meredith. He entered with a cry of '*There* you are!' and, as was his habit, made a beeline for Martin's position. Stella Holt rushed up and intercepted him.

He looked alarmed. 'Who the hell are you?' he said indignantly.

'There is a new single queuing system in operation from today, sir. Could I ask you to step back to the end of the rope, please?'

'Take your hands off me. I want to see Martin.'

A disembodied voice rang out. '*Position Number Two*,' it said, with an odd, squeaky inflexion. It sounded like a Swedish castrato speaking unnaturally good English.

'Who said that?' asked Mr Meredith, fearfully.

'There you are, sir, Position Number Two is available.'

'I want to see Martin.'

'He's operational,' she said, quite sharply.

'*Position Number Two*,' trilled the Swedish eunuch.

Harold Meredith thumped his walking stick down on the floor.

'Listen madam, I don't know who you are, or where you've come from, but this is my post office and I shall choose to see who I want.'

Stella Holt's tone hardened. 'If you go to Position Number Two you will be dealt with and out of here much more quickly.'

'What makes you think I want to get out of here quickly?' Mr Meredith protested. 'I'm not in a hurry. I like being here.'

Stella Holt had made dealing with Mr Meredith something of a personal crusade and she wasn't going to give up easily. 'Have you seen our video?' she asked him. She pointed out one of the video screens which was gently burbling on about licence renewals and commemorative issues. Harold Meredith peered up at it.

'I don't come to the post office to watch television, thank you,' he said. 'I come to the post office to get away from television.'

'It gives you suggestions for what you might want.'

'Oh, I know what I want,' said Mr Meredith. 'I want to ask whether or not I need to fill in the tax district number in my application form for transfer of my war disability pension to my brother-in-law's building society account.' Stella Holt gave up. Quite soon after that, gathering together her armoury of clipboards, calculators, compact cameras and portable telephones she left, with encouraging words and a fast-fading smile. She missed Mrs Harvey-Wardrell by a whisker. Which was probably just as well.

'That is quite ghastly!' boomed Mrs Harvey-Wardrell from as far back as the remains of the Easter egg mountain.

What Mrs Harvey-Wardrell saw before her was not a post office as she and generations of Harvey-Wardrells had come to know it. It was more like a freshly landed spacecraft. A stop-gap environment on the road to automation and eventually the final eradication of the human element from the whole process. She said as much to her small pale companion, a lady called Lettice Brockwell, who had a ginger moustache and one leg slightly shorter than the other.

Mrs Harvey-Wardrell, sporting a Barbour, deer-stalker and long green wellingtons, strode across the strip of grey carpet which was studded with the Post Office Counter Service logo, as if it had been walked on by someone with it stuck on their foot.

'*Position Number Two*,' squeaked the voice. Owing to some electrical fault the Swedish choirboy had moved up from alto to soprano.

'Whatever's that, Lettice?'

'It said "Position Number Two", Pamela.'

She spied Martin, who was desperately trying to look unconcerned, at Position Number One. 'What's all this Position Number Two business, Martin? This is a post office, not the *Kama Sutra*.'

'I'm afraid it's a standard feature now, Mrs Harvey-Wardrell,' said Martin lamely.

'Well, I think it's quite frightful. If this is the face of the future, the sooner we get North Square back the better. Four first class stamps for Tasmania please, Martin.' She turned to her companion. 'I shall have to have a word with Marshall. Do you know Marshall?'

'I don't think I do, no.'

'He's in charge of all the post office rebuilding. Awfully clever chap. Far too capable for this sort of job. Now those are air mail, aren't they Martin?'

'Forty-five pence, yes.'

'I don't want them traipsing round the Cape of Good Hope.'

'All foreign mail goes by air now.'

'Because it's most frightfully important that these letters get there as soon possible.' She turned to her companion. 'Jonty's developed frightful piles and my man in Harley Street says not to let anyone in Tasmania touch them. He's got to go to a chap in Melbourne.'

'Jonty out in Tasmania now?' her friend enquired.

'He's doing some frightfully hush-hush work on a new reservoir. Locals are up in arms and I think Jonty's time in the Falklands will stand him in good stead! Mouse loves it of course, but then she's always been an outdoor girl. Thank you, Martin. And I do hope you don't have to stay in this frightful place for long.'

Like a large steamship with a dinghy in tow the pair of them disappeared out through the sweetshop. For a moment the post office was empty.

'*Position Number Four,*' shrilled the Swedish soprano. Mary Perrick looked across sheepishly. 'I'm sorry, Martin. I pressed it by mistake.'

Martin had rarely been so happy to see his lunch hour. Not that it was announced any longer by the old wall clock, but that was a minor quibble. Thirteen hundred on the dot-matrix indicator or one o'clock on his watch, it marked a respite from the nightmare. He sat for a moment in the narrow, airless back room which had been provided for staff breaks. There were two spindly metal and plastic chairs on either side of the door and a shelf beside a wash-basin on which was a kettle, a box of tea bags, a jar of coffee and a stack of polystyrene cups. On one of the chairs Shirley Barker sat peeling a piece of cling film from around her lunch. Martin took his sandwiches from his anorak pocket and looked at them without interest. He had no appetite.

Shirley looked up at him, myopically. 'Not having your lunch, Martin?'

He shook his head.

'I've heard that about people who work in sweetshops,' she said confidingly. 'They lose their appetite.'

Martin looked at Shirley. 'Isn't this awful?'

'What?'

'Our *new* post office.'

'I think it's lovely.'

Martin made for the door. He dropped his ham and cheese sandwiches, unopened, next to the chair on which she sat eating. 'Have mine as well.'

'No, thank you, I'm a vegetarian. I don't condone the raising of animals for slaughter.'

'Then just eat the cheese,' he said, and slammed the door.

Twenty-three

Martin walked furiously out through the yard at the back of the shop as if he knew where he was going. He didn't. He stopped, then turned and made his way along an alley which led eventually to the High Street near the Market Hotel. He crossed the road and into North Square. The old post office was a sorry sight. The builder had moved quickly to board up the windows and the oak doors were scuffed and scratched and firmly shut. There was a noise of sawing and hammering from inside and this led Martin cautiously down Echo Passage. At the entrance to the site there was a gate which was open. Martin went in. A truck was drawn up close to the back entrance and workmen inside were tossing things through the window. As Martin drew closer he realised with a shock that he recognised much of what was being flung away. The long public writing desk, wrenched from the wall, scabs of plaster still stuck to its fixings, poked out amongst the debris with which the back of the lorry was nearly filled. Dismembered strips of what had once been a counter clattered on top of each other. A drawer whose contents he had once laid out so meticulously that he could tell a money order from a post cheque by the feel of its upper edge, hit the side of the truck with a jarring clang.

He picked his way across the forecourt. A warning voice sounded from an upper window. 'Oi!'

The back door was open. Or rather, gone. There was another, louder, shout but Martin darted quickly inside. The old sorting office was stripped bare, though the daily break rotas were still stuck to one wall, and the Theston Civic Theatre calendar which Elaine brought in each year was still hanging from its nail on the back of the kitchen door. Where once had stood the door that led from the staff room to the main office there was now a gaping hole. Martin leaned through it and looked around. Two men in hard hats with handkerchiefs tied around their mouths were working away with crowbars and hammerdrills demolishing the counter, ripping down the shelves and tearing out wires and piping. Nothing recognisable remained intact except the Newmark wall clock. It had stopped, of course, and was turned at an odd angle, but it still hung in its usual place. Choosing his moment Martin stepped forward, towards it.

'Oi! Get away from there!' A voice rang out through the din.

He turned and there was Crispin the builder.

'What the fuck d'you think you're doing?' he shouted, his narrow eyes tight with anger.

Two other men joined him. One held a sheaf of drawings in his hand and Martin didn't recognise him. The other was John Devereux. Martin could cope with Crispin's absurd anger. It was Devereux's cool half-smile that put the fear of God into him.

' 'ard 'at area this, Martin,' said Devereux. 'I'm sure Mr Crispin could spare one if you want to look around.'

There was a splitting crack and crash from somewhere above them. Martin ducked instinctively as a shower of rubble and plaster fell about him.

'I just came to see how the new post office was coming on,' Martin heard himself saying before a dust cloud rose from the floor and he started to cough.

The man with the charts looked bewildered. Crispin looked hostile. Devereux smiled sweetly.

'Well, Martin, that's what *I'm* doing.' He turned to the builder beside him. 'And it doesn't look too good, does it, Mr Crispin?' Crispin shook his head as Devereux spoke. 'There's dry rot and . . .' He snapped his fingers. 'Come on Joe, what else?'

'Metal fatigue on supporting columns, concrete decay and subsidence at the north-west corner,' Joe Crispin mumbled.

Devereux looked across at Martin. He spread his arms. 'Very bad. Going to take a lot of fixing.'

'How long?' Martin asked. He'd wanted it to sound like a genuine enquiry, but it came across harsh and brusque. If Devereux was angry he concealed it well. 'I'm glad to see you take an interest, Martin. We'll make sure you're the first to know.' Then he turned to Crispin, confidingly. 'Martin's working for us too, you know.'

Crispin nodded grimly. 'Well, he still shouldn't be in here without a hat on. It's against the regs. I'll get done,' he said.

'You know the way, Martin,' Devereux called after him, superfluously as it turned out. Joe Crispin gripped his arm tight and personally escorted him from the remains of the post office. Behind him there was another ear-splitting crash. When he turned round for a last look the Newmark wall clock had gone.

Twenty-four

Nick Marshall was disappointed in Sproale. He had hoped that he could rely on him to run Theston post office whilst he himself got on with the communications project. Now he was having to deal with his sentimental attachment to an outdated building and the man's perverse refusal to appreciate all that Nick had done for him in securing in record time, and at considerable expense, a brand new, state-of-the-art post office that would be the envy of small towns across Britain. Towns at the end of a queue which he and Devereux had so successfully jumped. Even when they'd taken him into their confidence and paid him good money, Martin had proved unable to help them with the simplest tasks – such as supplying information on the Rudge family. Nick had been left to pick up the pieces.

Still, Nick thought to himself, as he ran, loose and smooth across the Suffolk heathland, into a freshly risen sun, at least there had been pleasures along the way.

The time he had spent winning Elaine's confidence had paid off handsomely. Over candlelit dinners, drinks and intimate evenings beneath the paisley duvet, Nick had slowly and patiently pieced together the story of what had really happened to Frank Rudge all those years ago. And it was dynamite. His fish processing business had indeed collapsed when the new cold store was built twenty miles further up the coast. But the firm who had built the new processing plant had systematically paid off all the main operators along the Suffolk coast. Like others, Frank Rudge had been induced by liberal amounts of largely German money to go out of business. The fishing jobs in Theston went and in their place had grown Frank Rudge

Haulage and Rudge Padgett Properties.

The revelation that Shelflife had acquired this information had worked wonders on Frank Rudge. He had been persuaded, in return for certain assurances of confidentiality, to release his stranglehold on the land around the harbour. He had also promised to recommend to the next meeting of the Council Planning Committee that land-use restrictions on the area should be reviewed. All in all a highly satisfactory outcome for Shelflife and some interesting sex for Nick Marshall. Now the pieces were nearly all in place. It was essential no one lose their nerve.

He sprinted hard over the last hundred yards of soft, springy turf and pressed the stopwatch button on his wrist as he reached his car. He had broken his own record.

Nick Marshall made his next move carefully. At the end of the day's business, he and Martin were alone in the post office. Martin was checking through the day's counterfoils.

Nick leaned back from his terminal. He flicked at his hair and locked his hands across the back of his head. 'You know, I feel very good today, Martin. Very good.'

Martin didn't look up.

'You know why that is?'

Martin shook his head. He was counting.

'Because I think at last, even you, even you, Mart, are beginning to get used to this place.'

Martin slipped a rubber band around the counterfoils and dropped them into the drawer beside him. He looked Nick Marshall in the eye. He felt nothing but contempt for him now. 'It'll do,' he said. 'Until we move back.'

Marshall switched off his terminal. 'We won't be moving back, Mart.'

Martin paused in the act of picking out another batch of counterfoils. He took a deep breath. 'I wondered when you'd get around to telling me that.'

180

'Mart,' said Marshall, 'this is not in my hands. The old post office building was unsafe.'

'Who told you that?'

'It was in Crispin's report.'

'And you believed it.'

'What are you trying to say?' Marshall sprang athletically from his chair, hoping this panther-like movement might distract from the less graceful activity at the right-hand corner of his mouth. 'The cost of refurbishing that office was going to be astronomical. All the efficiency improvements and the modernisation that the people of Theston have a right to would have been jeopardised.'

'What about the Post Office?' Martin protested. 'Doesn't it have a duty to maintain its properties?'

'Mart, that building is going to cost half a million to get in shape.' He checked Mary Perrick's terminal and clicked that off. 'The Post Office doesn't have that sort of money any more.'

'Well who does?' asked Martin, helplessly.

'Well, there might be a potential buyer. Shelflife is talking to someone.'

Martin looked round at Marshall in disbelief. 'Who?'

'Nordkom.'

Martin nodded slowly. Nick Marshall met his gradually comprehending stare as brazenly as he could. If only his bloody mouth would stay still.

'The consortium that employs your company?'

Marshall interrupted. '*Our* company, Martin. Don't forget that.'

'That's very convenient, isn't it,' Martin said.

'Very convenient,' Marshall agreed.

'Except for the people of Theston.'

Nick Marshall moved away. His voice turned hard and practical. 'Martin, I appreciate your concern for selling stamps and chatting up old-age pensioners, but in a few years almost everything that happens in a post office will be handled automatically. There will be no need for people to come in here every other day and wait in a queue for twenty minutes until the person in front's stopped talking, just to have their docket stamped. People won't need to do all that.'

'They can sit at home instead, I suppose. Buy socks from the television.'

'Martin, if that's what bothers you, why don't you go and run a social club?'

'Because I run a post office!'

Marshall had never heard Martin shout before. His pink, cherubic face was not suited to anger.

'Look,' Martin's voice rose. 'I want to know what's going on!' He stood jabbing a finger at Marshall's crisp white shirt-front. You told me you wanted to make North Square the best post office in the county. 'You told me we'd never end up in the back of a shop. Now you tell me this miserable rent-a-post-office is the best you can do. Well, if that's the price to pay for your bloody project I don't want to be involved.'

Marshall watched and waited and slowly pulled in the line. 'But you *are* involved, Martin. You're a consultant.'

Marshall watched him. Martin was red in the face and breathing hard.

'We've invested in you, remember?'

Marshall flicked the combination on the safe, and turned, his hand on the light switch. 'Now we'd like some sort of return.'

The lights went off leaving Martin in darkness.

To cycle home, in a good sunset on a crisp clear evening at the beginning of spring, had long been one of the pleasures of Martin's life, but that evening he saw no joy in the majestic sweep of colour spreading far and wide across the sky.

The money. If only he hadn't taken the money. Never take anything you haven't earned his father always said, and Martin had been impatient with him. His father had been known to refuse tips at Christmas.

Now he could see that, as in many things for which he was ridiculed, his father had been right. The money was the root of all Martin's problems. It was the cause of his powerlessness. It was his enemy's strongest weapon. If only he had not picked up the money that night. If only. If only.

As he free-wheeled down beneath the railway bridge and then worked hard to get speed up Abbot's Hill, there seemed only one solution. He must give the money back. It would not be the end of the world. He could buy the chair another day. There would be other chairs, other opportunities.

It would also free him from the clutches of Marshall and Devereux and enable him to start some kind of fight back. Whatever happened, his preferred and habitual option was no longer open. He could not do nothing.

By the time he had crossed the bypass and negotiated the pockmarked surface of Marsh Lane his mind was made up. Not waiting to remove hat or coat or cycle clips, he ran upstairs, slammed his door shut and dialled Ruth's number. He was still catching his breath when she answered.

'It's Martin,' he said. 'I've made a decision.'

'Martin!' cried Ruth. 'The chair! It's here.'

Twenty-five

It lay awkwardly against the kitchen table at Everend Farm
Cottage. A single limb jutting out at a forty-five-degree angle
was wedged in a groove between the scuffed brown quarry
tiles. Its heavy wooden back leaned up against the table-top,
the corner of which stuck through the top two horizontal
supports.

Ruth leaned against the side of the kitchen doorway. She was
wearing loose cotton trousers and an embroidered waistcoat
over a black cashmere jumper. She held a cigarette in one hand
and a glass of whisky and melting ice-cubes in the other. 'Do I
detect an aroma of Ernest on the seat?' she asked.

Martin was squatting on his haunches, running his fingers
slowly along the lightly ridged wooden uprights. He ignored
the question. Indeed, he'd barely looked at her since he
arrived. She drew on a cigarette and watched him poring as
intently over the rough, timber surfaces as if he were examining
a newly discovered Rembrandt. As far as Ruth was concerned
the chair was a big disappointment. She wasn't sure exactly
what she'd been expecting when Roger and Kate
Morton-Smith had turned up on her doorstep. They were on
their way to an antiques fair in Norwich, and they'd swapped
the powder-blue Mercedes for a rented red van. There had
been a minor panic when Ruth mislaid Martin's money. She'd
put it away behind a loose brick under the sink and forgotten
which one.

When they had gone she had tried to raise some enthusiasm
for the graceless object, but had come to the inescapable
conclusion that it was a horrid waste of hard-earned savings.

Her relief at Martin's ecstasy on seeing it was tempered by a genuine concern for his sanity.

'Hell-o,' she called, as Martin prowled round it yet again. 'Anyone in there?'

'Here,' said Martin, taking hold of one of the arms, 'help me lift this.'

Ruth put the cigarette in her mouth and, eyes narrowed against the rising smoke, took the other arm of the chair.

'It's heavy,' she grunted.

Following Martin's instructions she helped prop it up against the sofa. It was too high at first but Martin found some bricks and laid one at each corner and together they lifted the sofa until it rested on the bricks and this brought the seat up to the right height to balance the chair.

Martin pushed it back on the sofa, as far as the central pole would allow it to go. Then he turned and slowly and respectfully lowered himself down on to it.

It was big and wide and at first he looked lost in it, but once he had settled himself, once he had hesitantly slipped the worn leather harness over his shoulders and around his waist, once he was sitting back, palms flat against the arm supports, spreading his back along the length of the wood, an extra-ordinary change took place. The transformation Ruth had seen once before in this room began to happen again, only much more vividly this time. Martin became slowly and perceptibly more substantial. His face lost the earnest frown with which he had arrived, his eyes grew wider but softer, the line of his jaw grew stronger, his slim chest widened. Even the sight of his toes barely able to touch the ground did not detract from the remarkable display of possession.

For a long time neither of them spoke.

Then, as slowly as it had occurred, the change began to reverse until it was Martin, pink-faced, smooth-skinned, shy apologetic eyes set wide in round, regular features, who sat before her once again.

'I've done it now,' he said softly. 'I've done it now.'

He had never really told Ruth much of what happened in his other life, his life outside Hemingway. It had been irrelevant. Once he was with her there had been so much else to talk about. Today he told her for the first time most of what had been happening to him these past few weeks. At the end he hung his head.

'I don't know how to deal with it. I've never been tested before.'

For the first time, Ruth felt she would have liked to put an arm around him. To be Grace and Hadley and Pauline and Mary and Marty all rolled into one. She poured a whisky and handed it across to him.

'It's not too late, Martin.'

He shook his head. 'I think I've missed my chance.'

'If you don't mind my saying so, that's Martin talk.'

Martin nodded and showed a trace of a smile.

'That's not a phrase your man would have used,' she went on. 'He would have said get amongst those bastards. Give them what they gave you.'

'It's easy in books,' said Martin.

Ruth persisted. 'You have one great advantage. They won't expect you to do anything.'

Martin gave a half-laugh, half-shrug. 'How does that help me?'

Ruth threw her cigarette into the fire and stood up. Then she took off her waistcoat and shifted the small pine dining table to one side of the room.

'You ever done martial arts?' she asked.

Martin frowned. 'You mean karate?'

'That kinda thing.'

Martin laughed soundlessly and shook his head.

'Well, it's big in the States. Especially for unmarried women living in New Jersey.' She selected a spot in the centre of the room. 'Now, what they teach you is to let your assailant make the first move and to use their movement to your advantage.'

She beckoned to him. 'Get up.'

'What?'

She took a stance, feet planted firmly astride. 'Get up!'

Martin did so, reluctantly. She moved round to face him. 'Now Martin, I know you're a pacifist but imagine I just called your mother a whore.'

Martin laughed and shook his head. 'What *are* you doing?'

Ruth's eyes blazed. 'Come on now. I just called your mother a whore, for Christ's sake.'

'Look Ruth, I don't want to do this.'

'Okay. Ernest Hemingway was a lying pansy who couldn't write for shit.'

Martin shook his head but he didn't smile.

Ruth taunted him again. 'He was a fat, sad, drunken old slob who couldn't even write a line for the Kennedy inauguration when they asked him to.' Martin said nothing.

'But he'd never have let anyone walk over him the way you let Nick Marshall walk over you. He'd despise you.'

He lunged at her. Ruth waited till he was almost on her. 'See. You let him come. Throw all he's got at you then –' she grabbed his arm, side-stepped and twisted his wrist, 'take him off balance and zap! He's on the floor with your knee in his neck.'

Which was indeed where Martin was, head squashed hard into the rug which smelt of dust and damp and talcum powder. Ruth was on top of him, her shin across the back of his neck, pinning him down.

Ruth congratulated herself. 'Hey! That was pretty good.'

'Eurghh!' said Martin.

'You okay?'

Martin grunted again and Ruth released him and stood up.

Martin rubbed his neck and Ruth put out a hand. He took it and she pulled him up on to his feet. He reached unsteadily for the back of a chair.

'Just remind me again why you did that?' he asked her.

Ruth reached for a cigarette. 'One, because I don't get enough exercise, and two, to demonstrate that a little guy can cause a lot of trouble if he knows how to move. Did you eat something?'

'I'm not hungry.'

'You will be.' She went into the kitchen in a businesslike way and called back to Martin. 'I bought some wine. Let's be civilised and plan your revenge over dinner.'

When the time came for him to leave they had drunk two bottles of red wine as well as a Scotch or two, and thoroughly reviled everyone concerned with the demise of Theston post office.

Martin quoted, verbatim, whole passages on the techniques of partisan warfare from *For Whom the Bell Tolls*. Between them it was agreed that, like its hero, Robert Jordan, Martin should take on the enemy from behind the lines.

His first task, they decided, had to be to select and brief someone who felt the way he did and who had a high profile in the town. Once such a figurehead was in place a campaign could be organised around them. The evening ended with an ambitious attempt to load Hemingway's chair on to the back of Martin's bicycle. This was an abject failure. They staggered back to the house with it, helpless with laughter. The chair remained leaning drunkenly across Ruth's sofa.

Ruth couldn't sleep that night. This wasn't unusual for her, but this time it wasn't words, names, dates and page references that kept her awake. It was a delicious, shameless, wholly unintellectual feeling of rank lustfulness. She knew, as she lay, on her back, on her side, on her other side, then on her back again, in the silent pitch darkness of the Suffolk night, that Martin Sproale wanted to fuck her and she wanted to fuck him and that it was going to happen sooner or later.

As she lay there, enveloped in this delectable fantasy and not knowing quite how to make the most of it, she began to laugh.

Quite quietly at first, then slowly and gradually louder and deeper and heartier until she feared she might bring the Wellbeings hurrying down the path. And this thought made her laugh even more. It wasn't a warm night, but Ruth was sweating through her loose black cotton pyjamas as she pulled herself up out of bed, wrapped a bathrobe around her, lit a cigarette and sat down at her desk to add a PS to the letter she had started that morning.

'PS Hem-fan update (hot off the presses!)

British men are not at all what they appear to be. Underneath every calm and quiet exterior there lurks a beast and beneath every beastly exterior lurks someone dying for mother's milk and an early night. Mild Martin has today turned into a passable impersonation of a Horseman of the Apocalypse. (*An* Horseman of the Apocalypse, sorry. Anne Horseman-of-the-Apocalypse – there's a new heroine for you.) Mart is hopping mad and looking for ass to kick. Why? The collapse of the monarchy? The imminent demise of the British currency? The ordination of women? No. What has turned Martin from mouse to Minotaur (does that work?) is that THEY HAVE MODERNISED HIS POST OFFICE. Apparently there are dark forces at work not a half-dozen miles from where I write who will stop at nothing until they have given him up-to-date facilities and worse still, provided them for other people as well.

The country is warming up. In every way.
Watch this space.
Yours for ever and a day,
Ruthie.

Twenty-six

On one of the first warm days of March, when the skies were blue and innocent as June, Martin Sproale could be seen cycling through Jubilee Park and down the gentle hill that led away from the centre of town down to the old merchants' houses on Mulberry Green. He stopped outside the most handsome of them. It was half past nine on a Monday morning and Martin, fired with enthusiasm for his new role as urban guerrilla, had decided to take a week of his annual holiday. Leaving his bicycle leaning by the hedge he crunched his way across the gravel to a columned and porticoed front door. He pressed a well-polished enamel doorbell on the bit where it said, helpfully, 'Press'. He cast a quick look in the direction he'd come from and was pleased to see his arrival appeared to have gone unnoticed.

The door was opened by a middle-aged woman with full grey hair only partially concealing a strawberry mark that spread down one side of her neck. She wore an apron and held a duster.

'Yes?'

'Is Mrs Harvey-Wardrell in, please?'

He was shown into a drawing room, filled with sunshine. The lady with the duster tut-tutted and pulled down a blind. She peered critically at the surface of a carved oak chest.

'That sun's a menace,' she said, and scowled at the great clear sky outside.

A moment or two later, the approach of Pamela Harvey-Wardrell was heralded by the sharp, urgent yelp of a dog and the sound of a slithery scrabbling of paws on freshly-polished floor. A voice rang out from the hallway.

'Hilda! Caspar shouldn't be here, and he knows that. Will you please put him in with Benjie. Oh, and those things in the billiard room are for the deaf.'

The drawing room door swung open. Mrs Harvey-Wardrell saw Martin Sproale bent double over the Turkish carpet.

'Are you all right?' she asked.

Martin straightened up breathlessly. 'Just taking my clips off.'

'Not at the post office?'

'No, I've taken a week's holiday.'

'Oh!' She threw her head back dramatically. 'How I envy you! Perry and I love to get away at this time of year. But alas he's frightfully busy and I've been roped in to organise the Oxfam evening. Would the post office care to help out? It would be awfully good if you could. A few packets of envelopes for the odds and ends stall?'

'Yes, I'm sure.'

'Most kind. The police have promised stickers.'

Mrs Harvey-Wardrell sat herself on the edge of a *chaise longue* and Martin noticed for the first time that she had rather good legs. She crossed them elegantly, absently fingered the pearls that hung down over the top of an expensive angora jersey and indicated Martin to sit as well.

He sat cautiously on the edge of a wing-backed armchair.

'It's the post office I've come to see you about, Mrs Harvey-Wardrell.'

'Oh yes.'

She listened to him with the same expression he had seen in pictures of white missionaries in Africa. Earnest and slightly distracted.

'I've reason to believe that if we're not careful we may never have our old post office back again.'

'You mean we'll have to keep using that neon-lit rabbit hutch?'

'It looks that way.'

'It's an excrescence.'

'Well, exactly, and knowing you feel that way, I wonder if you would be interested in, well, in leading a campaign.'

At the word 'leading' Mrs Harvey-Wardrell had shown momentary interest. Now her eyes narrowed suspiciously.

'Campaign? What sort of campaign?'

'To get the post office back into North Square where it's been for the last sixty years.'

'Well . . .' A cloud passed over Mrs Harvey-Wardrell's long and stately features. Martin thought to himself how remarkable it was that the upper classes did not just have bigger houses. Noses, eyes, ears and chins all seemed larger than the national average. 'Martin,' she said, 'Much as I abhor that abortion of a place where you work, there is a teeny problem.'

Martin was quick to reassure her. 'There's hardly any work involved, Mrs Harvey-Wardrell. All you would have to do is put your name to it.'

Mrs Harvey-Wardrell raised her eyes in saintly fashion as if what she was about to say was wretchedly hard for her. 'You have to understand, Martin, that I am not a totally free agent. My husband is, as you know, an extraordinarily successful economist, working at the very highest levels of international finance. But, Martin, he is not a sentimental man and I fear . . .' She paused on the word 'fear'. With her eyebrows and her upper lip raised and nostrils flared she looked for a moment like a horse refusing a jump. 'I fear he will be less moved by the desire to preserve the traditional tone of Theston post office, than to make a considerable amount of money by acquiring it for more profitable endeavours.'

Martin leaned forward, frowning. 'I'm sorry?'

'He's buying it.'

'Buying it?'

'Well, not buying it himself of course. He's arranging the finance. Apparently the Post Office top brass can't wait to get rid of it. Your friend Nick Marshall was round here in January asking for advice. Doesn't he tell you anything?'

Martin looked down, grimly. 'He tells me what I need to know.'

'I'm sorry, Martin. I would do something if I could.'

Martin shifted uncomfortably. He felt desperately foolish. Outwitted and cheated. And this had been going on since January? He rose from the chair.

'Well, I'm sorry to have bothered you, and I . . . . I'd rather you didn't mention my visit. Especially to Mr Marshall. It was only from the best intentions.'

Mrs Harvey-Wardrell accompanied him to the door. She seemed regretful.

'The menfolk make all these decisions. I suppose they know what they're doing. I'm told it's all going to be frightfully beneficial all round.'

Martin nodded ruefully. A Pekingese dog waddled towards them. She hoisted it into the air and nuzzled its snub face.

'Caspar, you're hideous.'

She turned to Martin. 'Try the vicar. He's frightfully keen on causes.'

The Reverend Barry Burrell liked to be called Barry. He was good-looking in an unforced way and was much disliked in Theston. His predecessor, Dr Wyngarde, had behaved in an impeccably vicarish way, speaking the old Prayer Book clearly, visiting the sick ineffectually and never preaching a sermon longer than twelve minutes. Barry Burrell's avowed aim was to be a hands-on rector. To this end he had paid special attention to taking the church into the community. He had held services in pubs and old folks' homes, blessed stock cars and once held midnight mass in the canteen of Theston Rubber Ltd. In return for these favours he hoped the community would come in to the church. Traffic wardens were encouraged to read the lesson, welders to bring their equipment to harvest festival and one of the local bus companies to sponsor the Christmas crib. He had a firm handshake and a close friend called Tessa.

He was unhelpful to Martin.

'Jesus Christ our Lord is the figurehead, Mr Sproale, not me.'

They talked in one of the side chapels at St Michael and All Angels. In the background Harold Meredith, their recently appointed vigilante, pottered, rearranging hymn books and trying to catch what they were saying.

'I'm one of the toilers in the vineyard,' Barry was telling Martin. 'If you would like me to come in to your post office and wash the feet of your employees, symbolically of course, I would. If you want to use our church for a service of reconciliation between the divisions of the restructured post office I would gladly offer it in His name, but for me to be a leader would be an assumption of powers that are only His to deploy.'

'What would you feel like, Reverend Burrell –'

'Barry, please.'

'What would you feel like, if you had to carry on *your* business in the back of a sweetshop?'

Barry Burrell liked a joke and he laughed heartily. Then he took Martin's hand, shook it warmly, disappeared into the vestry and closed the door behind him.

Martin heard the subdued sound of female laughter. 'Choir practice,' explained Harold Meredith.

Twenty-seven

For the next three days, as discreetly as possible, Martin canvassed the great and the good of Theston. He chose only those he felt would be sympathetic, but the response was disappointing. Cuthbert Habershon, the well-respected, recently retired District Coroner, was too busy growing roses. Dr Cardwell preferred to save the Health Service first and the Post Office second. Norman Brownjohn, the ironmonger, Theston's senior shopkeeper, was very keen for the post office to move from Randall's, but only as far as Brownjohn's. The one local worthy who offered unequivocal support was not on any of Martin's lists. Indeed Martin had deliberately tried to avoid him. Be that as it may, Harold Augustus Meredith had put his house and forty-seven years of experience in the Royal Army Pay Corps at Martin's disposal and, in the absence of any other candidate, Martin had reluctantly accepted. As soon as the details were finalised, Mr Meredith would begin to circulate a petition. But first the name of the campaign had to be fixed, policy formed, statements of intent drawn up. And it was already Thursday.

A squally March wind spattered the windows and rattled the roof as Martin pulled the Corona Portable Number 3 towards him. For once he didn't need to feel apologetic or inadequate. At last he had something important to write. Five hours later, when the wind had subsided, leaving low grey clouds and an early twilight, Martin slipped his finished work into an envelope and cycled over to Everend Farm Cottage. He needed Ruth's word processor and printer. He also needed her approval. Ruth read his prospectus carefully, but without making the noises he expected.

'Is it all right?' he asked anxiously.

'It's kind of long. All that historical stuff. I mean, who is this guy Padge? Was he martyred by the Romans or something?'

'He was the old Postmaster.'

'But he doesn't need *three* paragraphs, right? I mean this is a call to arms, not a novella, Martin. People don't have time to read more than a page.'

'They have time in Theston,' he said, defensively.

'Look, I know about these things, believe me. I have leafleted, Martin. Three Mile Island, Stop the Whaling, Nicaragua. I came into this world bearing leaflets, and I know two things. Keep it short and make sure you mention the phone number at least twelve times.' She riffled through his copious sheets of paper. 'You have no phone number here at all.'

'Meredith doesn't like the phone,' said Martin. 'He's eighty-two. He can't hear it ring.'

'Was he your automatic choice?'

Martin looked hurt.

'I'm sorry. Cheap shot. But is it wise to have old, deaf people running a campaign?' She tapped the end of her cigarette into the saucer of her teacup.

'There wasn't a lot of choice,' Martin explained. 'People were either busy, or they didn't want to get involved. Meredith knows the town, he'll go out collecting signatures. He'll work hard. I know that. He's got nothing else to do.'

'Okay. Let's say this eighty-two-year-old troublemaker hits the streets, what is he, i.e. you, asking people to do?' She flicked the pages. 'I mean looking at this I'm not sure if you want me to set fire to the new post office, chain myself to a bulldozer or boycott Chinese food products.'

Martin was getting thoroughly rattled. He had not expected to have to defend himself against Ruth, of all people. 'It's a serious attempt to warn people what is happening.'

'I know it's serious, Martin, but reading this you'd think the closing of Theston post office was the second worst thing this century after Hiroshima. What you need to do is decide what you want to achieve, and what you need to do to achieve it. D'you want money or marches or civil disobedience?'

Martin thought for a moment. 'Yes,' he said. 'Why not?'

'Why not what?'

'Why not all that? If that's what it takes.'

'Are you ready to go to prison?'

'I'd never thought of it like that, but – yes, if I had to.'

Ruth picked a shred of tobacco off her bottom lip. 'For a *post office*?'

Martin stared back defiantly. 'Yes.'

Ruth shook her head slowly and with admiration. 'You would too. You would.'

Martin seemed awkward with her compliment. 'If everything else failed,' he muttered. 'All I want to do now is collect enough signatures to force the Post Office to change its mind.'

Ruth raised her hands. 'Good, that's clear. That's cut a page and a half already. Now, next problem is the name.'

Martin felt on stronger ground here. Until he saw the expression on her face.

'Look,' Ruth said, 'I'm with you all the way. I love protesting. But,' she scanned the top of Martin's first page, ' "Theston People For Re-opening the Post Office in North Square" does not trip lightly off the tongue. Nor is TPFR a promising start for an acronym. So how about turning that around and trimming it down a little.'

'What's an acronym?'

Ruth looked surprised. 'For a man who's been in love with Hemingway for most of his adult life –'

'Hemingway never used fancy words.'

'*Touché.*' Ruth smiled. She went on more quietly. 'An acronym is something, you know, like UNICEF or UNPROFOR. Words made up from first letters, so people never have to say the whole thing. And that's what you need. Something nice and simple. Save Our Post Office? SOPO? Not bad.'

Martin objected. 'We've got a post office. It's the old one we want to save.'

'Save Our *Old* Post Office. SOOPO?' She shook her head. 'Not so good.'

'It's accurate.'

'That's not the point of an acronym.'

Martin threw up his arms. 'Well, why don't you just think of a word and fit the cause to it?'

'Stop!'

'Why?'

'No, that's it,' she said triumphantly. 'STOP. Save Theston's Old Post Office.'

'That would be STOPO.'

'Martin,' Ruth said icily, 'don't be a pedant.'

Twenty-eight

In the end it was Quentin Rawlings who came to the rescue. If it had not been for him STOP would never have started. Harold Meredith, though willing, was a far from ideal campaigner. His house-to-house technique was, to say the least, eccentric. His fondness for doorstep chats, indeed chats of any kind, slowed down his progress. Often, at the end of a visit, he would leave without having remembered to mention what he came for or, having mentioned it, would leave without his leaflets or his clipboard. By the time he returned the occupants had had time to slip out the back door or hide.

By the end of his first day he had obtained seven signatures on the petition and a promise of a stall at the next Conservative jumble sale. On his way home he decided to make one last call. Pushing wearily on a wrought-iron gate which hung half off its hinges, he found himself at the bottom of the path that led to the door of Hogarth House – family home of Quentin and Maureen Rawlings.

Pushing away a black and white plastic football with the end of his walking stick, he made his way to the front door. Hogarth House was not as pretty as it sounded, nor was it romantically named after the painter. It dated from 1907 and was one of three homes in the area built for the family of Maurice Hogarth, the sugar-beet king. It was tall and vulgar with unnecessary finials and fussy stucco mouldings that only served to accentuate its awkward proportions. The current owners had done little to the red and yellow brick façade other than let an adventurous Virginia creeper loose on it. This had become so prolific that in high summer it was quite difficult to find the front door at all. But in the middle of March the leaves were still in bud and Harold Meredith had little difficulty in locating not only the door, but also an antiquated pull-stop doorbell.

The effort required to pull it produced precious little reward besides dizziness and a faint tinkle from a distant room which Mr Meredith didn't hear at all. He was about to heave on it again when the blotchy green front door was pulled open and Quentin Rawlings stood there. He wore a stained white polo-neck tucked unsatisfactorily into a pair of mustard-coloured corduroys. His hair was unkempt. He looked as if he had just got out of bed. In fact Quentin Rawlings rarely got into bed. His life was centred around his anger, his typewriter and his determination to correct all the ills of the world before he reached retirement age. He stared truculently at Harold Meredith. 'Yes?'

'I've come about the post office,' said Mr Meredith. Quentin Rawlings emitted a short, sharp yelp, which caused Mr Meredith to start back in alarm.

'Don't talk to me about the post office.'

When Rawlings spoke he employed the same oratorical technique whether his audience was the local Labour Party, the National Conference, or his wife at breakfast.

'Did you know that out of twenty thousand offices in this country, eighteen and a half thousand are now owned by outside agencies? That in the last five years we have lost something in the region of one thousand sub-post offices, each serving an average catchment area of eight square miles each – that's a total of eight *thousand* square miles of rural Britain from which basic services have been denied?'

Harold Meredith opened his mouth to speak.

'Did you know that the Government, not content with splitting up the traditional, integrated multi-functional role of the postal services is proposing to sell each one separately to the highest bidder?'

Harold Meredith's mouth remained open.

200

'I mean is that not ludicrous? Parcels competing with letters competing with the people who sell stamps? Have you ever heard anything like it?'

Harold Meredith decided his mouth would not be needed and closed it.

'And what's more, I tell you that in this very town we live in they have decided to replace the old post office, without consultation and without *any formal announcement of change.*'

Mr Meredith raised a hand.

'What we should be doing here is not standing around letting them get away with it. We should be making a noise, creating a fuss, rallying opposition, telling the people of Theston what is happening under their very noses.'

'Well,' began Mr Meredith.

Quentin Rawlings jabbed a finger in his direction.

'Start a campaign to raise these issues.'

'Well,' repeated Mr Meredith.

'All you need,' went on Rawlings, 'is someone prepared to go round and do the leg work, knock on doors, visit the shops, and someone else prepared to create and co-ordinate a strategy. As it happens I've just completed a pamphlet on the subject. Are you interested?' Harold Meredith nodded helplessly. 'Wait here, I'll get you a copy.'

Some time later Mr Meredith retraced his steps along the mossy overgrown paving stones that led to the half-hung gate of Hogarth House. In his bag, in addition to his clipboard, spare pair of gloves and fifty undelivered STOP leaflets, were twenty-five unsold pamphlets by Quentin Rawlings entitled "Outrage! The Persecution of the Post Office'.

Rawlings remained under the impression that the STOP campaign had entirely originated from his chance meeting with Mr Meredith and Martin was quite happy not to disabuse him, especially as Rawlings seemed only too keen to call a meeting, to draw up a campaign plan and to work all the hours that God gave, insisting only that his name, together with a list of the

books he'd published, be printed on all official communications.

A first meeting of the core group was called for Saturday
morning at Hogarth House. Apart from Martin, it was
attended by Rawlings, his wife Maureen and Harold Meredith.
Rawlings urged that an important first step must be to mobilise
natural allies. The post office staff themselves would clearly be
anxious to protect their jobs and their future.

On his first afternoon back at work, Martin approached his
colleagues. He had a quiet word with each of them, suggesting
that they meet in the staff room immediately after close of
business to discuss an urgent matter. Nick Marshall had left
after lunch for yet more important meetings and said he would
not be back that day.

The tiny, claustrophobic area of storage space known as the
staff room was woefully inadequate for a meeting. Martin
pushed the door open, hitting Shirley Barker a sharp crack on
the knee. He flushed, apologised, looked around and was about
to welcome them all when he stopped abruptly.

'Where's Elaine?' he asked.

Geraldine took an upturned mug and rinsed it under the tap.

'I think she had to buy something before the shops closed.
She said it was urgent.' She smiled unconvincingly as she said it
and the others had stopped talking and were watching Martin
out of the corners of their eyes.

'Is she coming back, d'you know?'

'She said to carry on without her.'

'Well,' said Martin, feeling in his pocket for a handkerchief,
'some of you might already have noticed that there is a
campaign to stop the Post Office from selling off our old
premises in North Square.'

'What on earth for?' asked Shirley Barker. 'The Post
Office'll do what they want. That building we were in was a
death-trap, so I heard.'

'That's nonsense,' said Martin. 'That was a story put about by people who want to make sure we never come back. Now I don't know about you but as far as I'm concerned North Square was a one-hundred-per-cent better place to work in. There was space and light and room to move and above all, it was a centre for this community. There was none of this Customer's Charter rubbish about single queues and flashing lights and minimum counter times. We treated our customers well because we wanted to, not because we were told to. This –' he nodded contemptuously towards the door to the office, 'this is a cage, and if we let them have their way we'll all end up like bloody rats.'

There was silence. Shirley Barker affected shock, Mary Perrick looked embarrassed. Geraldine watched Martin from above her mug of tea.

'What I propose is that, as it is in all our interests, we try and help the STOP campaign.' He reached in his briefcase and drew out a bundle of slips of paper secured with rubber bands.

'What I'm asking you to do is quite simple.'

He pulled one of the slips out and held it up.

'Each of these pieces of paper contains the name of the campaign, the aim of the campaign and an address and telephone number. And all you have to do is slip one into every pension book, post office savings book, family allowance docket and anything else that gets passed over the counter. Obviously it's best not to do it when Marshall's around because he's . . . well he's management really, it would be an embarrassment for him.'

He looked around and began to slip the rubber bands off the bundles of paper.

'I'd like us to start tomorrow, if we can.'

Shirley Barker stood up. As she spoke, she gathered her handbag, coat and scarf together. 'Martin, I value my job and I find it very useful and I want to keep it. I don't honestly mind where I work.'

'With respect, Shirley,' said Martin, 'You are part-time. You spend a lot less of your life here than I do.'

Shirley pointed at the others. 'We're all part-timers here apart from you. Mary's a part-timer. Geraldine's a part-timer. And they're here because you got rid of John Parr and Arthur Gillis. Remember? Maybe you'd be better off starting a campaign to bring *them* back, rather than having a go at us.' She fastened her floral pattern headscarf, pursing and unpursing her narrow lips nervously. 'Arthur was a fine and decent man with years of working life ahead of him. Save the Post Office came a bit too late for him.'

She picked up her bag and reached for the door. When she went out it slammed shut behind her.

Martin stared at the door. Mary Perrick stood up. She was a softer, rounder, infinitely warmer sort than Shirley Barker, but the message was the same. 'I'd rather not get involved either, Martin. I need this job too. It doesn't pay much, but I'm thankful for whatever.'

She stood for a moment and spread her hands wide, then, with nothing else to say, nodded, smiled a quick, embarrassed smile, opened the door and went out.

Geraldine cradled the mug of tea in her hands and made no move.

Martin frowned. He thrust his lower lip forward. He slowly replaced the rubber bands on the slips of paper and returned them to his briefcase. Geraldine stood up and took her mug over to the wash-basin. Martin aimed a kick at the nearest chair.

'Why wasn't Elaine here? She's in the union. She was always much more of a fighter than me.' He looked up at Geraldine. 'She's a fighter, you know. She's a toughie is Elaine. I mean, we've worked together, side by side, for six years. Did you know that?'

Geraldine ran her cup under the hot tap. The water splashed off and some of it ran on to the floor.

'Damn!' Geraldine reached for a cloth.

'She'll support the campaign. Surely . . . won't she?'

'Well, don't bank on it.'

'Why ever not?'

Geraldine squeezed out the cloth and laid it carefully on the side of the basin. She looked at Martin. He was waiting for her to say something. He was hot. He looked tired. He looked as though he needed comforting words, but she knew that for some reason he trusted her and expected the truth.

'You've been shafted, Martin,' said Geraldine quietly. 'Elaine's with Nick. They're going out together.'

Martin stared back.

'They're an item, Martin.'

Twenty-nine

Ruth saw Ted Wellbeing trundle up the hill on his tractor. A seed drill reared up behind the back wheels, bucking and quivering and shedding clods of freshly turned soil as he negotiated the gullies left by a week of wind and sweeping rain.

Today she envied him. Envied him the outdoors and the mindless routine. As the sun climbed higher (on the days when it was visible) Ruth began to feel restless. She was ready to get away from other people's lives for a while and back into her own. For nearly a week she had been working hard trying to prove a theory of hers that Hemingway's preoccupation with the way hair was cut and the way it could be altered to change a personality began, not with gender confusion in early childhood, but from the time he met Pauline Pfeiffer. Of all the wives, of all the Hemingway women, Ruth felt closest to Pauline. Her vivacity, her bookishness, her slim, neat figure and dark features appealed to Ruth. So she had been trying very hard to prove that it was Pauline's obsession with her appearance, and particularly the style, cut and colour of her hair, that activated her husband's fascination with gender-bending. That it was Pauline who had led him to explore the subject in two of his most important books, *A Farewell to Arms* and, more particularly, in Ruth's favourite, *The Garden of Eden* – an odd, haunting, erotic tale not published until twenty-five years after Hemingway's death.

Unfortunately the facts were refusing to fit her theory. They were being highly obstreperous – appearing, disappearing and reappearing in all the wrong places. She sat at the window for a while, not writing, just watching the blue-grey sky turn white and then slowly darken. She stood and stretched and felt for the switch on the big yellow table lamp she'd bought herself as a Christmas present. Then she walked into the tiny bathroom and pulled the cord of the light switch. She looked into the mirror and was holding her own thick, dark hair back from her forehead when a knock on the front door startled her.

When she opened the door, Martin stood there. He had a sports bag over his shoulder and his face was hot from cycling. He looked dejected and helpless, which only increased her irritation at seeing him.

'I didn't expect you,' she said.

'I didn't think you ever expected me,' he muttered and she sensed that something was wrong.

'Are you busy?' he asked, looking in as if half-expecting to see others there.

'I'm writing, as ever,' she shrugged. 'The saga continues.'

'I'll go if you want. I just came to see the chair.'

Ruth laughed, lightly. 'Of course. I forgot. Come on in.'

She felt uneasy and embarrassed for him. They stood awkwardly for a while, then she said, 'Look, you go ahead. I'll fix a drink.'

She went into the kitchen and pushed the door half-closed behind her. For once she didn't want to talk Hemingway. She poured herself a drink first and sipped it unhurriedly, staring out at the sodden countryside, letting the slow warmth revive her.

When she came out of the kitchen, Martin was no longer there. In his place was a hunched, wary figure wearing a white tennis cap, grey sweatshirt and a light brown cotton jacket with a pattern of tiny check. He wore plain white Bermuda-length cotton shorts. His calves were bare and he sat, leaning forward, as if waiting. Ruth approached cautiously. The figure in the chair was concentrating on something in the middle distance. His face wore an ironic, self-mocking smile. She held out a glass of whisky.

'You want a drink?'

For a moment nothing moved, but when the figure slowly lifted his head, Ruth experienced once again the uncanny sensation of being with a stranger she knew well.

'I guess I look ridiculous,' came a voice that was slow and heavy and yet in which the smile remained. She said nothing.

'I don't look like a decent fellow should look, huh?'

He took the whisky from her and drank it back in one. Then he held the glass out again and watched her refill it.

He drank again, more slowly. This one was neat and he gasped at the after-taste. Then all of a sudden he looked up and breathed deep and beamed around him.

'Well, I look like this because this is the way I like to look most of the time. I look like this because, come tomorrow, I shall be in Havana and I shall be drinking cold beers with Mrs Mason on the deck of HMS *Anita*.'

Ruth caught all the allusions. In 1933 Ernest left Pauline behind in Key West and took a two-month fishing holiday in Havana. He met up with the beautiful, wilful, twenty-three-year-old Jane Mason, whose husband was working and couldn't go with her, and they fished together off a boat called *Anita*, which belonged to Joe Russell, one of Hemingway's Key West cronies. It was an episode of his life she and most Hemingway scholars had always wanted to know more about. A rare extramarital affair, known to have taken place, but still steeped in mystery.

Ruth poured herself another drink and sat down opposite him, one side of her face caught by the lamplight. 'Why are you going away so soon?'

'Because I worked goddamn hard at that book and I need to get it out of my system.'

'I worked hard to get this house ready for you,' she said quietly. 'You know how much money I spent?'

His face clouded. 'That's the only way you see these things. Through the end of a bank balance. So your father bought this house. Great. So you put in nice furniture, big curtains. Paint everything. Great. I do no more fucking writing because I have to sit around choosing curtains when I could be out on a boat chasing marlin with my real friends.'

'You call those bums you hang out with your friends?'

'They're simple guys. They drink and they gamble and they live off the sea. But I love them. Okay?'

'You love them more than me?'

'Maybe I do. Maybe they don't keep wanting to hang on to me and tidy me up and put me on display.'

'I just want to have you here in the house with me. I don't care if you wear nothing but a pair of sneakers and a leopard- skin loincloth, I'd rather I looked after you than Mrs Mason. I'm your wife, dammit. What happened? What did I do wrong?'

'You did too much. You tried too hard.'

'You loved me once. You loved me so much and I loved you and we went everywhere together and we made each other very happy.'

'If you say so.'

'You don't know?'

'I *do* know, for Chrissake, I do know.'

'You knew for a day. You knew for a week. Then someone more interesting comes along and I have to go along with that. I have to wait while you make your plans and then I do what you want me to do. Isn't that right?'

'No . . . no . . . It's not right.'

'You do what you want to do and I'm just supposed to fit in, right?

'No, no!'

'I'm the wife who has to stay home till the master returns.'

'No.'

'*My* writing is not worth shit.'

'No.'

'All you want is a body to be there when it suits you.'

'No!'

Ruth saw the sweat break out on his brow, but she couldn't stop now.

'Well, I'll tell you. You ain't as hot as you think you are.'

'Quit, will you?' His head swung angrily.

'Don't want to hear the truth, huh?'

'I said quit.'

'I tell you I could walk out that door right now and find a dozen guys who'd give me a better time!'

'I said *quit!*'

A cut glass ashtray flew towards Ruth's head. She ducked and heard it smash against the wall and fall in pieces to the floor behind her.

She straightened up.

Martin stood staring helplessly. 'Are you all right?'

She nodded.

He looked down at his hand, moving it slowly up towards him, as if sensing it for the first time. His voice, when it came, was small and bewildered. 'I'm sorry, Ruth. I'm sorry.'

'You okay?'

Ruth stayed where she was, eyeing him warily. She found herself taking breath in short, sharp gulps.

Martin shook his head, as if trying to clear it from a daze.

'I don't know what came over me.'

'It was my fault,' she said. 'This is a crazy thing to do.'

'I forgot,' he said. 'I thought you were – I thought you were someone else.'

'Someone besides Pauline?'

'Yes.'

'Want to tell me?'

Martin said nothing. Then he drew a hand across his eyes and looked down at the chair.

'I'm sorry. It's this thing,' he said, trying to wriggle free without toppling the chair. 'I must get up. I must get out of it.'

The wind was up again outside Everend Farm Cottage, but it was not hostile. It blew hard and slackened and the next time it blew less hard. The room was growing dark. Ruth took a brush and began to sweep up the pieces. It was a way of stopping herself shaking.

Martin climbed out of the chair. 'I better go.'

'You're going nowhere. Just sit right down again. I'll fix you some coffee.'

The coffee was strong and he felt it must be doing him some good. Ruth had a mug too and she brought it over and knelt down by the fire and she lit a cigarette from the fire and they both watched the new logs hiss and slowly start to take the flame.

'I've never done anything like that before. Honestly. Never.'

'I believe you,' said Ruth.

'Something inside. Can't explain. Something very strong.'

'Listen. If you wanted to hurt me that bad it's something that needs dealing with.'

'I didn't want to hurt *you*. You know that, don't you?'

'Sure,' said Ruth. 'But I wasn't being me. I was being Pauline and you were being Ernest. Then you stopped being Ernest and as far as you were concerned I stopped being Pauline and became someone else. Oscars all round I think. But let's not do it again.'

A burning log rolled towards them out of the fire. Ruth reached for a poker and pushed it back.

'I think I was in love with her,' said Martin, matter-of-factly. 'But I didn't know how to say it properly. So I did nothing. Now she's betrayed me. Sleeping with the enemy.'

The log spat back at Ruth, causing her to pull back. Her back came up against his legs. 'Goddamit. There's a sniper in there!'

Martin gave a short half-laugh. 'It's not your night.'

'I'll say. It's the English countryside firing back. Well I'm going to stay out of range.'

She relaxed back against Martin's legs. There was a pause, then Martin spoke, slowly. 'You're the authority,' he said. 'What would Hemingway have done?'

'I'm no authority. Not yet anyway.'

'Well, from what you've found out so far, Professor of Hemingway Women, what would he have done if he was me?'

Ruth considered the question.

'Well, once things began to go wrong between him and a woman, it was usually a sign he'd found another one he liked more.'

'Well, that's no help.'

'No other women in your life, then?'

'Absolutely not!'

Ruth drew her knees up under her chin and arched her back away from him. 'Well in that case,' she said with feeling, 'I think he would have been very disappointed in you.'

Martin smiled ruefully and stayed silent.

Ruth cleared away the coffee things and offered to fix some food, but Martin didn't seem interested in food. So she opened a bottle of wine and came back in front of the fire and they drank it together and she settled back in her favourite foetal position, knees drawn up, back resting gently, but firmly, against Martin's knees as he sat in the armchair, staring into the fire.

'Do you mind?' asked Martin, after a while.

'Do I mind what?'

'Do you mind that I'm, well, that I'm like this. I never used to tell anyone what I did. It was all private, between him and me.'

'I feel honoured, Martin,' she said, feeling free not to mean it.

'I was so excited about the chair. I wanted it so much because it would bring me closer to him and this is what happens.'

Ruth leaned back and drew on her cigarette. Martin watched as she blew the smoke towards the fire. It merged with the wood smoke and was snatched away towards the chimney.

'It doesn't affect you – to be Pauline?' Martin said to her after a while.

Ruth shook her head and blew out a trail of smoke. 'I can't be Pauline. I can read all her books and her letters and everything about her but I can't do what you do.'

'Why is that, d'you think?'

She paused, then tipped her head back. 'Because I think I'm nearer Mrs Mason.'

'But she was –'

Ruth grinned. 'The scarlet woman. Fast and loose and drank a lot and was a little mad to say the least.'

Martin looked at his glass. It was empty. 'I wouldn't know what to do with someone like that.'

Ruth smiled. 'Well imagine,' she said. 'You Papa. Me Jane.'

She threw her cigarette into the fire and pushed herself back against his knees. 'Open sesame!' she said, wriggling against them.

Martin offered no resistance. He slipped forward off the chair and on to the floor. She leant close up against his chest. He could feel the warm breadth of her back.

'It's always good to see you,' she said and she took his arms and wrapped them close around her. 'I like to see you.'

She clasped her knees and began to rock gently from side to side. 'You maybe should take holidays more often.' She could feel his hands open cautiously around her breasts, which were free and loose under her blouse. 'I'm always ready for you.'

They sat like that for a while, then he said, 'Me too, daughter.'

She felt the warmth of his face as it touched her cheek and the surprising softness of his lips against her shoulder. 'Me too.'

'Where shall we go tonight?' she asked. 'The Floridita? Chory's?'

'Too many Americans at Floridita.'

'It still does the best daiquiris in town.' She nuzzled her head back against him. He buried his face in her thick, dark hair. It smelt of aloes and the sea.

'We could go on to El Pacifico,' she whispered. 'Dance on the roof.'

'I prefer the girls at Chory's. You remember the one with the big lazy eye?'

She laughed. 'The one you called the wrestler?'

'That's the one.'

'Some girl.'

His mouth was now passing up and down across the back of her neck. She knew what was happening and she was pleased. She tipped her head forward, away from him, then leant it all the way back till it rested on his shoulder.

She spoke softly. 'We could go down to the Nacional for an absinthe and behave badly along the front.'

His hands slipped lower and she felt him lift her cotton blouse and she felt the warmth of the fire on her unprotected stomach and the soft play of his hands across her breasts.

'If it's a new moon,' she said, 'we could take the boat out and make love on the bay. I've always wanted to make love on the bay.'

His hands ran down wide and strong across her stomach. They had started shy but now their touch was assured. She eased her long legs apart as they ran on easily down.

'Old Gutiérrez wouldn't like that,' he said and she felt his breath on her neck as he spoke. 'They're bad, bad boys those sailors, but they're good Catholics and they'd rather see Papa fishing than fornicating.'

She laughed lightly and slipped herself free of her loose black trousers and with a quick lean forward pulled clear of her blouse.

'On the other hand,' she said, turning in towards him, 'we could try the church on the corner.' She reached for his belt. 'You ever made love in a church, Papa?'

'Hell no,' he grunted. 'Too cold.'

When they were both naked she lay along him and she could feel how much he wanted her. She felt his long soft fingers tracing the curve of her spine and the small of her back, as his lips moved slowly from her breasts down the narrow line of her stomach.

'Tell you what,' she said. 'Let's just stay here in the hotel.'

Thirty

There was a long and desolate stretch of beach south of Theston where the houses petered out and sand dunes covered in hard spiky grass ran twenty miles down the coast before they reached the next village. To get to it Martin had to skirt the walls of the harbour and pick his way carefully along the green and slippery causeway that led to the old pier. The smell of saltwater and seaweed was thick and cloying, and he remembered the days when there had been other smells here, of tar and fish and petrol. His father had often brought him down to watch the fishermen. They had stood, hand in hand, and watched the boats winched up the slipway on sturdy chains, green and shaggy with hanging fronds of sea grass. When he was old enough to come to the harbour on his own, he was told never to go further than this and never to set foot on the old, abandoned pier. Of course they all did and there were often boys, anxious to impress, who had picked their way through the rusting barbed wire and over the fence and out along the girders. Martin had always watched, never dared. One day he was watching when a boy called Fraser went out at low tide and reached the very end of the two-hundred-yard pier and held up one of the warning lights as a trophy and waved it in triumph. But he waited too long and the tide came in faster than he could make his way back and he lost his footing and they all saw him fall. After that there was much talk of dismantling the pier but, in the end, the approach was fenced off and left, and over the years nothing happened, except that the wooden fence posts were replaced with concrete ones and the barbed wire with razor wire.

This was now festooned, like the rim of the beach itself, with impaled litter and polystyrene cups thrown overboard from passing freighters. Martin walked carefully past it, across the shingle and up towards the low brick shelter which Frank Rudge had erected for the army's exercises and which they had never used. There was still the occasional, abrupt reminder of war when the Jaguars and Tornadoes from RAF Dentishall raced low down the coast and out to sea. But for most of the year there was little sound but the soft plump and swish of breaking waves and the hoarse rattle they made on the pebbles as they drained back to the sea.

Martin had sometimes come here with Elaine. It was a place where they could walk and not be disturbed.

Now he had come here alone, after work, for the same reason.

The previous night with Ruth had left him confused. He had never felt such powerful physical attraction, nor had he ever felt quite as fulfilled or as wonderfully, radiantly, pleasurably happy. He had to keep reminding himself of this because, as soon as he left the cottage, in the last, solid darkness that comes just before dawn, the delight and pleasure had disappeared as swiftly as the darkness itself.

With the daylight came guilt, embarrassment and apology. His mother said nothing, which only made things worse. He wanted to tell her all that had happened, but couldn't. At work he wanted to hide what had happened from Elaine, but he was pretty sure he hadn't. He walked along the beach now, pulling his coat collar close around his neck as a cool breeze suddenly gusted off the steel-grey sea and he wondered what on earth he should do next.

Sex with Ruth had been exciting. He had never been as close and intimate with anyone before. He had never let anyone do what she did for him before. What happened now? He reached a small headland and pulled himself up onto a shingle bank and sat and watched the sea and felt, not closer to anyone, but further away than ever before.

He didn't see Elaine straight away. First he saw Scruff, nose down, earnestly following some trail through the grass where the top of the beach met the sand dunes. The dog stopped and his tail began to work and he barked in recognition. Martin stood. He wanted to move but there was nowhere to go. A moment later he heard Elaine calling the dog. She stopped suddenly as she saw him. Her hair caught the breeze and her face looked cold and pinched in the raw sea air.

They faced each other without speaking. Then Elaine pulled out a pink handkerchief and dabbed away the drip she could feel forming on the end of her nose.

'What are you doing here?' she asked.

'What are *you* doing here?' said Martin.

'Taking the dog for a walk,' Elaine said, which was true, but she'd deliberately chosen to walk here so she wouldn't have to meet anyone.

'It's going to rain,' she said, nodding out to sea. 'D'you want a lift back?'

Martin shook his head. 'I've got the bicycle,' he said.

'Why don't you buy a car? It's about time.'

'Haven't got the money.'

She looked at him a moment. 'Not what I've heard.'

'What have you heard?' Martin asked. Scruff was jumping up, reaching for the top of Martin's legs, and Martin tickled the top of his head.

'I've heard Nick was quite generous,' said Elaine.

'Well, you'd know, wouldn't you,' said Martin, and he suddenly pushed the dog away. 'Get off me, Scruff!'

'What did you do with it?' she asked.

'What?'

'Your thousand pounds?'

Martin stooped and threw a pebble low towards the sea. Scruff hurtled after it. 'If you must know I bought a chair.'

'A chair! For a thousand pounds?'

'You wouldn't understand.'

'Nor would most people. Where did you find it?'

'I didn't find it. Ruth found it.'

'Oh. Well, if Ruth found it.'

Elaine turned and stared out at the sea. Scruff was splashing about at the water's edge, nose down, searching.

'She's got control over you,' Elaine went on, without looking at him. 'She's got you under her spell, hasn't she? I remember when she came in the post office that first time. John Parr laughed at her and said she looked like a witch. I remember it because I thought that was a cruel thing to say. But maybe he was right.'

'What's it worse to be then,' said Martin, 'a witch or a tart?'

Elaine's eyes blazed. 'What do you mean by that?'

'I know what you're doing behind my back, Elaine.'

Elaine shook her head. 'Your bloody back. That's all I ever saw, your bloody back.'

Martin turned away, bitterly. 'Well, I don't care,' he said. 'Whatever you do from now on, Elaine, it's all right with me.'

She looked at him suspiciously.

'You've made your choice. It's simple. You've chosen Marshall. You like him. I hate him, that's all.'

'Well, that's good,' Elaine retorted. 'I remember the time when you thought he was the best thing since sliced bread.'

Martin reached for a pebble and weighed it up. 'That was before I knew what was going on.'

He picked up a pebble and flung it low over the surface of the waves. It bounced once, twice and disappeared. Scruff barked in delight and scurried off after it.

'Well, you were right, for once,' said Elaine. 'We're lucky to have him here.'

Martin snorted derisively. 'What's lucky about having someone who wants to destroy our livelihood?'

'Oh God, Martin. Don't tell me you really believe all that Save the Post Office rubbish. He's given us a damn sight more efficient office than the one at North Square ever was.'

'Oh, it's rubbish is it?' Martin replied angrily. 'Wanting to keep a decent post office is rubbish?'

'Martin,' said Elaine, 'it's a building. That's all it is. A building. What we do can be done anywhere.'

The waves were growing larger and one spilled on to the beach quite close to them. Elaine scrambled higher up the shingle and stopped, looking down at him.

Martin scrambled after her. 'It's not just the building. It's what goes with it.' He was shouting now. 'We're like the milkman. We keep an eye on people. If someone doesn't come in for their pension or their allowance or their green giro we know about it. If anything's happened to them we can tell. They can tell us things too. We're the listening centre of the community.'

'Is that one of Miss America's phrases?'

'Oh, fuck off, then!' shouted Martin. 'You talk about me being controlled and twisted. You believe anything Nick Marshall tells you. Well if Ruth's a witch then he's a crook. A twenty-four-carat-gold crook. Just like your father used to be!'

Elaine stared out to sea, into the wind. A long dark rim of cloud was spreading from the eastern horizon. She turned and looked along the beach. She called to Scruff, who reluctantly sniffed his way along the pebble-strewn sand towards her. Then she glanced quickly at Martin. 'Well, I've some news for you. The post office is sold. They signed yesterday. We couldn't move back even if we wanted to. It's not ours. So you know where you can stick your stupid campaign.'

There was a distant noise, like the soft rolling of thunder.

Martin watched Elaine until she was over the other side of the harbour. He saw her hold the door of her car open and shout impatiently for the dog. Then she climbed in herself, without looking back. He heard the gears grate and wheels kick the gravel as she swung around and drove away fast up the low hill that led to the town.

He gazed out to sea for a long time. The sight of that huge sombre sweep of water was comforting. Its restlessness soothed and reassured. To the east the border of black cloud grew as an inoffensive blue and lemon sunset faded in the west. A persistent and strengthening wind agitated the surface of the water. A curtain of rain was approaching fast and thunder rumbled far out over the sea.

Martin sprang up and went tripping and sliding down the shingle. Then he half-ran, half-stumbled along the stony beach until he reached the barbed-wire fence and the broken remains of the causeway. There the first drops of rain hit him and by the time he reached his bicycle his coat was sodden and heavy, and the wind was screaming. There was no question of his riding so he walked along the road holding his bicycle as close as he could beside him, and that warmed him up and despite the sudden ferocious wildness of the storm he reached the centre of town feeling oddly exultant.

He wheeled his bicycle along Market Street and past the bright lights of the hotel, across the High Street and into North Square.

He stood in the swirling rain and looked across to the post office. Scaffolding shrouded the building and where the roof had once been a huge tarpaulin slapped and cracked and strained in the wind. Martin raised a hand and wiped the water from his face, then, mounting his bike, he rode round the two sides of the square and down through Echo Passage. He would have coasted into Phipps' Yard and come to rest, precisely, at the back steps of the post office, but the site was boarded up and the gates were padlocked.

He looked around. There was no one to be seen. He leaned his bicycle against the wooden security fence and made sure it was firm. Then he climbed awkwardly up on to the saddle, from where he could reach a projecting scaffolding bar. His coat had doubled in weight from the rain and it required all his strength to heave himself up by the bar until he could swing his feet on to the top of the fence and lever up the rest of his weight.

Once over the fence he ran along the scaffolding walkway until he reached a ladder, leading up to the next level. From there another ladder led to the roof level. Up here, where it was exposed, the rain stung his face and hands and the wind savaged the tarpaulin with such force that he could not for a moment move with any safety. He knelt on the wooden planks and clung to the rocking scaffold for dear life. The moment there was a lessening of the howling wind he ran quickly to the corner of the building and ducked down. A rope running through a grommet in the tarpaulin secured the roof covering to the scaffold.

When he saw how poorly the knot was tied he gave a mental note of thanks to Marshall for employing a builder like Joe Crispin, and began to tug away at the end of the rope. Then the force of the gale hit fair and square and he fell backwards as the tarpaulin bucked and sprang out of his hands. Released from the knot, it lashed and curled furiously over on itself like a scorpion in a fire, but did not break free. Martin scrambled along the scaffold boards, which shook and shuddered at one fierce gust, pitching him painfully against a pile of bricks. He fell back, his foot skidding out over a sheer drop to the street. He grasped giddily at the scaffolding bar and held himself from falling. He lay there panting. Sixty feet below he could see the rain in the lamplight sweeping across North Square. He was surprised to see there were vehicles passing and what he had thought were empty streets were dotted with people sheltering from the storm. Someone, beneath the awning of the Market Hotel, seemed to be looking up towards him and he heaved himself back on to the scaffold and crouched down, bent double against the sodden duckboards.

The rain lessened, then came again with swift, torrential force. Grabbing the rail he slipped and slithered the last few feet. He reached the corner and found another knot, but this one was tightened by the extra pressure and he could not release it. A bus pulled up right below him. He flattened

222

himself against the boards and waited as it disgorged its passengers. In between the high-pitched screams of the gusting wind he could hear voices quite clearly. The image of Robert Jordan, flattened against the floor of the forest as the Fascist cavalry advanced towards him, came, thrillingly, into his mind as he clung for dear life to the swaying, storm-racked scaffold.

Then the wind fell and he wrenched the tarpaulin down with all his strength and tore at the knot, knowing one sudden gust might fling him from the roof. At last the rope was free and, bent double, he scuttled back along the scaffold. He had reached the top of the ladder on the second level before the wind came again and he tumbled down and fell on a stack of timbers. He dragged himself up and flung himself towards the fence. Above the shrieking of the wind he could just make out the sound of splitting fabric and a scattering of dislodged bricks as they fell into the yard. He jumped quite painfully to the ground and reached for his bicycle. The pedals whirled furiously until he took control and then he cycled away and did not stop to look back until he reached the top of Victoria Hill.

Like the whirling cloak of an operatic villain, the tarpaulin flapped and swirled angrily in the air above the post office. Then, as he watched, it rose up one last time, somersaulted, ripped free and tumbled messily across the low gables of the fine Georgian houses on Market Street until, lashed on by more ferocious gusts, it licked and slapped and tumbled its way over the rooftops before wrapping itself around the massive chimney breast that rose from the roof of the old Masonic Hall. Here it held fast for a while, then the wind dropped and it sank, slowly and groggily, to disappear from sight behind the fancy crenellated parapet.

Martin felt a surge of pure and inexpressible delight.

Thirty-one

On the morning after the storm Martin overslept for the first time in sixteen and a half years. When he came down Kathleen was packing up his sandwiches. Martin rushed about the kitchen. His head was squeezed tight with pain. It felt as if a bullet were lodged inside, but he knew it was vodka. He had virtually emptied a bottle on his return. It had been his way of celebrating.

'Where's my briefcase?'

'Where you normally leave it.'

'Where's my hat?'

'On the radiator.'

'Oh, God.'

He was halfway down the bypass when he remembered he hadn't shaved.

He cycled perilously fast and was rounding the corner of Bishop Street and within sight of the back entrance to Randall's when he saw Harold Meredith hurrying up the street towards him. He turned his head away and crouched low on the bike. Harold Meredith waved his stick and shouted. 'Martin!'

It was no good. Martin uncoiled himself and slid to a halt.

'Very good news!' shouted Mr Meredith. 'About the campaign!'

Martin looked quickly around and raised his finger to his mouth.

Mr Meredith came up close to him and dropped his voice to a loud whisper. 'I'm glad I've caught you. I missed you earlier in the week.'

Martin began to wheel his bicycle towards the gate of Randall's yard. 'I'm late for work, I can't stop now,' he said.

'I had a bright idea. I put those little forms you gave me into every hymn-book in church!'

They had reached the gate.

'Mr Meredith,' said Martin, reaching for his key, 'I'm late, I must –'

'I put out a hundred at communion and two hundred at matins before that vicar found out.'

The pride in his voice only made Martin feel worse. He unlocked the gate.

'Three hundred altogether I put out.'

The church clock struck nine. Martin had never been late for work. Not once in sixteen and a half years. He had no option but to push the gate gently shut. Harold Meredith stuck his stick in the gap.

'Two hundred and ten replies, Martin. Two hundred and ten replies! All wanting to save the old post office.'

Martin thrust the gate open again. He looked down at Mr Meredith. The old man seemed to have shed at least ten years. His eyes were bright. His chin stuck out defiantly. Martin wanted, suddenly, to hit him. To knock him down. Anything to stop him.

'I'm thinking of putting them in the bus. Driver wouldn't notice and there's no conductor any more.'

'Mr Meredith –' Martin repeated, wearily.

'I'm on my way to tell Mr Rawlings. He'll be pleased.'

The pain in Martin's head was now so intense that he could control himself no longer. 'It's too late,' he screamed. His voice began a slowly rising crescendo. 'Don't you understand? It's too late! We have been scuppered! Shafted! Stitched up and sold down the river! The campaign is over. The post office has gone forever, Mr Meredith.' Even as he shouted he felt the girdle of pain loosen. 'And we the innocent of Theston have been shat upon. Shat upon from a very great height!'

He was wiping his lips on the sleeve of his anorak when he heard a discreet cough from close behind him. It was Nick Marshall.

'I think we need to have a word, Martin. Inside.'

Nick Marshall followed Martin into the staff room and turned and leaned against the door. He pushed a hand through his hair, put an arm out against the wall and stood frowning, his body poised and taut, trying to contain his impatience. He cleared his throat tersely. 'Glad you could make it today, Martin.'

Martin's pain was now almost completely gone and he was beginning to think more clearly. 'I'm sorry about all that.' He shook his head. 'I didn't feel at all well this morning, Nick. I've not been myself for a few days.'

'So I hear,' Nick smiled darkly. 'You've been the organiser of a campaign.'

'Campaign?'

'What's it called, Mart? "STOP"? Is that it? Very clever.'

'That was a grass-roots campaign, set up by others, Nick.'

'Not what I heard. Not what I believed either. Eighty-year-olds don't go printing stuff like that, calling themselves names like STOP.'

'They do if they feel strongly enough, and he wasn't alone. There's plenty of people out there who think like him. We don't want to lose a post office that worked perfectly well.'

'So it *was* "we".'

'All right, I happen to agree with them. But that doesn't mean I ran the campaign.'

'Stop lying, Mart. It doesn't suit you. I was told by an impeccable source. Someone who knows you very well.'

Martin nodded grimly. 'Someone who used to know me well, but who now knows *you* a lot better from what I hear. And you're welcome. At least the Elaine Rudge I used to know didn't betray friends.'

'Elaine's not the traitor, Martin. You are. A decision was taken for the best interests of the post office in Theston. You are an employee of that post office.'

As he spoke the side of Marshall's mouth began slowly but

surely to flicker into life. He rushed a handkerchief to the danger area. 'Or were.'

From his pocket he produced an official-looking white envelope which he handed to Martin. 'When you get home, read this,' he said.

Martin tore the envelope open. There was a folded sheet inside, embossed with the Peterborough-designed company logo. Martin read what it said quite quickly. He looked up. Nick Marshall was staring intently at the wall, as if looking for barely visible life-forms.

Martin concentrated hard on keeping his voice from shaking. 'You can't do this. I've been sixteen years with the Post Office. You can't do this.'

Marshall turned to the door. 'It's a month's notice. Full pension.'

'For what? For wanting to help the customers?'

'That's the way you see it, Mart. The Post Office sees it as industrial sabotage, and that could cost more than your job.'

Martin gasped in disbelief. 'Industrial sabotage? For helping collect a few names? I mean, what are we coming to?'

Marshall produced something else from his pocket and held it up. It was a bicycle clip. 'I expect you were wondering where this had got to. I know how much clips mean to you, Martin.'

'So what, it's a bicycle clip. You find bicycle clips all over the place.'

'Not often on scaffolding, fifty feet above the ground.'

'You can't prove anything.'

'We could try though, Mart, and if we did, you would lose more than your job.'

Marshall became brisk. He didn't want to be in this small airless room doing this. He was a scientist, an engineer, an inventor. He had done his best to learn about human behaviour but it was a slippery, awkward, time-consuming thing, unstable, irrational, unquantifiable. He moved past Sproale and reached for the door.

'By all means stay the full month,' he said, 'but I should tell you that as from Monday morning Ms Rudge will be my Assistant Manager.'

Thirty-two

At lunchtime that day, John Devereux and Nick Marshall met at Nick's flat for one of their regular briefings.

'Nicholas, my lad, I sometimes think there's someone Up There working for us.'

The loss of the tarpaulin covering on the old post office was one of several bits of good news for Devereux that morning.

Geraldine served them coffee then opened up her notepad and sat ready.

Marshall checked some notes. 'The surveyor reckons there's a couple of thousand pounds worth of direct damage, replacement of materials etc. plus another thousand in man hours lost – drying out the timbers, that sort of thing.' He handed the notes across to Devereux. 'It looks very rosy.'

'Negligence?'

'Of course, and just at the right time. Crispin was cheap and did as he was told, but now Nordkom have bought the building they'll need someone who knows what they're doing.'

He broke off and turned to Geraldine. 'Don't write that down.'

She drew a line through the last sentence.

Marshall held his hand out. 'On second thoughts, give me the page.'

Geraldine tore it off the pad. 'Don't you trust me?' she asked.

'I don't trust anybody. Especially after last night.' Marshall crunched the paper into a ball and threw it across the room. It landed in the waste paper basket without touching the sides.

He went on. 'That roof damage means we can legally have

him out by the end of the week and get Stopping's boys in.'

'Stopping? Is he owt, as they say where I come from?' Devereux looked across at Geraldine and added, 'That's spelt O-W-T. It means is he any fucking good?'

Marshall shrugged. 'He's the Mayor. We promised him some of the action – don't write that down either, Gerry. In fact don't write anything down till I tell you.'

Geraldine tore out another page, screwed it up and sent it arcing into the basket. Devereux nodded approvingly. 'Not bad for a woman. Do you know a woman that can throw, Nick?'

'What?'

'In my experience women can't generally throw.'

'I've always been good at games, Mr Devereux,' said Geraldine sweetly. 'Especially when balls are involved.'

Devereux smiled uncomfortably and crossed his legs. He couldn't suss out this girl. She looked great and talked like a lorry driver but he'd never met anyone who'd laid a finger on her.

'John?' Nick was looking at him. 'Are you with me?'

'Yes?' said Devereux, abstractedly.

'I said we have good news on the installation. The DTI licence is through. Under development rights there's no limit on masts under fifteen metres.'

'That's . . . er . . .'

'Forty-five feet. We can start transmitting with half that.'

'Sounds good.'

'I've been in touch with Telemark. They're the installation specialists. Norwegian. They can have a mast, two transmission dishes, and three pole antennae in place within three months.'

'That's soon.'

'It's important, though, John. We have to stay ahead of the game.'

'I'm not sure the new Post Office companies will be ready to complete by then.'

Nick shook his head despairingly. 'They should be planning now. *We* have, for God's sake. Anyway, if the Post Office isn't ready by then we'll have to look somewhere else.'

'Hey! Careful, Nick. We're partners, remember. And I'm your employer.'

Nick smiled. 'By the way, John, how is your Dutch coming on?'

Devereux laughed. 'Dutch! Those bastards speak English better than I do. Mind you, a refresher trip to Amsterdam wouldn't go amiss.' He winked at Geraldine, who ignored him.

Nick Marshall spoke with hardly a pause. *'Die Engelse boerenlul heeft drie miljoen gulden teveel betaald.'*

Devereux laughed again. 'What's that mean? I have two sisters and the fat one fancies you? Sorry! You won't approve of that, Geraldine.'

Geraldine smiled and said, 'It means, "The English asshole has paid three million guilders too much." ' She paused.

Devereux looked from one to the other. He gave an uneasy half-smile. Marshall smiled back.

'Not the sort of thing they're likely to say in English, you see John.'

Thirty-three

At about the time that the Manager of Theston post office was meeting with the South East Area Co-ordinator beneath the lifeless prints of podgy galleons and chunky foreshortened *Cutty Sarks* that dotted the walls of his flat in Atcham, an unusual sight was to be seen at the holiday town of Hopton, six miles due east on the edge of the North Sea.

Behind the disintegrating pebble-dash façade of the Lifeboat Inn the ex-Assistant Manager of Theston post office was ordering a third round of Devlin's Old Magic Ale with a whisky chaser. His sky-blue anorak lay unzipped to reveal a v-necked grey and yellow flecked sweater, a white shirt and a grey tie spattered with the initials of his recent employer. His neat and well-pressed trousers were secured by two bicycle clips to a pair of green and maroon paisley-patterned socks.

He had arrived less than half an hour earlier at this old, tired pub perched precariously on the edge of the crumbling cliffs between Theston and Lowestoft. He had been drinking doggedly since then. Strangers rarely chose this pub and Trevor, the barman, concluded that wherever his anoraked visitor came from, there must be something seriously wrong.

This did not distress Trevor, indeed it rather cheered him up. He had lost track of the times he himself had drunk to forget, and as a barman he was grateful to those who took their sadness quietly and caused him no trouble.

Trevor was in his mid-forties. He was a philosophical man. Life had been a series of failures and each one he had accepted more philosophically than the last. His job here was perfect. A failure working amongst failures in a pub that was slipping slowly into the sea. He pressed a measure of Bells into a whisky tumbler and set it on the bar alongside the beer.

He took the money. 'Everything all right?' he asked unhopefully.

Martin nodded and did not look up.

'I tell you,' said Trevor, taking a cigarette out from behind his ear, 'if you could lay all the problems I've had in my life end to end, they'd stretch from here to bloody Lowestoft.' He struck a match and lit the cigarette. 'But I don't let them worry me. Quite the contrary.'

Martin took the beer and drank deeply. Trevor noticed.

'I draw inspiration from them. You know what Jesus said. "Come unto me all ye that are heavy laden and I will give you rest." Well, I like that,' he said, dropping the dead match into a chipped ashtray. 'But then I'm more heavily laden than most.' Out of the corner of his eye he saw Martin dispose of the Scotch in one swallow. Classic symptoms.

Trevor sighed heavily. 'It's nothing to feel bad about. Failure. It's meant to be. Whatever's happened to you has happened to somebody else at some time so you might as well just accept it.' He pulled on his cigarette, taking the smoke gratefully into his one remaining lung. 'Otherwise what do you do? Kill yourself.'

Martin slowly lifted his head. Through the numbing haze of alcohol there shone a sudden shaft of light. A ray of hope. A beacon in the darkness, an answer among questions, a something in the nothingness. A hovering, beckoning embraceable Holy Grail that would cleanse all his wounds and wipe away all his tears.

Killing himself was so startlingly clear and simple a solution that Martin felt a powerful surge of elation. He looked with new and grateful eyes on the grim surroundings of the Lifeboat Inn. He took in the bristle tiles on the floor and the flock wallpaper on the walls and the formica tops of the tables. The sounds of sharp cackled laughter, boozy argument, and droning television commentary merged into an indistinct cosiness. The smell of tobacco, beer and HP sauce fused into a cheap, familiar fug.

He could think himself in Sloppy Joe's in Key West or the Café des Amateurs on the Rue Mouffetard. Hem had loved bars. Bars provided almost everything Papa had needed. A drink, a glass, a table to write on, an audience to talk to, an opponent, a lover, an argument, a story.

Having made up his mind to kill himself, Martin was suffused with such fondness for the place that he decided one final pint would not go amiss. He consumed it with gratitude, and Trevor took quiet, if misguided, pride in the fact that his simple wisdom had saved another lost soul.

Martin peed for a long time, ran his hands under a thin trickle of cold water, held them for quite a while under a condom machine until he realised it was not the hot air dryer, found the hot air dryer, failed to make it work, wiped his hands on his trousers and made his way unsteadily out into the crisp fresh air.

As his bicycle bumped and rattled across the car park and on to the main road he felt himself a heavyweight at last. A potent, uncontainable force about to be released from trivial rounds and common tasks to play a final, apocalyptic role. He blatantly gave no hand signals as he turned left, flagrantly ignored a red traffic light and rode quite shamelessly across the path of an oncoming bus.

Martin found himself, still alive, on a road he was not familiar with. It wound inland from Hopton between fields and farms. He put his head down and cycled fast and emphatically along the wrong side of the road.

After a minute or two it became clear that he had chosen for his last great gesture of defiance a thoroughfare entirely devoid of traffic. He pulled up alongside a five-barred gate, out of breath and no longer clear as to where he was or why he was where he was. Wherever it was. He waited, panting, for his head to swim back into focus. As it did so, something caught his eye, off to the left in the field on to which the gate opened.

The light was flat and waning but there was unmistakably something there. He looked again. Then out of the shade it came. A magnificent long-backed, short-legged, thick-shouldered Friesian bull. Martin felt a head-burning rush of appalled excitement. He had watched bulls before. He had hung on gates and thought about what it must take to be a matador. Uncountable times he had felt the sweat break out on his palms as he contemplated illustration number forty-three in Carlos Baker's biography: 'Ernest (in white pants) in the "amateurs", Pamplona, 1925.' There was Papa, in the bull-ring, unprotected, skipping like a schoolboy round the swinging, jabbing, treacherously curved horns, whilst Spaniards rushed about and screamed and shouted and pointed. Now, in a field on the Suffolk coast, Martin was seized with the conviction that at last the moment had come for him to experience that thing which terrified him most. How neat, how perfect, how absolutely right that he should perish this way.

A wind had freshened from the north-west and clouds were piling in – angry, grey and low. He licked his lips and took a long, deep breath of farmy air. He began to climb the gate. It swung as he mounted it and he noticed that it could easily have been opened by slipping a length of loose red twine over the gatepost. He vaulted over and dropped onto the rich springy turf. Closer-to, the bull was a truly awesome creature. In fact it was massive. Far bigger than it had looked from the other side of the gate. It stood about two hundred yards away, flicking its tail and swinging its great heavy head in a gesture that suddenly brought to mind his father trying to shake sea-water from his ear after bathing. Martin could hear the wind now, catching at the scrappy branches of a dead elm, rustling at the hawthorn hedge. He edged a bit closer, eyes fixed on the bull.

How would it charge? Pawing the earth first or suddenly and without warning? How would the impact be? A mighty thundering weight, living daylights smashed out of him, followed by blackness and oblivion? Perhaps he would be tossed. He had seen pictures of gored matadors, flung through the air like blown litter. Perhaps he would hit the ground, his back broken, his body limp and helpless, his eyes waiting to be gouged out by vengeful cloven hooves.

Martin moved closer still. Then, for a moment, his courage failed him. Perhaps it was enough just to be in the same field as the prodigious beast. One of those that Papa had described as being 'afraid of nothing on earth'. Perhaps that was enough. Just to have been there. It was certainly quite something to tell people. A lot of people would never even have got this far. Oh, no. He could certainly leave it at that without any fear of being thought to have let anyone down. Certainly not. But then something took hold of him, some spectacular madness, some final lunging desire to have done with it all. He found himself running forward, waving his arms and screaming at the top of his voice.

He must have covered ten or eleven yards when out of the corner of his eye he saw that he and the bull were not alone. In the opposite corner of the field there were at least a dozen more huge creatures watching and waiting. Martin stopped screaming abruptly. A chill *frisson*, a sudden, sharp awareness of the possibility of real fear, pierced his alcohol-shrouded senses. But it was too late. The bull ahead of him turned, tossed its colossal head and began to charge.

Martin stood stupefied. It was charging away from him. And as it did so, all the other bulls turned and charged away as well, thundering as fast as they could to the furthest corner of the field. At the same time he heard a shout from the gate. 'What you bloody think you bloody playing at?'

Martin turned in the direction of the voice, feeling now like the bull he had just disturbed. A mud-streaked Land Rover had drawn up by the gate and a small, angry man with a face the colour of a nasty wound stood there. A young, curly-headed boy was beside him.

236

The farmer's face was ugly with rage.

'Afternoon,' said Martin hoarsely.

'What in bloody buggeration are you bloody doing in there, you bloody bugger?'

The little boy, who can't have been more than six or seven, giggled.

'I . . . er . . . I thought that one of the bulls was about to get loose. I was trying to keep it in the field,' tried Martin.

'What bulls?'

Martin indicated the cowering herd in a corner of the field.

'Where in God's name were you brought up?' retorted the farmer, ferociously. 'Bulls have bloody balls, you silly bastard.'

He regarded Martin with frank contempt. 'I suppose you wouldn't know what those are.'

The curly-headed boy giggled again. The farmer pointed angrily into the field.

'Those buggers are bloody bullocks. They haven't a bollock between them. And I'm not going to get them bloody fed if stupid bloody buggers like you start waving their bloody arms and yelling and putting the fear of bloody God into them.' Then he stopped and looked at Martin suspiciously. 'Are you one of those hunt saboteur buggers?'

Martin shook his head. He ached all over and he could feel the first drops of rain.

The farmer persisted. 'You bloody look like one. All bloody scrawny and smooth. Well, you're all the bloody same you buggers. You can't be real men, so you get in the bloody way of those who bloody are.'

Martin reached the gate and a moment later mounted his bike. So urgent was his desire to get away from this place that his foot slipped and the pedal spun round and cracked him hard on the shin. He thrust his left foot down to steady himself and felt it slither away on a lurking patch of bullock ordure. He toppled, quite slowly, into the hedge.

The curly-headed boy giggled.

Thirty-four

Martin woke up with a jolt. He lay, fully clothed, holding his breath, straining to hear a repetition of the sound that had awoken him. It came again, preceded by a shrieking gust of wind. He pulled himself up. His head swam. Without putting the light on he made his way unsteadily to the window and slammed it shut as another gust cracked into the side of the house.

As he turned he caught himself a hard, disabling blow on the corner of the safari table. He clutched his thigh and sank to the floor cursing.

He lay there until the pain wore off, then dragged himself across to his bed, leaned against it and reached up to switch on the light.

What it revealed was not a pretty sight. At least he had remembered to remove his shoes, which lay mud-caked where he had thrown them, beneath the hand basin. His anorak was nowhere to be seen. Maybe he had removed it downstairs. His soiled post office jumper and crumpled shirt had screwed themselves up around his body as he slept. His trousers were creased up along his thighs.

He remembered arriving back home, damp and dirty. He had gone straight upstairs, telling his mother he wanted an early night. That must have been six thirty or seven. He turned the Ingersoll traveller's clock towards him. It was two o'clock.

The wind rose to a scream then fell away again. He clambered to his feet and began to pull off his jumper and his shirt, his still-damp trousers and his underpants until he stood before the mirror naked, save for the paisley-patterned stockings on his feet.

His body was white and smooth. His shoulders were wide and skinny like a coat hanger. His chest was concave and hairless and his skin freckled a little at the shoulders. His stomach bulged, round and compact, and skimpy reddish brown hair ran down towards his groin. He was quite startled to think that it was this body that had brought Ruth such pleasure only two nights ago. There must have been some mistake.

He ran water into the basin and doused his head and washed beneath his arms. He dried himself carefully and pulled on a clean pair of underpants. Then he opened his wardrobe and flicked methodically through the hangers.

He selected a military outfit. Though Papa had never been a soldier he had been in a lot of wars as a reporter or an ambulance driver and Martin felt he would approve of the khaki shirt, serge trousers and combat boots that he took down from the top of his cupboard. To round it all off he clipped around his waist a German army belt which was as close as he could get to the *Wehrmacht* belt that Hemingway often wore. This one too had '*Gott Mit Uns*' engraved on the buckle, and he had found it in an army surplus store behind Colchester Barracks.

On the table he laid a US army helmet of the sort Hem was holding in the photo he had of him with General Barton and Colonel Chance on the Western Front in '44. He took a bottle of tequila and a glass from the cabinet together with a small bag of sea salt and a hardening week-old lime he had been saving for just such a moment as this.

He sat down, sliced the lime and put the pieces on a saucer in front of him. Into another saucer he tipped a small pile of the salt. Then he took the tequila and poured a measure into a thick, heavy-bottomed bar glass. He looked up. 'No going to bed tonight, Papa.' He raised his glass to the big, sad, grainy figure in the photo on the wall. The half-closed left eye regarded him appraisingly. The big wide open right eye watched and said nothing.

Martin wetted the back of his hand and spread salt on it. Then he drank the tequila in one and, as soon as he felt the burn, licked the salt, then took a piece of the lime and chewed on it. He felt grateful for the kick of the salt and sharp stab of the lime as it killed the hard unpalatable taste of the alcohol. Martin grimaced then looked up again at Hemingway.

He felt a sudden swelling of pride. 'I broke the law last night, Papa.' He grinned modestly. 'I broke the law. Not an easy breaking of the law either.' His head warmed with the tequila. 'A fucking difficult breaking of the law. I climbed up scaffolding fifty feet high in an overcoat to break the law. I climbed up scaffolding fifty feet high in an overcoat *in a force eight gale* to break the law ! You may laugh, but I could have fucking killed myself!'

Martin began to laugh uncontrollably. 'I could have fucking killed myself, Hem.'

Slowly he recovered. He finished the tequila and took another.

'Look at us. Just look at us, Hem. Why do we do such fucking stupid things? Why do we have to go looking for trouble?' He jabbed his hand at the photograph. 'It's all your fault. I didn't go looking for it. I was happy. I had a job with prospects. I had –' his voice tailed off, 'all sorts of things.'

Martin stood suddenly and awkwardly. He kicked the table leg as he moved out past it and the helmet hit the floor with a thud and rolled away. He froze. His mother woke at the slightest sound. She'd probably have been lying awake listening to the wind anyway. She always lay awake when the weather was bad. He held his breath and was relaxing it when he heard a door open and a voice sound across the landing. 'Are you all right, Martin?'

Martin collapsed into a chair. He tittered to himself. 'Yes, I'm all right, Mother. I'm dressed as Ernest Hemingway, I've had two neat tequilas and I've just knocked an American army helmet off the fucking table.'

'Martin? Are you sure you're all right?' she called again.

This time he shouted. 'Yes, I'm all right.' He got up and went to the door. 'Something rolled off the bed!'

There was a pause, then he heard her door shut. He stood motionless for a while, arm out against the door. Then he shook his head and turned back into the room. He took another shot of tequila and swung round to the photograph. 'Mothers!' He looked up and shook his head. 'You hated yours, didn't you, Hem? You hated her because she drove your father to suicide. Isn't that what it was all about? That bitch Grace. Mm?' He paused. His head began to spin. He steadied himself on the mantelpiece and took a long, deep breath. 'I'm sorry. These are very personal questions, but I . . . I need to know a little more about you. I feel there are things you've been keeping from me. Like failure. I want to know what to do about failure, Papa. Because *you* failed, didn't you? In the end, you failed. You failed in style. You blew your brains out on your own front porch. Double-barrelled English shotgun pressed so hard against your face you blew away most of your head. Early morning. The time you loved. The time you wrote best. The time you wrote about so fucking beautifully.'

Martin felt a sudden, irresistible wave of self-pity which hit him like the crash of the gale against the windows. Though there were no tears he could shed at the moment, Martin knew he had hit bottom.

His eyes met Papa's. 'We're so alike, aren't we? So alike.' He spread his arms out, slowly, feeling the length of the mantelpiece. Then he raised his head and stared into the unblinking, enigmatic eyes above him. 'I used to think that you were everything I wasn't and I was everything you weren't. But the great thing is –' He stopped. The room swung viciously. 'The great thing is we are one and the same, Papa. Failures.'

Thirty-five

Martin bowed his head and his fingers lightly clasped each end of the mantelshelf. For a while the only sound he could hear was the wild coming and going urgency of the wind, which flapped and slapped at the windows and sang in the chimney. His eyes closed and the alcohol warmed his blood and beguiled his brain.

He woke sharply. The sound of the wind had become violent and hostile. The feel of the smooth tiled surface of the mantelpiece was cold and heavy against his forehead but when he tried to pull away from it, he found himself unable to move.

Then quite suddenly he felt the unmistakable pressure of a hand upon his head. It was a substantial hand. The soft part of it covered the crown of his head and the long thick fingers stretched down to the nape of his neck. The pressure was strong and steady and palpable. He felt no fear at its touch, only a sweeping, encompassing calm. The solid, unequivocal promise of protection. Then he no longer heard the wind hooting and whooping and howling beyond the house. He heard only a slow, steady voice, pitched neither high nor low, and the voice was real, as real as the mantelpiece he clung to and it spoke slowly and clearly and firmly to him. It was telling him that there was much to do and a long way to go and that Martin was needed to complete what he himself had never been able to do.

Martin desperately wanted to be able to reach up, to grasp the hand and hold it tight, but when he did so it was gone, the voice was gone and the sound of the wind returned.

Very slowly he raised his head from the fireplace. His eyes

travelled cautiously upwards. Up, past the cluster of Hemingway postcards that leaned against the wall at the back of the mantelpiece, up across the art deco face of a clock that once stood in the foyer of the Palace Hotel, Madrid, and up, finally, to Hemingway's photograph on the wall. He shut his eyes. Then, he opened one eye, very slowly, and checked the right hand. It was where it had always been, held low by his side, the pencil still projecting loosely from it. He opened his other eye and let it run, ever so carefully, up the scroll-handled chest of drawers until it came to rest on the left hand. It, too, was motionless, lightly clenched on the curling sheaf of handwritten pages that lay on the writing board.

'It wasn't your hand, was it, Papa?' Martin whispered, and Papa smiled and shook his head and, as he did so a quite extraordinary thing began to happen. The whiskery white beard began to disappear from Papa's jaw. The upper lip sprouted a ginger moustache and the broad high cheek bones rounded out. The strong, straight nose grew a bump or two, the eyes became smaller, lighter and merrier. Finally the hair turned into an unruly shock of red. Pillar-box red, as they used to say in Theston. And the smile grew wider and the eyes gazed down on him full of laughter and anticipation as Martin remembered they did on Christmas mornings when he sat in bed surrounded by the contents of his stocking, and he knew there would be no front door slamming shut before dawn, no empty mailbag flung angrily down on the table in the early darkness of winter afternoons. And the smile grew into a laugh, a long, full, uncomplicated laugh. The laugh that he had almost forgotten.

He so much wanted the laughter to continue, he so much wanted it to go on and on and never stop, but as he watched he could see that familiar desperation creep back into the eyes and he knew so well what would follow.

And the laughter died and the smile set and the hair turned white and thin again and the ginger moustache became a beard again, and that was also white. And the nose widened and straightened and strengthened. The cheek bones once more stood out broad and high. And the eyes grew darker and wider and all that was left in them was the fear and the entreating.

Thirty-six

Following her night with Martin, and because she had heard nothing from him, Ruth had taken to walking, on the lengthening evenings, often many miles from Everend Farm Cottage. She had never been much of an outdoor girl – she'd always been the studious, bookish, library-ish type, but she had begun to feel claustrophobic in the cottage. She would pick her way down the muddy farm track, cross over the lane at the bottom and follow the direction of a signposted bridle-path. The farmer whose land it used to be had sold out to a management company and they had grubbed up the hedges and ploughed over the footpaths. But Ruth had bought herself a pair of green wellington boots and, delighted with their invincibility, tramped over the warm, flinty furrows and through stretches of shallow standing water until she reached a stream. She followed this for a mile or two until it flowed into a wide estuary. Grey herons rose lazily from the reeds and at a certain time each evening a flock of brent-geese flew in, low and in perfect formation, to land with growling cries and skidding splashes on a nearby inlet.

The more Ruth walked and thought, and the longer Martin's silence went on, the more convinced she became that the old pattern was re-establishing itself. Her voracity, his retreat – something spoiled once again.

She ran and reran the events of that evening in her mind, trying to answer the question of what had taken place. Who exactly were the two people involved? Had she been with shy Martin or the gruffly confident stranger whom Martin could become? Had he been making love to the fastidious intellectual

Ruth Kohler or the unapologetic adulterer Jane Mason? Had his lover been Ruth Kohler for whom sex was so complicated, or Jane Mason, to whom it came so easily?

The inescapable fact remained that on that night she had deliberately ceased to play the role of the Pauline Pfeiffer she so admired and had chosen to be the woman who had helped destroy Pauline's marriage. Was all this not just confirmation of her own inability to enjoy a physical relationship unless some risk of danger and destruction was involved? The more she thought about it the more something quite fundamental troubled her.

She had hitherto always gone along with the prevalent feminist view that men were by and large the more destructive agents in this world – the warriors, the fighters, the rioters, the gangsters, the strippers of rain forest and the droppers of bombs, and that women, more concerned to protect and preserve what they had brought into the world, were by and large the more constructive.

Did not the fact that she had slipped so easily into the role of a woman she knew to be destructive, simply mean that she, Ruth, could be equally destructive, and that the capacity to be destructive was in essence no weaker in women than men?

One evening, a week after she had last seen Martin slipping out of her door, long-legged, blue-anoraked, red-bobbled into the pre-dawn silence, something crystallised in her mind and she hurried back through the fields. By the time she reached the cottage, the sun had gone and the familiar rolling grey clouds were approaching from the west. She tugged her boots off impatiently and, not waiting to pull off her coat, reached for the light switch and sat down at her writing table. She pulled the neat pile of manuscript pages towards her and started leafing through them.

What she had feared was true. The more she read of her chapters on Pauline, the less they made sense. The more she looked at the period of their marriage the more she could see

246

that her assumption of Pauline's productive, wholesome and wholly beneficial artistic influence on her husband could not be borne out by the facts.

In the years between *A Farewell to Arms* and *For Whom the Bell Tolls*, all of them spent married to Pauline, Hemingway had written a succession of books and stories many of which were regarded as inferior stuff. The much-praised *A Farewell to Arms* was written, it was true, as they basked in the heat of first love, but the book itself was an evocation of an earlier love affair, with another woman in another place. *For Whom the Bell Tolls*, the next great novel he wrote eleven years later, was dedicated to Martha Gellhorn, the woman for whom he finally left Pauline.

Darkness fell and her eyes grew tired as she flicked through the sheets – some two hundred or so – which covered this period. The conclusion was inescapable.

Ruth had assembled a case that was skewed, inadequate, simplistic. She must take the evidence and rearrange it. It was a formidable task and time was running out. It was now nearly April and her book was supposed to be completed by the beginning of July. New research would have to be done, perhaps a third of the text rewritten.

She sat back and lit a cigarette. She stared out of the window into a dark black night and her gaunt reflection in the glass. She rubbed her eyes, reached for the first Scotch of the day and made a decision that seemed to solve many problems.

The next day, Ruth's canary yellow Datsun could be seen negotiating the rutted surface of Marsh Lane on its way to Martin's house. Inside, Ruth took one hand from the steering wheel to steady the bouncing, lurching fishing chair that was her excuse for breaking the silence. It was a warm, still Sunday afternoon. Kathleen Sproale was in the garden and watched her draw up. She told Ruth that Martin was out on his bicycle somewhere and wouldn't be back for some time. Then she straightened up and tapped her trowel on a stone to free the earth from it.

'I've just about done now,' she said, with a quick smile. 'I've no more energy.'

Her smile was a little brave, it seemed to Ruth.

'You prefer coffee, don't you,' said Kathleen, pulling off her gardening gloves and moving towards the house.

They sat in the kitchen and looked out across the marsh grass and the sedge and the trailing willow trees that swung mournfully in the soft balmy breeze.

'It's the best time of year, I always think,' said Mrs Sproale. 'Spring.'

'I don't know how you live here in the winter,' said Ruth. 'It's bad enough at Everend Farm, but at least there's some shelter.'

'I sometimes wonder myself,' said Kathleen. 'But Martin's father always liked it. Didn't like the town. Said he saw enough of it on his rounds.'

'What did he do? Your husband.'

'He delivered letters. Postman.'

'Martin never talks about him.'

'No. Well, he died when Martin was seventeen.'

'Was he ill?'

Kathleen nodded. 'He'd been ill a while.'

Outside the window a swarm of black and yellow siskins had discovered the bacon rind on the bird table and were mounting a series of darting attacks.

'That must have been a real shock for Martin.'

Kathleen's soft watery eyes turned sharply on Ruth, then quickly away. 'Well, I should think that's why he doesn't talk about it.'

'Maybe he should go and see somebody. Get some advice.'

Once again Kathleen's eyes met hers. She spoke scornfully. 'A psychiatrist?'

'Well, some kind of therapy. Why not? I was in analysis for a while. It helped.'

248

Kathleen's gaze turned to the bleak flatness outside. She spoke softly, but almost to herself. 'Didn't help his father. He was sent from one psychiatrist to another like one of his own parcels.' She stared hard out of the window. 'Didn't hear a bloody word from any of them after he'd gone. Excuse my language, Ruth. None of them had a word to say for themselves.'

All at once Ruth felt cold. 'How did he die, Mrs Sproale?'

Kathleen stayed staring out of the window. She was breathing hard and her mouth was working as if trying to form some difficult word. 'I don't tell people that,' she said eventually.

'It might help if you did.'

The kitchen clock struck the half-hour. Mrs Sproale turned to Ruth briskly, almost pugnaciously. She brushed the flat of her hand across the table top as if to remove imaginary crumbs. 'That was seventeen years ago. I'm more worried about his son now.'

She stood up abruptly, speaking rapidly as she deposited the imaginary crumbs at the sink.

'All that Hemingway nonsense. I used to think it was just harmless but now I think it's poisoning him. I sometimes want to burn that room of his. All those bits and pieces of someone else's life. I hear him up there every night now, talking and shouting. I've heard him swearing sometimes, and there's no one else there. Just him.'

'He's been through a hard year.'

'But whose fault is that?' To divert her anger Kathleen seized a bundle of cutlery that was draining on the rack. 'He could have been engaged to Elaine Rudge, he threw that away.' She began to sort the cutlery vigorously. 'He could have been Manager of that post office one day, he threw that away. He was everybody's friend, everyone in Theston knew him. Now he either stays upstairs or he's out for hours on his bicycle and never tells me where.'

She heaved a sigh and stood for a moment, leaning her arms on the draining board.

Ruth turned and looked out over the reclaimed marshland that ran flat to the sand dunes and the sea. A poet could probably deal with that, she thought, but as an academic she found it an untidy and arbitrary landscape. Aloof and unfriendly. It reminded her, ominously, of the symbolism in *A Farewell to Arms*. How Hemingway contrived the book so that all the scenes of death and disaster had happened on the low, flat, land, and all the scenes of love, life and hope were set in the clear air of the mountains. There were no mountains round here.

There was a noise at the side of the house and Martin appeared at the door. Ruth was shaken by the sight of him. He wore the white tennis hat she recognised. Beneath it protruded a thatch of fine sandy hair. His eyes were red-rimmed and bloodshot and a line of thin stubble ran along his jaw. He wore a shapeless sports shirt and long, baggy check shorts fastened with a length of rope. He seemed bigger than she remembered and shabbier too. Though his slow, deliberate movements betrayed little, the colour that rose quickly to his face indicated his surprise at seeing Ruth. ''Lo,' he nodded, shortly, leaning against the doorway.

Ruth was uncomfortable, and Kathleen, sensing this, began to busy herself, gathering up the cups from the table.

'I brought the chair,' said Ruth.

Martin didn't seem to take this in. 'The chair?' he said, thickly.

'Your chair. It's in the car,' Ruth pointed. 'Only just. Had to take a seat out. Mr Wellbeing helped.'

Suddenly Martin began to respond. He pushed himself away from the door and looked towards Ruth with a look of disbelief. 'My chair.'

Ruth nodded.

Together they eased it from the back of her Datsun and with

some difficulty carried it upstairs. His room was strewn untidily with books, papers and bottles. The bed was unmade. Once they had put the chair down, Martin quickly pulled the sheets and blankets up and over the bed and thrust a couple of bottles back into the cabinet. Then he straightened a little awkwardly. As he stood and watched her, it seemed to her that the expression in his eyes was almost the same as the expression in the eyes on the photograph on the wall behind him. Wary, once wise, now a little afraid.

Martin gave her a quick, nervous smile and began searching for a place for the chair to stand.

'How are you doing, Martin?' she asked, deliberately not looking at anything too closely.

'Good,' he said. 'Good. I've been making lists of everything.'

'Lists?'

'You know. All the ships he sailed on. All the injuries he had. All the hotels he stayed in. All the rivers he fished. There's a lot to do.'

He pulled two chairs together and began to arrange the fishing chair between them.

'Do you want a hand?' Ruth asked.

'Yes . . . yes . . . thanks.' He spoke quickly, nervously again.

They pushed the chair into position. He didn't sit in it right away. His fingers brushed lightly along the armrests and lingered across the rough, worn back supports, as if renewing acquaintance with an old friend.

'I hope you don't mind me coming round like this?' she asked him, cautiously.

'No.'

'I came to see you in the post office a couple of times but you weren't around.'

'No. I don't work there any more,' said Martin, quickly, dismissively. He took hold of the arms of the chair and leaned his weight on to it.

'You left?'

Martin stood back, looked down at the concoction of wood and leather and metal balanced uncomfortably against the thick shoulder of an armchair. He nodded admiringly.

'You *left* the post office?' Ruth repeated.

Martin looked up as if hearing the question for the first time. 'I was asked to leave.'

'Why?'

'Because of the campaign.' He turned towards her and looked up, with a nervous smile that faded quickly. 'You can't keep things like that a secret in Theston,' he said.

Suddenly and unexpectedly Ruth found herself too upset to speak. Tears filled her eyes in an aching rush. Martin turned away, embarrassed, the way she had hoped he wouldn't be, staring uncomfortably out of the window. As she angrily fought back the tears Ruth was in a sense relieved. If his response had been friendly and physical who knows what she might have said and done.

'I'm sorry.' She shifted. 'It's all been my fault.'

'What for?'

'For opening my big mouth. For getting you into chairs and campaigns.'

Martin turned back to her and wagged a finger. He seemed suddenly to have regained confidence. He heaved himself into the chair. It swayed precariously. 'The battle's not over.'

He grinned, broad and wide and pushed himself hard against the unyielding wooden back. 'The battle's not over, Ruth. We'll start another campaign. Only this time we'll run it ourselves.'

Ruth smiled. She reached in her bag and searched briskly for a cigarette. 'You'll have to do it without me this time,' she said.

Martin's face clouded. 'Why?' he asked.

'I'm going away for a while.'

His frown deepened. 'How long?'

'However long it takes to finish my book.' She lit up and inhaled hard.

'I thought you'd nearly finished.'

'So did I. But –' He watched as she tossed her head and stretched her long neck and threw a column of smoke high into the air as she had the first day he set eyes on her. 'I was wrong,' she said flatly.

Martin lay back in the fishing chair and took in what she had said.

'I'll be in Oxford,' she went on. 'I need the libraries. I've got to find a whole lot of new stuff.'

'How long?'

'Six weeks. Maybe two months. As long as it takes.'

Martin nodded slowly. He seemed about to speak, then quickly, abruptly, his mood changed. 'Can we go for a drive? There's something I want to show you.'

They drove down to the bypass and across into Theston, avoiding the centre of town and coming out on the hill above the harbour. Here Martin asked her to pull over and park. They got out of the car. He had brought with him an old pair of marine binoculars. He led her a little way down the hill to where they could see the harbour more clearly, and raised the glasses to his eyes.

In the short time since he had been there with Elaine, the place had been galvanised. Vans and trucks painted with the lightning-bolt logo of the Telemark company were clustered around what had once been Frank Rudge's cold store and processing warehouse. This was now scaffolded and a light-weight aluminium frame was already in place on the roof. Even though it was a Sunday there were men working, securing a fabric skin across it. A line had been marked out towards the pier and trenches were being dug. Beside the trenches lengths of pipe were piled ready and a huge drum of cable dominated one end of the site. Council contractors had begun laying a new and wider tarmac surface to the harbour approach road.

But today Martin was looking elsewhere. He took down the

binoculars and handed them to Ruth. 'There, look.' He pointed excitedly. 'In the harbour.'

Ruth adjusted the glasses and focused on a long, graceful motor yacht with a black tinted perspex screen and a white streamlined hull and superstructure. A line of four portholes led to a name on the bow that she could just pick out. *Nordkom IV*. It was a glamorous boat, incongrous and dominating in the harbour.

Martin whispered to her. '*Pilar!*'

'Oh come on!' Ruth grunted derisively. '*Pilar*' had character. That's just a playboy boat.'

But Martin was hardly listening. His eyes were fastened on it, as it rocked gently, lazily at anchor. She could see beads of sweat on his temple. He spoke softly and urgently, without a glance towards her.

'Imagine being out on that. Outriggers in place, lures dropped. Riding a ten-foot swell, in the fighting chair, a five-hundred pounder circling on the line. Reeling in slow and steady. Hours sometimes.'

Ruth knew nothing about boats and fishing. She hated *The Old Man and the Sea* and found Santiago the fisherman the most dismally sentimental of all Hemingway's heroes.

'They blow them out of the sea nowadays, don't they?' she said sourly.

Martin didn't hear her. He was gazing at the boat. It was as if she had already gone away.

Thirty-seven

One month to the day after he had received his letter of dismissal, and three weeks after Ruth had left for Oxford, Martin Sproale returned to Theston post office. He presented an extraordinary aspect. His hair had grown thick and bushy. His face had fleshed out and much of it was now concealed beneath a thickening pale red beard. His shoulders had grown broad enough to hold a wide beige sweatshirt, which hung way down over a billowing pair of cotton shorts. He wore grubby espadrilles and no socks. The whole effect was of a weird distortion, as if Martin's long, rangy frame was seen in a fairground mirror. This, at any rate, was how it looked to Elaine who happened to be between transactions as he appeared, hovering at the handmade chocolate counter and glowering through at the long line of Monday morning post office customers.

Since Martin had been sacked there had been rumours in Theston that he had gone away or even that he was seriously ill. These were contradicted by reported sightings of him on the hill overlooking the harbour. Though all confirmed that something had snapped, nothing quite prepared Elaine for the wild, shambling figure who was now approaching the ten-deep queue which coiled obediently around the rope and stainless-steel cordon.

'*Position Number Four.*' The high, strident tone of the earlier announcements had been traced to a fault in the system. The tape had now been readjusted and the voice was deeper and more vibrant. The Swedish eunuch had been replaced by an elderly tragic actress.

Martin went straight to the head of the queue. There was some shuffling and much whispering among those customers who recognised him. The wide-bosomed middle-aged lady at the front of the queue was not one of them. She shot a withering look of disapproval as Martin took up position alongside her. 'Do you mind?' she said sternly. 'There is a queue, you know.'

Martin leaned in towards her. 'I'm disabled.'

She eyed Martin sceptically, glancing quickly down at his lower half. 'I'm sorry to hear that, but there is a queue.'

He leaned in closer. 'Cambodia. With the UN. Clearing land mines.'

The lady was not convinced. 'You look all right to me.'

'Internal,' Martin whispered.

'What?' she asked.

'My stomach has been almost entirely replaced.'

'*Position Number One*,' the voice announced, tragically.

As the woman made to go forward Martin held up a carrier bag. 'My stools,' he said. 'They were meant to go off yesterday.'

He moved swiftly to the counter. Shirley Barker was at Position Number One. She could not disguise a mixture of shock and distaste at Martin's appearance.

Martin pushed aside a few matted strands of hair and regarded her cheerfully. 'Hello, daughter,' he beamed.

'Hello, Martin,' Shirley replied cautiously. 'How are you?'

His eyes searched behind the counter.

'It must be a nice change not having to get up at six thirty every morning,' Shirley ventured warily.

Martin nodded enthusiastically. 'Means I can get up at six, when it's barely light enough to see the pine trunks and the soles of your feet are wet from the dew on the stones, and the touch of the air from the sea promises how the day will be. It's the best time to write.'

Shirley was aware of disapproving faces behind the rope. 'What is it you wanted, Martin?'

256

He sighed heavily. 'I want the same as anybody else, daughter. I want to know that I've taken care of the big things. Like love and hate and fear. And that I haven't done too bad at the small ones either. And when the time comes to make my peace –'

She interrupted. 'D'you want stamps or anything?'

Martin stopped and looked sharply across at her. She felt a strong intimation of hostility. 'I want to see Geraldine please,' said Martin.

'Well she's at the end there. She's occupied.'

'Will you tell her I'm here?'

Shirley had recovered her composure by now. She fingered the brooch at her throat. 'Look Martin, there are a lot of people waiting in that queue.

'I don't care how many people are waiting in the queue,' Martin replied quietly. He leaned closer. 'Get off your goddamn ass, go down that goddamn counter and tell Miss Cotton to get the fuck down here. Fast!'

Ever since she had started work at the new office, Shirley Barker had been longing for an excuse to press the security alarm button. In her imagination she had always seen it magically producing two or three burly ex-marines abseiling down from the roof to rescue her. She was considerably disappointed that security appeared, after a short delay and a little nervously, in the shape of Alan Randall, sporting a new leather sports coat and a spotted bow-tie.

Martin felt a tight grip on his elbow. 'Come on now, Martin. Let's talk about this outside.'

Martin turned angrily and pulled his elbow sharply away. 'Do you mind!' he shouted. 'I've come here for postal services. I don't want sweeties. I don't want dirty magazines. I want to talk to one of the employees of the Post Office service of this country.'

'We are running a business here, Martin,' said Randall firmly. 'You will be dealt with in strict rotation.'

Alan Randall was a confectioner and abhorred physical violence, so when Martin hit him it was a completely new and unfamiliar sensation. One moment he was the voice of reason, the next he was lying flat on the floor. He didn't feel anything other than faintly ridiculous, and the fact that Hettie Loyle, a woman half his size and with an artificial hip, should be helping him up only made things worse. He rubbed his jaw as he had seen them do on television and assured all and sundry he would survive.

'What was that all about then?'

Martin sat, long legs squeezed uncomfortably beneath one of the dainty round tables of the Theston Tea Shoppe. Geraldine sat opposite him. She was wearing a purple chenille sweater which she had pulled hastily over her company blouse as they had left the post office. With one hand she twirled a lock of hair – which had grown recently and changed colour from ash blonde to light auburn, and with the other she rotated her spoon slowly round a mug full of pale brown coffee.

'Well?' she asked again. 'What was so important about seeing me that you had to slug someone?'

Martin looked up. Geraldine could see his eyes were red-rimmed and unhealthy. Too much booze or too little sleep. Maybe both. He was certainly in bad shape.

'I hate that place,' he began. I hated it the first time I saw it and I hated it when I worked in it –'

Geraldine nodded quickly. 'Martin, after what just happened I'm sure the feeling's mutual.'

He lowered his head again, then peeped up at her with a quick, coy smile. 'It was a good punch, though.'

Geraldine took a sip of the coffee. It was warm to tepid, which was how she liked it. When she spoke she tried hard to balance exasperation with consideration.

'Martin, we would all have been pleased to see you. There was no need to come in looking for trouble.' She couldn't help adding, 'Trouble is out today, anyway, he's meeting the bankers.'

Again Martin shook his head scornfully. 'I came for you.'

Geraldine narrowed her eyes. 'Why me?'

Martin looked her in the eye for the first time. 'Because of the boat,' he said.

Geraldine was about to drink again, but the cup stopped halfway to her mouth. She frowned. 'I'm sorry, Martin,' she said. 'Did I miss an episode?'

'The boat I've seen you on. In the harbour.'

'You've seen me on a boat?'

Geraldine felt suddenly uncomfortable. Not with the boat so much as the seeing. His look of concentration intensified. 'Sure. I watch that harbour every day. I watch what's going on. I watch who's there. I know when Devereux comes. I know when Nick comes. I know when the boat's in and who it brings here.'

'So?'

Martin's eyes met hers. She saw something in the back of them, some remnant of what had appealed to her that night at Marshall's. Some odd light that burned.

Martin continued, slowly and precisely. 'I want, more than anything else, to go out in that boat.'

Geraldine was aware of having to get back to work. She glanced at her watch and made to speak. Martin cut in quickly. 'Do you understand?' he asked her. 'I want to go on that boat. I want to go fishing.'

Geraldine gave a half-shrug, half-laugh. 'Martin, I don't want to see you get in any more trouble. Just forget all this mess. Forget all these people. Take a job somewhere else. Honestly. There is nothing else you can do and no way I can help you.'

'I want to go out and I want to go deep and I want to feel just what it's like.' The pitch of his voice rose again. 'You understand, don't you? I know you do. You're not like the rest of them, Geraldine. Are you. Are you?'

Geraldine watched him pityingly. He was a sad sight. A battered, bruised, beaten man. He was not bad or wrong, he was just hopeless. But it was not her fault. She was not particularly happy with the work she was doing, but she did it and she did it without complaining. She also did it well enough to have been given, amongst other things, the responsibility of liaison between Shelflife and Nordkom each time the yacht made one of its increasingly frequent visits across the North Sea to Theston. She had been brought up with boats and she knew exactly what Martin meant about the excitement of being at sea, but whatever his delusions were, she could not satisfy them.

'I'm sorry Martin, there is no way I could get you anywhere near that boat.'

In any case, *Nordkom IV* was no fishing boat. It was a state-of-the-art, seventy-five-foot motor yacht built in Sweden for Nordkom at a cost of one and a half million pounds. She was a beautiful ship, but she was not for recreational purposes. The sun-lounge, the jacuzzi, and the integrated bathing platform were rarely used. *Nordkom IV* was an ocean-going boardroom, able to cover the one hundred and thirty miles from Rotterdam to the English coast in the space of one planning meeting.

To let this threatening, wild-eyed derelict anywhere near the pristine white powder-coated steel hull, let alone the solid teak-strip deck or the twenty-foot-long polished mahogany boardroom table, would not be sensible.

Thirty-eight

In the twenty-five years of her life Geraldine Cotton had rarely done the sensible thing. If two courses of action were presented to her she would evaluate them as to what she probably should do and what she probably shouldn't do and invariably she chose the latter. She blamed this entirely on her parents who had devoted two otherwise promising lives to being sensible. They had made a sensible marriage and bought a sensible house and taken sensible jobs to which they could drive their sensible cars. They had sensibly had three children whom they enrolled at sensible schools in the hope that they would grow up to be as sensible as themselves.

It had nearly worked. Geraldine's sister George, older by four and a half years, was a Human Resources Officer with one of the most sensible companies in Britain. She had been married for eight years to an intelligent, hard-working loss adjuster with an unblemished record of marital fidelity. They had two delightful children and were planning a third. Her brother Giles was a geography teacher at a school for largely sensible children in the Thames Valley. He had recently joined the Ecology Party but, despite this encouraging trend, had dashed Geraldine's hopes by becoming engaged to a terminally sensible girl called Sheila who worked as a Centralised Billing Query Co-ordinator for South-Eastern Gas.

Geraldine had become aware of wanting to do things that were not sensible from the age of six. She had decided to climb the massive sycamore tree at home as soon as she was old enough to do so, not just because it was massive but because it overhung the garden of the house next door. But her curiosity had misfired. What she had seen Mr Marsden doing to Mrs Marsden through an upstairs window of the house had so surprised her that she had lost her footing and plunged through a greenhouse. She was badly cut and very shaken but conscious enough to be able to tell her parents that Mr Marsden appeared to be a cannibal.

The incident had given her an appetite for parental disapproval. This sustained her through her teens at a mixed boarding school (her choice) where she developed a passion for rugby football, and afterwards through a diploma course in engineering at a little-known Scottish polytechnic. From twenty-one onwards she had had relationships with one or two boys, and several girls. She had been at various times an actress, an acupuncturist and a television aerial installation engineer. She was clever, well-qualified and resourceful, but she was still not sensible.

Her job with Shelflife Ltd had come along at the right time. She had just turned twenty-five. She had made a promising start in fringe theatre in London. But after a longish run as a rape victim, work had dried up and three months later she had answered the advertisement which led her to John Devereux and Shelflife. The prospect of a year by the seaside as a PA with a new telecommunications company sounded intriguing, appealing and not entirely probable. The sort of challenge she liked.

However, the activities of Shelflife were not quite what she had expected. In fact, they were becoming murkier by the minute. They had purchased the old post office for a knock-down price and sold it on to the Nordkom consortium, of which they were a part, also at a knock-down price, but not quite as knock-down as the price they'd paid for it. The Mayor of the town had been offered preferential building contracts in return for preferential treatment of Shelflife's submissions to the council. Following revelations at one particularly unpleasant dinner at Marshall's flat, Councillor Rudge, the awkward, independent Chairman of the Planning Committee had been blackmailed into silence. The support of local bigwigs like Peregrine Harvey-Wardrell had been bought with attractive share option 'sweeteners'.

The pattern of deceit was becoming remarkably predictable and the one thing that depressed Geraldine was predictability. This was the only reason she could think of for not banishing Martin Sproale's rambling, incoherent behaviour from her mind. That and the fact that he had clearly ceased to be a sensible person.

A week after Martin's spectacular visit to the post office, *Nordkom IV* came once again to Theston harbour bearing its cargo of executives and multi-media experts from Holland. Once the boat was moored up, Devereux and Marshall and assorted advisers joined them and meetings were held throughout the day in the master stateroom. In the evenings when the executives and crew had gone ashore to sample the local beer or the clubs of Norwich and Ipswich, Geraldine would be required to come on board with the cleaners and bring food supplies for the next day.

One evening, after the cleaners had finished, she was left alone on the yacht. It was a warm summer evening in mid-May and the sun lingered until well after eight o'clock. Geraldine climbed the half-dozen steps that led up to the flybridge. A set of immaculate, barely used striped canvas chairs had been laid out, and on the low table between them was a pair of binoculars. She picked them up and, adjusting the focus, scanned the harbour and its approach roads. Sure enough, there on the steeper of the two hills that led into the town, was a tall, oddly shaped, unmistakable figure wearing a red-bobbled, royal blue knitted hat, his wide shirt flapping in the wind. His arms were raised in a mirror image of her own and she knew he was watching her too.

For the next two or three weeks, whenever the boat was in, she noticed him there. His position barely changed. Sometimes he would appear to take out a notebook and jot things down. Sometimes he would not have any fieldglasses with him. He would merely be standing and watching.

Geraldine knew she could simply ignore Martin or even report him to Nick Marshall, but the more time went on the more she found herself identifying with his dogged and hopeless persistence. She began to find something admirable, even inspiring, in his refusal to face reality. In her mind he became the indomitable figure on the shore, the first Indian to see Columbus, the Celtic warrior watching the last Romans leave Britain.

One evening he was no longer to be seen on the hill. As she drove the rubber dinghy which was used as a support craft across to the harbour steps having completed her day's work, she felt oddly bereft. She made the boat fast and began to walk up the harbour steps when she saw him standing a few feet in front of her. This was the first time since his visit to the post office that he had made any attempt to approach her. She drew a quick breath. 'I was wondering where you'd got to,' she said.

'Well?' he said. 'Can I come aboard then?'

Geraldine smiled and shook her head.

'I can't take you aboard. You know that. If they find out –'

He replied quickly and decisively. 'They won't find out.'

'No, Martin,' she repeated firmly. 'If they come back and find you there, bang goes my Christmas bonus.'

He took a step towards her. 'They won't. They left fifty-five minutes ago in two cars, both taxis from Norwich. They'll be at the Blue Beat Club in Queen Street or Rocco's on Cow Hill. The journey averages one hour seventeen minutes each way. On four previous trips to Norwich they were back at 1.09, 2.12, 2.17 and 3.07.'

'You're crazy,' said Geraldine. There was a trace of envy in her voice. Martin, gross and dishevelled, his hair now long and wild as an Old Testament prophet, shook his head and stared back.

'Please?'

That was the first of several times that Martin went aboard. He knew exactly when it was safe and Geraldine, realising that this was the unorthodox company she craved, warmed to this shambling, driven figure. She showed him around the boat. Told him what worked how and where. But that was not enough for Martin. He liked the wheelhouse and the charts and the promise of the sea beyond the harbour wall. He wanted more than just to be aboard.

Thirty-nine

'*A new era begins today for the town of Theston in Suffolk.*'

Ruth Kohler reached forward and adjusted the volume control on her radio. Only since taking the flat in Oxford had she come to know the illicit pleasure of soaking in an English bath. She lay back to enjoy the first cigarette of the day, wreathed in the ash-flecked bubble stacks of Elizabeth Arden Celebration Gel.

'*At midday today, Dennis Donnelly, the new Minister for Technology, will open the first stage of a major new European telecommunications centre financed by the Dutch multi-media giant, Nordkom BV.*'

And by lunchtime, said Ruth to herself, Ruth Kohler, visiting Professor of English, would be returning to Theston having completed major new work on her ground-breaking study of one of the century's most controversial literary figures.

'*There have been strong rumours that Nordkom favour a link-up with the enormous resources of the British Post Office, if, as expected, privatisation proposals confirm the Government's decision to allow the commercial freedom Post Office bosses have demanded for so long.*'

It was nice to be going back to the centre of the universe, thought Ruth. Oxford was fine, but nothing ever happened. She grinned to herself. She was looking good and feeling good and she was determined to stop agonising about things. She would call Martin when she got back and they would play the rest by ear. She had even found a decent bottle of grappa, though she had had to scour Oxford to do so.

'*It's three minutes past seven,*' the radio voice sang through the soapsuds. *'Stay tuned for the Dick Arthur Breakfast Show.'*

A hundred and thirty miles away to the north-east of Oxford the soft throb of two eleven-hundred horsepower MAN 12 diesel engines weakened and died. An anchor chain clattered down through its hawse pipe and the long slim bow of the motor yacht *Nordkom IV* swung gently round in a light North Sea swell, until it pointed due north-west toward the tall, handsome flushwork tower of St Michael and All Angels, Theston.

Through a low-lying band of sea mist the observer on the hill could just make out a small motor dinghy put out from the harbour, driven by an athletic young brunette wearing bulky yellow waterproof trousers and a yellow and black windcheater bearing the Nordkom logo.

A few minutes later five men in well-tailored lightweight suits disembarked from the yacht into the dinghy. Behind them came half a dozen crewmen in sweatshirts and white chinos. One or two of the suits held mobile phones, all carried briefcases. The distant sound of men laughing together drifted across the water.

The dinghy reached the harbour wall as two silver-grey Mercedes estate cars slid into view. The men, still laughing, one or two hanging back to exchange banter with the woman at the helm, mounted the steps. Then they climbed into the waiting cars which drove off to the north in the direction of the town.

The observer kept his glasses trained on the dinghy. After a long and inexplicable pause, he saw what he was waiting for. Three short flashes of light issued from it. He moved quickly down the hill toward the long, low concrete shelter set back on the deserted stretch of beach to the south of the harbour.

He checked his watch as he went. It was twelve and a half minutes after seven. They had half an hour.

★

July 2nd was not the brilliant midsummer day Nick Marshall had hoped for. An easterly air-stream spread dull grey weather over Theston and now there was mist to contend with as well. 'We'll be lucky if we can see the bloody mast,' he muttered as he pushed open the door of the Portakabin.

He and John Devereux arrived at the harbour at a quarter to eight. Nick Marshall had already run seven miles and felt keyed up, but in control.

'It's a wee bit early. The sun'll burn this lot off,' Andy Glenson assured him. Glenson, a small, cynical Scotsman, was the foreman of works. He'd trained on the oil rigs, in the boom years of the seventies. He'd seen money made and lost. The third man in the cabin was Matt van Haren, the technical manager for Nordkom.

'You'd better be right, lad,' said Devereux. 'If Princess Diana paraded up the beach stark bollock naked she wouldn't get as many TV crews as we've got coming here this morning.' He ran his fingers down a list on the table in front of him. 'What's going on? Are we offering free lunches?'

Nick Marshall didn't smile. He ran his tongue over his lips. 'Everything all right, Matt? No last-minute hitches?'

Matt van Haren was slim and fair-haired with a moustache he was trying to extend to a fuller beard. He was only a year or so older than Nick Marshall. He wore a black and yellow PVC jacket over a teeshirt. A walkie-talkie hung from his waist. 'It was tight, I tell you. But we made the final connections last night.'

'So we have. . . ?' asked Nick.

'Three pole antennae.'

'That's good.'

' . . . and two transmission dishes,' van Haren went on. 'Both linked now with Zandvoort.'

'You've checked it out?'

Van Haren nodded. 'I had them on the line one hour ago, everything is fine.'

'And the onward links?' asked Nick. 'All in place?'

'All in place, Nick. Don't worry, we have done this before.'

'Not here you haven't,' said Devereux, reaching for a plastic cup and tapping the still-gurgling coffee machine impatiently. 'You don't know this country, Matt. There are going to be a lot of buggers out there hoping we'll fuck it up.'

Glenson laughed gloomily.

Van Haren spread a hand towards the window through which the spiky profile of the communications mast could be seen no more than three hundred yards away, rising from the superstructure of the old pier.

'This makes good sense for our business, I think?' asked Matt. 'We are all of us part of the European Union, after all.'

Glenson laughed again. 'Excuse me, Jimmy!' he said to Matt. '*You*'re part of Europe. We're part of Britain.' He tapped his forehead. 'It's not to do with aerials and tunnels, Matt, it's in the brain. And that won't change for a long, long time.' He turned to Nick. 'I mean, if we really *believed* we were Europeans we'd have a Dutchman to open this for Christ's sake. They've done all the work!'

'Oh come on, Andy,' Nick said, with a touch of impatience. 'Not now.'

'Why do we have to make do with some pillock from Whitehall for a job that's nine-tenths financed from Rotterdam?' Glenson went on. 'I mean, let's have Ruud Gullitt or Marco van Basten or Queen fucking Beatrice, excuse my language, Matt.'

'Marco van Basten and Ruud Gullitt were not available, Andy,' Nick said with a touch of asperity.

'And Queen Beatrice said if *you*'re on't job she's not coming near the fucking place,' added Devereux.

There was laughter, but Glenson persisted. 'But isn't that crazy?'

Marshall made for the door. 'Not *now*, Andy, we've got a lot to do. Bring the radios.'

He went out into the damp, briny air. Behind him Glenson was warming to his theme. 'What is the first thing they see in Holland when the world's first voice-activated video phone link is established? Some prat who was Minister for Film and Basketball until yesterday. I mean, come on, Nick, there's got to be a better way.'

Their voices trailed off into the mist.

Martin Sproale held his breath and watched as the four men left the cabin. The mist was a blessing. They had taken longer to get the goods aboard than expected and they were in danger of being spotted now the site was opening up for the day. To his relief Devereux and Marshall soon climbed into Devereux's car and drove away into the town. The other two men, the two wearing hard hats, disappeared into the main building.

With one supreme effort Martin pulled his awkward, bulky cargo clear of the rail on to the deck of the *Nordkom IV*. Below him Geraldine kept the outboard idling, ready to move. They were on the starboard quarter of the yacht, facing out to sea, out of sight of the harbour, but a pale sun was already beginning to disperse the mist and there was a lot to be done.

Martin hardly had time to savour the pleasure of finally seeing his chair on a boat. He dragged it across the teak plank floor of the deck and stowed it behind a bulkhead at the top of the stairs that led down to the saloon.

He heard Geraldine's urgent whisper. 'I've got fifteen minutes!'

Martin glanced toward the harbour. There was still no one in sight. 'All right!' he hissed back. 'Coast's clear.' As cautious as she could be on the throttle, Geraldine eased the dinghy around the stern of the vessel. Here she was exposed and she knew that anyone watching now could threaten the whole operation. She had not felt her heart thumping like this since the last very silly thing she'd done. Which was either free-fall parachuting or skiing blindfold or telling her parents she was in love with Freda Mitchell. She couldn't remember which.

As the dinghy's soft rubber side bounced gently against the sheer white hull, there came the sound of a badly fitted door scraping open on the harbour and Glenson and van Haren emerged from the control centre. They pointed towards the pier from which sprouted the slim, lightweight carbon-fibre communications mast, with its formidable array of dishes and assorted antennae, only a hundred yards from where *Nordkom IV* rocked on a gentle ebb tide. They began to walk purposefully towards it. Martin threw himself down onto the deck. Geraldine grabbed hold of a fender and pulled herself back and along the hull.

Their voices came nearer.

'I mean, I'm a European patriot, Matt,' Glenson was saying in his hard Glaswegian accent. 'I wanted a few flags on this one, you know. All the European countries, stuck on the wee mast.'

They were out on the pier now, picking their way across the steel-strip walkway that led to the tower. If they reached it they would be able to see both sides of the *Nordkom IV* from where they stood. Geraldine clung to the hull, tucking herself tight in below the gunwale. Martin lay uncomfortably spread-eagled on the cool, polished surface of the deck. Suddenly one of the men turned. It was the Scottish one.

'Oh Christ! Look at that.'

Geraldine held her breath.

'What's the problem?' said the Dutchman.

'Devereux's back. Probably wants the fucking mast moved two feet to the left.'

The voices fell silent for a moment, then the sound of Glenson's low cursing receded and a minute later Martin allowed himself to peek above the bulkhead. The three men disappeared once more into the Portakabin.

Half-crouched, he ran across to the starboard side and beckoned Geraldine forward. As she approached the stern he wriggled himself along the deck and, only at the last minute, when she shouted 'Ready', did he duck up, grab the cable she was pushing up through the hawsehole and make its looped end fast around the solid brass bollard. He took the first cable firmly, but the next one shifted away from him. As he grabbed for it again, he felt the first direct rays of the sun, spilling through the mist.

Geraldine was angry. 'Martin, for God's sake, we practised this.'

At the second attempt, Martin secured the line. As he did so there was a shout from the shore and he flung himself once again to the deck, hugging the cables.

'Gerry,' the shout from Devereux echoed round the harbour. 'Where the hell are you!'

Martin heard Geraldine's equally powerful voice shout back. There was not a quaver in it. 'Forgot my make-up! Had to go back. I'm heading over now.'

Then more softly, 'Martin?'

'Yes?'

There was a pause. He heard the flat of her hand slap against the hull. 'Good fishing!'

A moment later he heard her gun the outboard and head for the shore. The tide was receding fast now. No one would return to the *Nordkom IV* until it turned again, well after the ceremony. He was alone.

Three and a half hours later Nick Marshall, having attended a morning of briefings and itchy, but successful, last-minute negotiations, was waiting on the quayside for the arrival of the Minister. At the Market Hotel he had changed into a brand new Hugo Boss petrol-blue gaberdine suit, complete, after a short and bitter argument with John Devereux, with non-matching Post Office Counter Services tie. He glanced anxiously around the site. Opposite him, in a small enclosure, were gathered the official guests. The Harvey-Wardrells were to the fore, she looming a good six inches above her husband, Peregrine. He was not a big man at the best of times but today he was almost entirely concealed beneath the brim of his wife's straw hat, which was so wide and of such a vibrant red that she stood out like a mediaeval Cardinal. By comparison the rest of the guests were unremittingly dowdy. Squeezed in with the Harvey-Wardrells behind an officious little blue and white striped rope, were such worthies as young Dr Cardwell, holding the hand of his dumpy wife Jane (they had met at a blind tasting), Cuthbert Habershon, the old coroner, standing uncomfortably side by side with his busy, unsmiling, replacement Eric Moss and his vigilant wife Bridget. Lord Muncaster was behind them, sporting an elegant light-grey worsted suit bought from the Rudges' nearly-new stall, and alongside him, the Reverend Barry Burrell and his close friend Tessa.

In a separate enclosure the members of the Town Council, with the notable exception of Frank Rudge, jostled with the likes of Alan Randall and Norman Brownjohn for a view of the proceedings. Ernie Padgett sat hunched forward on a chair at the front with his big, massively coiffured wife Brenda standing beside him, her hand lightly resting on his shoulder. Frank Rudge claimed to have been suffering from chest pain and had stayed at home, as had Kathleen Sproale, who hated any sort of occasion. Harold Meredith and Quentin Rawlings had been denied official invitations, and they stood, grim-faced, up on the hill with the public.

It was to that hill that Marshall now looked, having consulted his watch, for first signs of the arrival of the Ministerial party. A sizeable crowd lined the route. Foremost amongst them was Elaine, standing with her mother and Mary Perrick and Shirley Barker from the post office. Seeing them provoked in him a sharp and profound sense of irritation at the whole charade of the last year. If only the Government had had the courage of its convictions the Privatisation Bill would have been in place a year ago and he would not have had to waste nine months of his life pretending to work in a post office. The calibre of those he had been dealing with had not given him great hope for the future. The Elaine Rudges and the Shirley Barkers. Either they wanted to be screwed or they wanted help with the crossword. They were completely uninterested in the wider issues. Ask them how you might change their lives for the better and they would suggest getting engaged or buying a new lawnmower. Small town Britain had been a great dis-appointment to Nick Marshall. Still, soon he would be out of here, rightly acknowledged as a man of universal vision. Christ had spent time in the wilderness. He had spent time in Theston.

He looked out to sea. The mist had cleared, and the sun was now taking on the higher cloud. The company yacht rode splendidly out in the deeper water alongside the pier. It was a fine ship, a symbol of what could be achieved by those blessed with vision and foresight and daring. Glenson was right. The businessmen it had brought over were far more important to the future of telecommunications than the Minister of Technology or the Mayor of Theston. He smiled quietly to himself. He'd already held informal talks, as they say, with the Dutch boys. They liked him. Liked his style. Liked the fact that he'd bothered to learn the language. Once this link was up and running Devereux and Vickers wouldn't see him for dust.

There was a stirring in the crowd now and he looked back towards the hill. A police car came into view and at a discreet distance behind it a black Ford Granada. TV crews shouldered their equipment in readiness.

Dennis Donnelly, the Minister, was the new name on the political scene. The coming man. He had only recently been plucked from the bowels of the Heritage Department and some said his promotion to Technology was only the first step in a rapid upward progress through the ranks of government. Donnelly was a man of principle. His principle was to support the Prime Minister in whatever he did and whoever he was, until such time as he himself had acquired enough power to withdraw that support and become Prime Minister himself. Donnelly had many advantages. He was still young, only thirty-eight, he was not particularly intelligent and he had never once slept with anyone but his wife. The only cloud on the horizon was that she had slept with lots of people and, despite his stern words, had shown no sign of desisting. She was probably at it now. Whilst he was in Suffolk heralding the dawn of a telecommunications revolution, she was probably being pinioned to the floor by some huge black telephone engineer. Dennis Donnelly put these unsavoury thoughts from his mind as he stepped out of his limousine and started to smile. He was greeted by Ken Stopping in one of his last mayoral duties, and taken down the line to shake hands. They all liked the Minister. He seemed a straight-talking type, greeting everyone like a long-lost friend.

Stopping's speech of welcome was short and unmemorable, severely hampered by his inability to say the word 'telecommunications'.

Then Maurice Vickers stepped forward. His lazy eye gleamed somewhere off to the left as he spoke of opportunities grasped and horizons widened and new dawns risen for a Post Office soon to be free of commercial restraints.

He skilfully avoided any controversial issues such as the total destruction of the traditional post office, and Nick, whose legs were aching now with the waiting, was greatly relieved when Vickers climaxed in suitably apocalyptic style and the great moment came for the eager Minister to be placed in front of a video camera and his likeness transmitted by telephone line to a voice-activated computer in Zandvoort. This would, all being well, send live pictures simultaneously to a dozen major financial centres on the continent of Europe and beyond.

Nick felt a curious and unexpected *frisson* of pride as the

Minister stepped forward. He heard the applause of the crowd roll round the harbour and he knew that most of it was for him. They didn't know it yet, but soon they would. Soon the name of Nick Marshall would be as well known as Marconi or Alexander Graham Bell, or even Bill Gates. Certainly it would be far, far better known than that of Dennis Donnelly.

The Minister settled himself at the microphone with shameless ease. He spoke with plausible spontaneity, glancing skilfully but carefully at the text his civil servants had prepared for him.

'I am delighted and proud to be here in Theston today to inaugurate an installation which will open up a new era in telecommunications. This will be the model for hundreds of similar installations up and down our beautiful coastline.' He made a quick mental note to sack whoever it was in the department who had inserted the word 'beautiful'. 'I am assured that when this operation is complete there will be a link with Europe, both by cable and satellite, which will be capable of handling two hundred megabits of information *per minute.*'

This impressively meaningless statistic echoed metallically around the harbour and was greeted with polite, if self-conscious applause.

Ruth heard the applause on her car radio as she pulled off the A45 beyond Ipswich and began to negotiate the series of roundabouts that led to the Theston road.

Elaine heard the applause on the hill but did not join in. She wondered if she had been the only one to notice the activity on the gleaming white yacht that rode out beyond the harbour in the first rays of the midday sun. It appeared that there was a figure on board, moving some heavy object towards the stern. Something about the way the figure moved troubled her.

Elaine was not the only one watching what was happening on the *Nordkom IV*. As the applause died, Geraldine Cotton, forced to stand in a tight charcoal-grey two-piece suit amongst the ranks of minor local celebrities, knew that in a very few moments Martin would have lifted the cover on the teak-strip deck and revealed the brass-topped shaft into which deep-sea fishing seats were secured.

Most other spectators were watching the Minister and marvelling at his youth and relative beauty.

'The construction of this centre is a tribute to all those involved,' Donnelly went on. 'The Post Office engineers, the technical team, the construction workers, the vision of the Mayor and council of the borough of Theston and of course our friends across the water.' He paused, expecting applause, but none came. He would get them on the next paragraph, marked, in the margin, 'Direct appeal to the public'. He took his voice up an octave and tried hard to make his eyes water, as he had seen Meryl Streep do so often and so well. 'Let us not forget that today, as the eyes of the world are upon us, we are here to celebrate a British achievement. A triumph of British ingenuity and British foresight. This truly is our chance to show that Britain can lead the world into the new era of international communications. With pleasure and pride I declare Theston International Telecommunications Transmission Centre open.'

Then a lot of different things happened. The Minister pulled a blue cord which drew a curtain back from a plaque bearing his name and the intertwined logos of Nordkom BV and Post Office Counter Services Ltd. The television crews swung round to focus on the new mast, Theston School Band struck up 'Rule Britannia', and out to sea a bright orange maroon soared into the air above *Nordkom IV*. As heads craned skywards, there came the throaty roar of powerful engines starting and, before anyone knew what was happening, the pristine seventy-five-foot vessel swung in a tight half-circle and headed out to sea. There rose from its stern the silvery line of a cable. Then another similar line sliced up beside it through the light swell. Together they rose above the surface of the water as the engines throttled forward to the shrieking pitch of a power boat. The cables tightened, the engines roared and, almost in slow motion, the communications mast rocked, leaned and with a sickening crack ripped away from the pier, toppled into the sea and disappeared beneath the grey-green waves.

The cables strained, snapped and twisted viciously across the water. The yacht sprang forward, shot through the waves and out to sea. A moment later, on satellite video links in major financial markets on the continent of Europe and beyond, the flashing white hull of *Nordkom IV* could be seen to make contact with the solid clinker-built fishing boat *Lady Mary,* and rear up and out of the water, high and spinning like a child's top before it landed and exploded in a bright yellow star burst.

By the time the Air–Sea Rescue helicopter flew over the area two lifeboats were already on the scene. Wreckage of the *Nordkom IV* was scattered over a wide area. The fisherman from the *Lady Mary,* by the name of Derek Adland, had been found, still alive, in the water. When he was brought ashore he could remember little. He repeated, over and over again, that the boat had come straight towards him, that it had made no attempt to take avoiding action. He could only conclude that whoever was at the wheel was out to kill him.

The coastguard said nothing at the time. He knew Martin Sproale and he knew Kathleen, and he knew that there had been no one at the wheel when the boats collided. The steering was locked on, the wheel was lashed tight to the floor with a powerful leather strap, found, on closer inspection, to be a German army belt of the type issued to the 1st SS Panzer Corps, circa 1944.

A few weeks later Ruth was sitting at her laptop at Everend Farm Cottage. It was hot for early September and she had opened all the windows. The smell of late summer drifted in.

A wheaty, dusty, pungent smell. She had typed a last chapter-heading two coffees ago. She hated conclusions. They sat there like sirens, luring the scholar onto the rocks of pomposity and complacency. Now let's have the solution, they seemed to say. Now tell us what it's all about. The letters chattered up. Silver on blue:

> The final event of Hemingway's life is the one many now
> consider the most predictable. Such a glib judgement
> should never diminish the scholar's duty to examine, from
> every perspective, the circumstances which led a man, still
> widely popular, still respected by many close friends, still
> loved by the woman who had seen him through so much,
> to take his own life on that brilliant summer's morning
> in—

Her concentration was broken by a knock on the door. She turned. This was the time Mrs. Wellbeing usually called, interrupting her with some offering or other—ducks' eggs perhaps, which Ruth didn't like, or strawberries, which she did. She rested her cigarette on the side of her new ashtray and went to the door. It wasn't Mrs. Wellbeing. It was the postman, and he had a letter for her. It had an American stamp on it. She thanked him, exchanged a word or two about the weather—people were talking of another drought—and pushed the door to.

Inside the envelope was a folded page of notepaper. As she opened it a tighter, less scrupulously folded enclosure slipped out. She bent to the floor, retrieved it and began to smooth it out on the table. It was torn from a newspaper. A story spread over the whole page, beneath the headline 'Key West Celebration Ends On High Note.' 'As the Hemingway Days Festival drew to a close after a riotuous week, it was generally agreed that this year's winner of the Papa Look-Alike competition was the best ever. English newcomer Martin Sproale could have fooled the family.'

To prove it there was a photograph alongside. It was uncanny. The beard, the build, the tight white T-shirt and the creased khaki shorts, the stance, the set of the eye and the jut of the jaw. She knew it so well.

Ruth did not need to read the letter. She laid it on the table and stared out the window of her cottage to the airless, browning fields beyond.

There wasn't much in it anyway.

'Ruthie,' it read simply, 'Legends never die!'